BITTER ORANGE

This Large Print Book carries the
Seal of Approval of N.A.V.H.

BITTER ORANGE

CLAIRE FULLER

THORNDIKE PRESS
A part of Gale, a Cengage Company

Farmington Hills, Mich • San Francisco • New York • Waterville, Maine
Meriden, Conn • Mason, Ohio • Chicago

19 Feb 2
B+T
31.99(30.39)

LIBRARY OF CONGRESS CIP DATA ON FILE.
CATALOGUING IN PUBLICATION FOR THIS BOOK
IS AVAILABLE FROM THE LIBRARY OF CONGRESS

ISBN-13: 978-1-4328-6045-5 (hardcover)

Published in 2019 by arrangement with Tin House Books

Printed in Mexico
1 2 3 4 5 6 7 23 22 21 20 19

In memory of
Joyce Grubb
(9 August 1910 to 4 July 2004)
&
Joyce Grubb
(8 April 1907 to 26 June 1982)

ONE

They must think I don't have long left because today they allow the vicar in. Perhaps they are right, although this day feels no different from yesterday, and I imagine tomorrow will go on much the same. The vicar — no, not vicar, he has a different title, I forget — is older than me by a good few years, his hair is grey, and his skin is flaky and red, sore-looking. I didn't ask for him; what faith I once had was tested and found lacking at Lyntons, and before that, my church attendance was a habit, a routine for Mother and me to arrange our week around. I know all about routine and habit in this place. It is what we live, and what we die, by.

The vicar, or whatever he is called, is sitting beside my bed with a book on his lap, turning the pages too fast to be reading. When he sees I'm awake he takes my hand, and I'm surprised to find that it is a comfort:

7

a hand in mine. I can't remember when I was last touched — not the quick wash-over with a warm cloth, or the flick of a comb through my hair, these don't count. I mean properly touched, held by someone. Peter, possibly. Yes, it must have been Peter. Twenty years ago this August. Twenty years. What else is there to do in this place except count time and remember?

"How are you feeling, Miss Jellico?" the vicar says. I don't think I've told him my name. I take in *Miss* Jellico, roll it around inside my head like a silver ball in a game of bagatelle, letting it bounce from one pin to the next until it drops into the central enclosure and rings the bell. I know exactly who he is, but his title, that remains elusive.

"Where do you think I will go? Afterwards?" I spring the question on him. I am a difficult old bird. Although perhaps not so old.

He shuffles on his chair as though he has an itch in his pants. Maybe the flake extends under his clothes. I don't want to think.

"Well," he starts, bending over his book. "That depends . . . that depends on what you . . ."

"On what I?"

"On what you . . ."

Where I end up depends on what I con-

8

fess, is what he means. Heaven or hell. Although I don't think he believes in those places, not any more. And anyway, we're talking at cross purposes. I could drag out the conversation, tease him, but I decide for now not to play.

"What I mean," I say, "is where will I be buried? Where do they put us when we leave this place for the last time?"

He slumps with disappointment and then he asks, "Do you have somewhere in mind? I can make sure your wishes are passed on. Is there anyone you'd like me to tell, anyone in particular you want at the service?"

I am quiet for a time, pretending to consider it. "No need to hire a crowd," I say. "You, me, and the gravedigger will be enough."

He pulls a face — embarrassment? awkwardness? — because he can tell I know he isn't a real vicar. He is only wearing the getup — the dog collar — so they will allow him to visit. He has asked to see me before and I have refused. Now, though, with our talk of graves, I am thinking about bodies: those which are below the ground and those which are above. Cara and I, sunning ourselves at the end of the jetty on the lake at Lyntons. She in a bikini — I'd never seen that much of someone else's skin all at once

9

— and me daring to lift my woollen skirt above my knees. She reached out until her fingers touched my face, and she told me I was beautiful. I was thirty-nine when I sat on the jetty, and in my whole life no one had ever said I was beautiful. Later, when Cara was folding the tablecloth and putting away her cigarettes, I leaned over the green water of the lake and was disappointed to see that my reflection hadn't changed, I was the same woman, although for a while that summer, twenty years ago, I came to believe her.

More images come then, one superimposed on the next. And I abandon chronology in favour of waves of memory, overlapping and merging. My final look through the judas hole: I am kneeling on the bare boards of my attic bathroom at Lyntons, one eye pressed to the lens that sticks up from the floor, a hand covering the other to keep it closed. In the room below mine, a body lies in the pinking bathwater, the open eyes staring up at me for too long. The floor is puddled and the shine of wet footprints leading away is already disappearing. I am a voyeur, the person who stands at the police tape watching someone's life unravel, I am in the car slowing beside the accident but not stopping, I am the perpetrator returning to the scene of the crime. I am the lone mourner.

Judas hole. I had never come across that word until I came here, to this place.

How long ago?

"How long?" I must ask the question aloud because a reply comes from one of the Helpers. No, not Helper; what's the name for her? Care Help? Assistance Helper? My wasting disease has eaten away more than flesh: it has taken any memory of last week as well as the names and titles I was told an hour ago, but it is kind enough to leave the summer of 1969 intact.

"It's eleven forty," the woman says. I like this one; her skin is the colour of a horse chestnut I might have picked up in late September and discovered in a jacket pocket in early May. Louder she says: "Only twenty minutes till lunch, Mrs. Jellico." She pronounces it Jelli-co, as if I might be a manufacturer of puddings: Mrs. Wagner's Pies, Mr. Kipling cakes, Mrs. Jelli-co's . . . what? I have never actually been *Mrs.* Jellico; I have never married, I have no children. Only here, in this place, do they call me *missis.* The vicar has always called me Miss Jellico, from the first time I met him. The vicar! I realise my hand is empty and he has gone; did he say goodbye?

11

"Twenty years," I whisper.

The memory of my first sight of Cara stirs me: a pale, long-legged sprite. I hear her shouting outside on Lyntons' carriage turn. I stopped cutting up my bathroom carpet and crossed the narrow corridor to one of the empty rooms opposite mine. Under the attic window, a lead-lined gutter edged by a stone parapet was packed with decaying leaves and the sticks and feathers of ancient pigeon nests. Far below, Cara was standing on the dry fountain in the middle of the carriage turn. The mass of her hair was the first thing I noticed — almost solid with its dark, tight curls and centre parting, hiding all but a strip of her milk-white face. She was shouting in Italian. I didn't know the words; the closest I have come to understanding Italian is the Latin names of plants, and most of these have faded now. A test: *Cedrus . . . Cedrus . . . Cedrus libani,* cedar of Lebanon.

Cara's bare feet balanced on Cupid's thighs, while one of her hands gripped the robes of a stone woman as though she were trying to wrest them from her, and in the other she held a pair of flat ballet pumps. I winced at the damage she might be doing to the already marked and chipped marble. I half hoped the fountain might be a Canova

12

or one of his pupils, although I hadn't yet examined it properly. Cara was wearing a long crocheted dress and, I was certain, even from my distance, no brassiere. The sun had nearly set on the other side of the house and her body was in shadow, but her head, where she tilted it back to look up, was vivid. I knew her already: hot-blooded and prickly, bewitching; a flowering cactus.

I thought she was shouting at me, up in my attic. I have never liked loud sounds, harsh words; I've always preferred the quiet of a library, and back then I couldn't remember anyone raising their voice to me, not even Mother, although, of course, things are different now. But before I could reply, though goodness knows what I would have said, the sash was raised in one of the stately rooms below mine, and a man stuck out his head and shoulders.

"Cara," he called to the girl on the fountain, giving me her name. "Don't be ridiculous. Wait." He sounded exhausted.

She shouted again, arms waving, mouth working, fingers pressed together, hands pushing her hair over her shoulder, where it didn't stay, and then jumped off the fountain into the long grass. She was always nimble, Cara. She came towards the house and went out of sight. The man vanished

13

back inside, and I heard him running through Lyntons' empty and echoing rooms, imagined the dust rising and settling in the corners as he passed. From my window, I saw him burst out of the front door onto the carriage turn just as Cara was pushing a bicycle at a trot through what was left of the gravel and simultaneously putting on her shoes. When she reached the avenue, she pulled up her dress and jumped on the bicycle like a circus acrobat jumping onto a moving horse, something I could never have managed then and certainly not now.

"Cara!" the man called. "Please don't go."

We watched her, he and I, swerve around the potholes along the avenue of limes. Pedalling away from us, she let go of the bicycle with one hand and stuck up two fingers in reply. It is difficult to recall the exact emotions which accompanied those sightings of Cara, after everything that happened. I was probably shocked by her gesture, but I like to think that I might have also been excited by an anticipation of my own reinvention, of possibility, of summer.

The man walked to the gates, which were eight feet tall and rusted open, and struck his palms against *Lyntons 1806* coiled in the ironwork. I was intrigued by his frustration; had I witnessed the end of their relationship or a lovers' tiff?

I guessed that the man was about my age, ten years or so older than Cara, blondish hair flopping over his forehead, and a way of holding himself as though gravity, or the world, had got the better of him. Attractive, I thought, in a worn-down way. He shoved his hands into his jeans pockets and as he turned towards the house he looked straight up to my window. Without knowing why, since I had every reason to be there, I slid back into the room and ducked below the sill.

Lyntons. Just thinking the word raises the hairs on my arms like a cat that had seen a ghost. But the Ward Assister . . . not that . . . a new white woman I don't recognise, with a white plastic apron covering her uniform, sees my open mouth and an opportunity to feed me a spoonful of overboiled broccoli. I press my lips together, turn my head, and let another earlier memory come.

Mr. Liebermann's handwritten directions: a scrawl of place names, arrows, and minor roads. An English market town, a church, a cattle grid. I struggled off the bus at the stop before the town and walked back the way I had travelled, to a narrow lane with tufts of grass growing along the middle. On

15

the paper, Mr. Liebermann had written *Stop here for the view* alongside an unnamed track that turned in beside a derelict lodge, although I learned later that he hadn't been to Lyntons himself. I suppose he thought I would be driving, but I have never held a licence, or had a lesson, never driven a car. I put down my two suitcases and considered leaving them under a hedge and returning for them later. I was hot in my raincoat — easier to wear it than to carry it — as I rested, leaning on the dented estate railings to catch my breath.

A mile away, beyond the parkland dotted with mature specimen trees, the house — Lyntons — balanced at the top of a green bank. It extended back into shadow, but the view I had was of wide stone steps leading up to a magnificent portico where the afternoon sun buttered eight immense columns which rose to a triangular pediment. I could have been looking at the English cousin of the Parthenon. To the left of the house, the sun reflected off the panes of the glasshouse Mr. Liebermann's letter had promised, while behind the buildings the land rose steeply to wooded hangers — a geographical feature of that part of the country: ancient woodland clinging to the sides of steep scarps which twisted and turned for several miles. Close by, a stream trickled through water meadows pockmarked with the imprints of cows' hooves, until it was hidden between overgrown bushes and shaggy trees. I glimpsed the glitter of a lake, and although I couldn't see it, I imagined the place where a bridge must cross the water. I had a thought, a shiver of excitement, about what kind of bridge it might be, given the age and style of the original house and what I had read about it, but I hadn't voiced the possibility to anyone. There wasn't anyone who would have listened, not then anyway.

In my bed, in this place, I think of bridges, and crossing water, and the ferryman, and wonder if I will have a premonition of my death. For all I know, everyone does — a bird inside a room, a chained fox, a watchful hare, a cow giving birth to twin calves — but only the unlucky recognise it for what it is.

Another Assister Carer, the friendly girl with the acne — Sarah? Rebecca? — combs my hair. She's younger than the others, I can't see her lasting long, but she's gentle and she doesn't do the inconsequential chatter as most do. When she's finished, only a few strokes required now, she holds a mirror up to my face and I am shocked all over again at the woman who stares back: her sunken cheeks, the mottled skin like tea stains on parchment, the scraggy neck. In the mirror, the woman's mouth opens and I see pale gums receding from yellow horse teeth, and as I recoil, my arms flail and the mirror is pushed away. The girl's grip is weak or she doesn't expect any strength from me, and in her surprise she lets it go. It hits the end of the bed, although of course it doesn't break but goes spinning off across the room. The girl is telling me to keep still, to calm down, to lie back, but now she isn't so gentle. A warm wetness spreads under me and she presses the buzzer and I hear the squeak of rubber shoes on linoleum in the corridor. A sharp stab of pain in my arm and once more I am in the attic at Lyntons.

I am in the attic at Lyntons, and when it is obvious that the man has gone back indoors I finish hacking across the middle of the bathroom carpet with my botanical sample knife. It was a beautiful knife, the handle curved to the shape of my palm, and the blade wide and short; I liked to keep it sharp. I don't know where it is now.

In a corner under the window I pushed my fingers down next to the skirting board

18

and pulled hard enough for the carpet to snap off in quick jerks, releasing a cloud of dust, and pitching me backwards from my squatting position onto my bottom. A layer of other people's skin, particles of desiccated insects, and plaster from the cracks in the ceiling settled over my face and hair.

The carpet was patterned, light-brown squares and reddish circles. At the edges it was grey with dust, and around the toilet bowl it was stained a poisonous yellow. I tugged and heaved and rolled the two halves over themselves into the middle of the room, exposing the floorboards beneath. The bathroom was large — three paces from bath to sink and the same from window to toilet — and must once have been a maids' bedroom. From the centre of the low ceiling a dusty lightshade hung on a plain flex. I didn't care how frightful it was, the bathroom and the bedroom next door were mine, for a summer at least.

There was a rap on the door to the attic at the end of the corridor, and I stopped, still on my hands and knees, hoping if I stayed motionless for long enough the person would go away. Sometimes, in the past, I had longed for company, but now, as someone literally came knocking, my thoughts scattered, and the beat of alarm at

19

the idea of talking to a stranger pulsed in my throat. The knock came again, and while I was levering myself up on the lip of the bath, I heard the door open and then the man I'd seen running after Cara was standing in the bathroom doorway, a little breathless from taking the spiral staircase.

He studied me, and I realised my botanical sample knife was in my hand and Mother's silk scarf still covered the bottom half of my face, tied there to keep the dust from my mouth.

"Hello?" he said, taking a step backwards. Closer up I thought he looked sadder, more handsome, the lines in his face smoothed out.

I pulled down the bandana, swapped the knife from one hand to the other and back again, uncertain what to do with it.

"Sorry," I said, because I knew the word would be expected.

"You must be Frances?" He held out his hand. Perhaps I seemed confused, gauche, because he added, as though I might myself have forgotten, "You're here to survey the garden architecture for Liebermann?" It was a moment before I took his hand, dry and as large as mine. I let it go quickly. "Peter," he said, introducing himself. "I'm sorry I wasn't around when you arrived, but it looks like you're making yourself at home?" He smiled, laughed almost, at the knife in my hand. I met his eyes and looked away, focussing on his lips, full for a man. His attractiveness made me feel all the more cloddish.

In one of his letters, Mr. Liebermann had explained that he had also commissioned someone to report to him on the condition of the house and its fittings. I had been expecting Peter but hadn't given him a thought, or if I had, I'd imagined him to be elderly and alone. "Sorry," I repeated, holding the knife behind my shorts — wide men's shorts from the Army & Navy store. "I was cutting up the carpet." As well as apologising I had learned that it helped to state the facts when I couldn't think of anything to say.

"I didn't see your car." While he spoke Peter's hands moved, circled around each other, pointed, illustrating his words.

"I came by train and then the bus," I said. "The number thirty-nine. It was twenty-eight minutes late." From his expression, it seemed I'd said too much, had maybe been rude. It was so hard to get it right, the way other people had conversations, back and forth with no effort. I wondered, not for the first time, how it was done.

21

"You should have sent a telegram," Peter said. "I'd have been happy to collect you from the station." He looked past me into the bathroom and carried on talking. "And sorry you had to hear all that, earlier. There's no missing Cara when she's in one of her moods. But you mustn't worry." I hadn't been worrying, I wondered if I should have been worrying. "She'll have gone into town. She always comes back." He laughed again. It sounded as though he was reassuring himself. "What are you up to in there?" He pointed. "The attic rooms are rather dingy. I think an old retainer must have been living in them, a nanny or a butler. Nothing's been looked after. You should see the mess the army left, graffiti like you can't imagine."

He came into the bathroom and looked about without any sign of embarrassment. "Army?" I said. I knew all the ways to keep the other person talking.

"Lyntons was requisitioned. Forty-Seventh Infantry Regiment. Americans. Apparently, Churchill and Eisenhower discussed the D-Day invasion in the blue drawing room. Goodness knows what a mess they made of the gardens. The soldiers I mean, not Churchill and Eisenhower, although you never know. Anyhow, you'd better prepare yourself. Liebermann did suggest that you have the rooms downstairs. They are grander, and I was hoping that Cara and I would be staying in the town but, well . . . my circumstances changed." He smiled. I liked him for talking so I didn't have to. "There's only this bathroom and ours downstairs fully working. I hope you don't mind too much being up here in the attic."

I saw him staring at the two halves of rolled-up carpet.

"There was a smell," I said.

In his final letter, Mr. Liebermann had enclosed a key to the side door with his directions, together with instructions to make my way up to the attic rooms. When I'd opened the door at the top of the spiral staircase that first time, the stink had punched me on the face: a reminder of those last few days nursing Mother. A mix of boiled vegetables, urine, and fear. "I didn't think Mr. Liebermann would mind if I took up the carpet."

"Oh, he won't mind." Peter flapped a hand in dismissal and went to the window, still talking. "Liebermann has no idea what's in the house and what isn't. He sent me an inventory, but nothing matches. There was meant to be a neoclassical chimney piece by Wyatt in the blue drawing room, but there's just a gaping hole. The grand staircase which was supposed to be marble inlay is definitely scagliola, and now that the damp and mould have had their way it isn't worth saving, but the upsides are that the cupola is magnificent and I found dozens of bottles of wine in the basement that aren't listed." He winked and then bent, hands on knees, to look out of the low window. "Probably corked, mind you. The inventory could be for a different house. I'd assumed Liebermann had visited before he bought Lyntons, but now I'm not so sure. Did you find the bedding we put out for you?" He didn't wait for an answer. "What a view."

My two rooms were on the west side of the house, just below the roof and chimney stacks. It was a floor of a dozen or so rooms leading off a corridor that ran north to south. All the west-facing windows looked out onto a glorious view over Lyntons' ruined gardens, the paths hidden by overgrown box and yew, a tangled rose garden, fallen statuary, and the ravaged flower beds, to the parkland, the mausoleum, and, beyond, a dark treeline and the hangers in the far distance.

"Have you walked around the grounds

yet?" I asked. "Or been to the bridge?" I wanted him to say that he hadn't so that whatever was there would be mine to discover alone, while at the same time I hoped he would tell me that he had seen the bridge and it was Palladian, so that I no longer had to brace myself for disappointment.

A Palladian bridge: understated architecture built to join two banks. Most often topped with a temple: stone balustrades and columns, pediments and colonnades under a lead roof, with coffered ceilings and statues. A water-cooled summer house open at either end, and built by the wealthy to stroll through or ride their carriages across. The bridge I imagined rose above the lake and spanned it with five elegant arches, while a spectacular open-sided temple grew upwards from the balustrades. The whole would be satisfyingly symmetrical, but with fine and intricate carvings on the keystones. It wasn't just a bridge, a means to move from one bank to the other, but a place built for love, for assignations, for beauty.

Peter straightened. "There's a bridge, is there? I keep meaning to go down to the lake for a swim but I've had plenty to keep me busy in the house, what with Cara and the wine cellar."

He kicked at one of the rolls of carpet and

laughed. "Getting rid of a couple of bodies, are you?"

Two

When I wake I am alone. My stomach growls and I think I must have missed lunch or breakfast, or both, but it's a drink of water I need most. They have left a beaker for me on the bedside table but I can only move my eyes towards it. My limbs will no longer do what my mind commands. The people here have changed my sheets and my nightdress, and I am ashamed to think of them touching my sick body, its pink and brown patches and atrophied muscles. I once heard someone say that you are supposed to get more comfortable in your own skin the older you become, more forgiving of its folds and creases, but it's not true. I used to be a big woman, *voluptuous* Peter once said. Now my flesh has melted away, but the skin remains and I lie in a puddle of myself. I close my eyes and turn my head to the window; the colour through my eyelids is rose madder. I return.

The day is new, the light is gold and green, and I am back in my attic bathroom. In my memory the sun always shines at Lyntons; the few drops of rain and rumbles of thunder we had never amounted to anything. It is my first morning and I am going to the lake. First though, I scrubbed the bath, the sink, and the toilet, and swept up the hairs left behind from the pieces of carpet, which I had lugged down the stairs and outside, heaving them onto a rubbish pile I had nosed out behind the stables. I clipped on Mother's Hattie Carnegie earrings and checked that her locket hung around my neck. Odd, perhaps, to get dressed up for a walk, but I liked to wear them to remember her, to be able to put a hand to my ear or my throat, and recall her voice and the way she used to look at me with love, before my father left.

While I was retying a shoelace, one of Mother's earrings flew off my ear as though we three — me, Mother, and the earring — knew they didn't suit me. A circle of rhinestones with a green Peking glass centre made for someone with more petite lobes. The earring scuttled across the bathroom floor and I chased it; a glittering mouse disappearing down a gap between the boards. I pulled off the other earring, put it on the shelf next to my talcum powder, and stuck my fingers into the hole, pushing my hand down until my knuckles jammed against the wood. There was only warm air. But a board was loose, moving against its neighbours. I tucked my fingers under and was surprised when it lifted out, exposing the joists beneath. In the wide spaces between, a silt beach was strewn with lost objects. The contents of a tiny shipwreck washed up on dark and gritty sand: pins, a rusted razor blade, a button, two hair grips, a few dirty beads from a broken necklace, and the earring. It rested against a metal tube, the diameter of a fat cigar, sticking up from the dust. I tried to pluck it out but it was firmly attached. The tube twisted and extended up above the floor — a short telescope. I licked my finger to clean what appeared to be a small glass disc in the top, and I lowered my face to the tube to look through.

What I saw was another bathroom from above, larger than mine and more imposing: a roll-top claw-footed bath and a scrolled sink, both of them warped and turning in on themselves as the lens distorted the view. The door was open and a yellow tongue of morning sun from the adjoining room licked the floor. On the back of the sink was a bar of new soap in a china dish, and beside it, on a small table, pots, perfume bottles, and toothbrushes were jumbled together. I watched while the door opened wider and a man came in. It was only when he stopped in front of the lavatory that I realised it was Peter. I jumped back, putting my palm over the top of the tube, and keeping still and silent as if he might at any moment look up and discover me. I recalled what he had said about how the rooms below were going to be mine, and I was grateful I'd been given a couple of converted servants' quarters with an army-issue bed topped by a thin mattress.

I remained motionless until I heard the toilet flush, then I twisted the tube down and replaced the floorboard.

Mr. Liebermann had sent me an inventory too, of sorts: a page enclosed with his directions as well as the key. It was a sheet torn from Lyntons' sale particulars:

A Neoclassical Mansion including Entrance Hall, Music Room, Drawing Room, Gun Room, Sitting Room, Dining Hall, Smoking Room, Billiards Room, Boudoir, Saloon, and Ten Bed and Dressing Rooms, Five Bathrooms, and Staff Accommodation. Seated in a Magnificent Timbered Park of 764 acres with Ornamental Lake, Fountain, Parterre, Walled Kitchen Garden, Classical Bridge, Orangery of Outstanding Design, Stable Block, Model Dairy, Ice House, Grotto, Mausoleum, Sundry Follies inc. Obelisk etc., and range of outbuildings. All in a state of some disrepair.

Mr. Liebermann had scribbled over it in pencil, circling *Fountain* and underlining *Classical Bridge* three times.

I had received his first letter with its American stamp and postmark a month after Mother was buried. A coincidence but a lucky one. With her death, the alimony my father had been paying her stopped, and although Mother left everything she had to me, surprisingly little money remained after I'd paid for the funeral and settled other bills. The apartment we lived in, a portion of a London house, was rented.

I believed it would be exciting not to know where I would go or what I would do next for the first time in thirty-nine years. We had a routine, Mother and I, which never varied, and I had imagined that being able to eat when I wanted, go to bed when I wanted, do anything I wanted, would make me free. I believed I would be transformed. I'd been preparing for Mother's death for ten years — every time I came home from the shops or the library, I unlocked the front door uncertain of what I would find. After she was gone, I was ready to leave too. I wanted to be rid of the memories of those years which were soaked into every surface: the chair she monitored the road from while waiting for me to return, the desk where she sat to write her regular letters to my father asking for more money, the bed where I nursed her and where she'd died — which, when I stripped the sheets, smelled of her and made me cry.

I was ruthless. I invited the local antiques dealer in and told him he could buy what he liked. He hummed and tutted and shook his head while I showed him around the rooms. The furniture was too dark and heavy, he said, the market had all but disappeared for our old-fashioned Victorian items. Still, he took everything including her old haute couture clothes that she'd saved from her previous life, bundling them into boxes, saying he wasn't hopeful about finding them a home. He paid me less for the whole lot than one dress had cost. I knew it, but I wanted everything gone. He left her underwear, a couple of pieces of cheap jewellery, and one evening dress that I kept for myself. I didn't think about the future, not then. I had no doubts something would turn up, and I was right, it did.

A few months previously, an article I'd written about the Palladian bridges at Stowe and Prior Park had been published in the *Journal of the Society of Garden Antiquities.* They had printed several of my pieces over the years, although they didn't pay since it was an obscure periodical read, I thought, by probably only half a dozen academics.

But it must have reached a wider audience, because one day I received a letter from a Mr. Liebermann forwarded by the journal, who wrote to say he'd purchased an English country house and gardens.

Dear Mrs. Jellico, As an expert on bridges and garden architecture in general, I wonder if you would consider visiting an English country mansion and its estate, which I have recently purchased, and giving me your professional assessment, his letter had started. I wouldn't have called myself an expert; everything I knew had been self-taught, aside from my year at Oxford. I had always spent my free time in the British Museum library, sitting in my usual chair, reading, making notes, and writing little history articles for pleasure. I'd not visited any historical sites outside London, at least not since my father had left.

I replied to Mr. Liebermann the same day with my acceptance of his offer — a commission, a chance to get out of the city, and, most excitingly, the possibility of surveying a classical bridge in real life. I didn't sleep properly until I received his reply. We settled on a fee and an arrangement for me to stay in the house, and I agreed to write him a report by the end of August on the items of architectural interest in the garden.

For my final week in London I booked into a King's Cross boarding house, my clothes in one suitcase and my books and what was left of Mother's belongings in another. I spent the nights awake, listening to the comings and goings of the girls on the street, and the days on my familiar seat in the British Museum library, reading everything I could find about Lyntons. Pevsner had only a page and a half, mentioning the pathos of the main portico, and using the dismissive tone I had come to enjoy, saying that the staircase was *of no interest.* The book touched on the follies in the grounds, and the orangery, but didn't mention a bridge. The estate church was listed too, but the interior was *disappointing* and the monuments *sentimental.* However,

I did learn that the neoclassical house was built at the beginning of the nineteenth century around an earlier brick one. I ordered up the relevant issues of *Country Life* but found nothing surprising, only a few dull photographs of chimney pieces, the portico, and the lake. One article mentioned a book of drawings, and this led me to a diary written by a woman who had stayed at Lyntons during the summer of 1754. She wrote at length about the tough pheasant served at dinner, how cold and shabby her bedroom was, and that no servant had answered her summons to come and light a fire in the grate. She also wrote about the classical bridge with its *fyne arches* that spanned the water.

I went to the lake that first morning, leaving through the side door, walking around the front of the house and passing under the portico's immense columns and down the wide steps. The formal garden of what once must have been ordered plants and hedges had grown up towards the house, swallowing the bottom steps, brambles cracking the stone and infiltrating the gaps. Valerian and rosebay willowherb had self-seeded, lilac bushes were leggy and untended, the flowers brown, while a rampant honeysuckle, or

Lonicera, outclimbed the bindweed, or *Convolvulus.* At one time, I imagined, the lake and the bridge would have been visible from the house, but now I cut myself a switch to beat my way through the undergrowth, following the shape of a path bordered by nettles that led to a row of Nissen huts, the domed roofs smothered by ivy. When I peered through the punched-out windows, it was clear from the smell and the mess that they had been most recently used as chicken sheds.

As I passed between monstrous rhododendrons either side of a series of worn steps, the stone pink with dropped and fading flower heads, I couldn't help but imagine what I might discover: a Palladian bridge more elegant than those at Wilton or Prior Park, wider even than the bridge at Stowe; and unlike Stourhead, mine would have a temple on top. See? Already it was mine. It would be my discovery — I didn't give one thought to Mr. Liebermann, not then — I would write an article which wouldn't just be published in a society's journal; it would be published in *The Times.*

I came out downstream, where the land had been excavated into a broad basin that slowed the water and would have given the impression to the owners and their guests that they were viewing a lake and not a dammed and manipulated stream. To my right, the water snaked out of sight around a bend, and when I stepped onto the bank, a raft of ducks rose up from the green water, flapping and squawking. I turned left, walking through a strip of tangled saplings, the ground rutted where the track must have been scoured by tank manoeuvres, although it was already colonised by grasses and ferns. The lake winked at me through the trees.

A few yards on and I had my first uninterrupted view of the bridge at the head of the lake. It was not as I had hoped. There was no temple on top, only more scrubby bushes and tangled plants growing across it from both banks. There were arches, but they weren't fine. I considered turning around, but I thought I might as well stand on it just to consider it done. A narrow deer path led over the bridge and I followed this, whacking at the brambles and their berries with my stick as they tried to catch at my clothes and skin. On the east side, the stream was sluggish, slowed by debris that had collected against the stones — branches, leaves, and a white scum that swirled about the surface. It was a sad, dank place, but when I turned from it and gazed out over the lake, the water was clear down to the weed, and in the centre the motionless surface caught the sun and the sky and threw them back to me.

I continued over the bridge and along the opposite bank, ducking under branches and using my switch, walking to the other end of the lake where it narrowed back into a stream, and I crossed a slick weir above a small man-made cascade. I sat here while the sun rose higher, and attempted to draw the bridge and lake in my sketchbook. I was used to being alone and mostly content with solitude even when in the middle of a London crowd, but here, sitting by myself beside Lyntons' lake, I was conscious of the couple up at the house and found myself wondering what kind of people they were.

Later, I walked the rest of the grounds and looked at the follies and some of the buildings: the obelisk, the mausoleum, the grotto, the kitchen garden, and the model dairy. I poked my head into musty storerooms, the icehouse, and the stables, unseen creatures running from the light and my heavy footsteps. The rest of the morning I sat on the little bed in my room with my papers on my lap and my books spread about me on the floor — there was no table or chair —

writing up my notes, redrawing my sketches, and creating a map of the grounds with the follies marked in relation to the house.

I washed my underwear and stockings in the bathroom sink using the block of soap that had been left there, its scent gone and its surface cracked, and draped the clothes over a string hung above the bath. Late in the afternoon I heated half a tin of pilchards in tomato sauce on a stove that had been put in my room, together with a few pieces of cutlery and crockery. I placed one of my suitcases on top of the other, put a spare pillowcase over them, and laid out knife, fork, and plate. Sitting crookedly on the floor in front of the dining table I had created, I ate my dinner.

After I had washed up in the bathroom sink and put everything away, I returned to my work. The next time I looked up, the light in the room was apricot from the lowering sun. I stood and arched my back, stretching and twisting my neck, and crouching at the open window, I looked over the grounds, trying to imagine how they might have been when they were first laid out — the distant fields green and un-ploughed, the oaks and cedars with their limbs intact and their bases clear of nettles. A time when every view from the house had been designed to create an idealised English landscape of vistas and open spaces framed by the dark rising hangers.

A smell of cooking came from below, garlic frying in butter, something meaty, and my stomach groaned — half a tin of pilchards was not enough. I leaned out of my window to inhale the aroma and as I looked down I saw a foot on the windowsill below mine, glimpsing grubby toes with newly painted green nails before I quickly withdrew my head. I wondered how one got to know one's neighbours.

For supper I finished the heel from the loaf of bread I had brought with me, and the tin of pilchards. I would have to go to the town the next day if I wanted to eat.

The air in the attic was soupy even with the window open, and I lay under a sheet in my nightdress thinking about who might have lived in the room before me and who had slept in the one next to mine before it was converted into a bathroom. Had a prying manservant who wanted to observe his mistress fixed the spyglass in the floor, or had a degenerate son, perhaps, thought it would be fun to ogle the family's guests? Just as I was imagining the requisite madwoman locked in the attic watching life going on below her, I heard a shout, a woman's voice — Cara's. I sat up and a light was switched on in the rooms below mine; the glow visible through my window and when I poked my head out of the window, Cara and Peter's bathroom light was turned on too. She yelled something in Italian, spitting out the words. Peter's reply was loud but measured:

"Please, Cara. It's late, can we not start this now."

She shouted back at him, her foreign words carrying outside into the night.

"In English, please," Peter said.

Cara screeched, an animal in a trap. There was a crash, glass breaking or china smashing, that made me momentarily pull in my head as though she were coming for me. A door slammed and my window frame shuddered in response, and somewhere below, Cara began to weep, still shouting through her hiccups, trying to catch her breath, making no sense. One of them yanked the windows closed and I didn't hear anything else, but my thoughts were drawn back to the spyhole in my bathroom floor.

I knew of course right from wrong. My father, Luther Jellico, had instilled it into me before he left and then Mother had continued in her way: payment will always be due for any wrongdoing, don't lie or steal, don't talk to strange men, don't speak unless spoken to, don't look your mother in the eye, don't drink, don't smoke, don't expect anything from life. I knew there were rules I was supposed to live by but it was an intellectual knowledge, a checklist to be ticked off against each new action, not inherent as it appeared to be for everyone else. There was nothing on the list about spying. I went to the bathroom and lifted the board without compunction. I knelt on the floor and looked through the hole.

Cara was curled on her side on the bathroom floor wearing a nightdress, her face obscured by her hair, the corkscrew coils wild. Her knees were pulled into her chest and her head lay on Peter's lap, her breast heaving out an occasional sob. He wore pyjamas and sat with his back against the wall, legs straight out in front. He stroked her hair, his head lowered over hers, and I marvelled at the love I thought I saw in that motion, a mutual giving and receiving I had never known. After a few minutes she sat up and covered his neck and face with little kisses while he remained stiff and upright, as though waiting to see whether she would suddenly change and lash out at him with a claw. She kissed him on the mouth, pressing her lips to his while her hand, a wedding ring on one finger, moved across his thigh and into the gap in his pyjama bottoms. I didn't look away, I was curious. Before her fingers were inside the opening, Peter gently took hold of her wrist and pulled her hand away. Cara hung her head, her body shaking with sobs. He stood her up, lifted her into his arms, and, as if she were a child or an invalid, carried her from the room.

THREE

The next morning, without any breakfast, I worked on my notes, and by the time I left the house the day was already hot, my palm sticking to the plastic handles of my string shopping bag. I hadn't been able to find my hat and could only think I must have left it on the bus. I crossed the weedy carriage turn and started the long walk down the avenue. The surface was pitted and full of potholes probably made by the army trucks that must have rumbled down it for the last time many years previously. The sun was fierce on the crown of my head and already I was thirsty. At the far end, in the distance, half a mile away, someone was coming along the avenue on a bicycle, and a moment later I realised it was Cara, head lowered and legs working to pedal up the slight slope to the house. What was one supposed to do in such circumstances? I had seen the colour of her nightdress — baby pink — knew the high keening wail she made when she cried, and yet we had not been introduced. Mother would have stopped and made polite conversation, pretending she had heard and seen nothing. Of course there was the weather. I could mention how blue the sky was or ask whether Cara thought it was going to rain, but I wasn't confident that I could look in the eye someone whose hand I had seen moving into her husband's pyjamas. Perhaps I could ask her whether she had anything I could drink. By now Cara had come around the left-hand bend, and I could see she was wearing a green headscarf tied under her chin, and sunglasses. Her knees, below the same crocheted dress she'd worn yesterday, pumped up and down. I imagined the bottle of lemonade she might have in her basket, cold from the refrigeration unit in one of the town's shops.

I wiped a damp palm on my skirt, ready to shake her hand when she stopped, and continued walking towards her. My words, *How do you do, I'm Frances, I'm here to examine the garden follies,* seemed like pebbles in my cheeks, dull things that would plop from my mouth and fall to the ground. I could hear the old man's wheeze of the bicycle's suspension and the rubber limp of her under-inflated tyres on the stones of the avenue, and I could see her cheeks, flushed from the exertion.

Then, when she was almost level with me, I walked off the paved surface and into the grass, and stood behind the nearest tree, pressing my back flat against it. I couldn't even pretend that she wouldn't have seen me.

As she rode her bicycle past, Cara trilled the bell, raising some crows into a cawing flap. I stayed there until she had time to reach Lyntons, get off the bicycle, hammer on the front door, and disappear inside, time enough for my blush to fade.

At the end of the avenue the main track turned sharp right towards the road, the way I had arrived. But straight ahead in the direction of the town, a footpath led between two fields, much overgrown and full of the buzz of insects. The sky was matt blue and the sun continued to shine, drawing all the liquid in my body to the surface, where it collected under my arms and in my cleavage; if Cara had passed me now, I would have knocked her off her bicycle to get at the fictional bottle of lemonade in her basket. I decided I was closer to the town than to Lyntons so I pressed on, thinking about the long glass of water I would ask for when I reached the tea shop; there had to be a tea shop.

When the fields ended, the path widened but grew darker, overhung with yews angling inwards until their branches intertwined overhead like a wedding arch, and I walked under them, a bride without a groom. The banks rose on either side, the earth track worn down, exposing the brown bones of the trees' roots. I was grateful for the shade, and it wasn't until a semicircle of daylight became visible ahead, and then an iron gate with a graveyard beyond, that I realised this avenue of yews must have been the one that generations of Lyntons had walked, ridden, and for a final time been carried along, supine in their best clothes, to the estate church mentioned in Pevsner. The gate was locked in place by knee-high grass, but beyond it, headstones leaned and butterflies zigzagged between a buddleia and flowering thistles. I shoved at the gate, pushing and flattening the couch grass enough to be able to squeeze through the gap. Here, at the back of the churchyard, the graves were untended; moss and rain had eaten away the dates and the names until the people beneath were no more than worn capitals. I followed the graves forwards in time and found four Lyntons lying together: two

Dorotheas, a Charles who had died aged twenty, and a Samuel who had lived for a year.

I took the path that tracked around the church, past another yew, its waist almost the tower's thickness, and a heap of grass cuttings, dead flowers tossed on top, the whole smelling of rot and warm vegetation turning slimy. On the northern side of the church, the vicar, in a black cassock, stood amongst the stones. His face was obscured as he bent his head above the pages of a book. Beside him an older man holding a cap rested on a long-handled spade. The two of them were standing over an open grave.

I kept close to the building and went around to the front door, which was unlocked. I hadn't been in a church since Mother's funeral, but the smell of beeswax and the air, as cool as running water, were familiar and friendly. Then, I had cried all through the service and the hymns. I wasn't able to stop even when the vicar was saying a few words or when the handful of Mother's elderly friends who had come were singing, although I wasn't certain whether my exaggerated weeping was from self-pity or horror that Mother was actually dead.

This church was beautifully plain: pews,

whitewashed solid walls, a wooden ceiling. I didn't think it was disappointing. I went down the aisle, slipped through a door into the vestry and was opening a cupboard above the sink when I heard a voice behind me.

"Can I help you?"

I turned; the vicar was standing in the doorway, the Book of Common Prayer in his hands. His eyes were bagged as though he had missed several nights' sleep, and his hair was pulled back from his face in an odd style, but most disturbing was his dark beard. I hadn't met a vicar before who wasn't clean-shaven.

"Sorry. I was after a glass," I said. "For water."

"I'm afraid you need to bring your own vases for flowers, and there's an outside tap for general use."

"I mean to drink."

He went past me and pulled back a cloth curtain strung below the sink, took a glass off a shelf, filled it from the tap, and handed it to me. "Mr. Lockyer saw you come in through the back gate." He looked me up and down, and I was aware of myself: a middle-aged woman rather thick around the waist, hair greying and her throat bobbing as the water went down. But I must have

49

passed whatever test he had set for me because he held out his hand and said, "Victor Wylde."

I hesitated, moved my hand that was holding the glass forward, withdrew it, and gave an embarrassed laugh before placing the glass on the drainer. My hand went out again, and withdrew again so I could wipe my palm on my skirt before I shook his hand.

"Victor?" I said. "Victor the vicar?" The words slipped out without thinking and he rolled his eyes as if he'd heard the joke many times before. "Sorry," I said. "Frances Jellico. How do you do?"

He must have already noticed my ringless fingers because he said, "Miss Jellico," with a nod of his head. "Are you one of the people camping out at Lyntons?" He fetched a handkerchief from a pocket hidden in his cassock and I had a sudden horror that he was going to use it to wipe his palm where we had shaken, but instead he dragged it around his neck and stuffed it back in his pocket.

"I'm writing a report on the follies and the garden buildings," I said.

"It was a Lynton we were burying. In fact, it was the last Lynton."

"I had no idea there were any still living."

"Well," he said. "There aren't any more. All of them are in the ground now." He reached up to the back of his neck, undid a hook or a button, and before I could turn away, pulled at his dog collar, the whole coming out from under his cassock with a sort of bib attached. I had never given much thought to the vestments of clergy, but this was so shocking he might as well have reached up his skirts and removed his underpants. I looked towards the sink, stumbling over something else to say.

"He . . . he . . . didn't have any relations?"

"She," the vicar said from behind me. There was the rustle of clothes being removed, his voice muffled while he took something over his head. "No relations, no friends as far as I could tell. It was just me and Mr. Lockyer, the gravedigger, and her of course. The last Dorothea Lynton was quite a character. Bloody cantankerous and forgetful. A difficult old bird." Coat hangers clanged together.

"My goodness," I said, not certain that vicars were supposed to gossip about their parishioners in that way. "Still, Mr. Wylde, she's gone to a better place, wouldn't you say?" It was a phrase I'd heard Mother use. I glanced over my shoulder. The vicar had removed his cassock, and underneath he

51

was wearing jeans and a long-sleeved tee shirt like the ones my father had owned, but unlike my father's this had a sunburst pattern across the front in pinks and yellows, tie-dye I thought they called it.

He raised his eyebrows. "If it makes you happier to think so. And Victor, please." He smiled, took the glass from where I had left it on the drainer, filled it from the tap, and bending over the sink, poured the water over the back of his white neck. "God, it's hot out there," he said, straightening. "Dorothea tried living at Lyntons again a few years back. She converted one of the attic bedrooms into a bathroom apparently so that some elderly woman she took with her could live up there, like a proper old-fashioned maid. I don't think they lasted a month. I'm surprised you're managing. Is there even electricity and running water?" He put his hand up to his hair behind his head and in a nifty movement slipped an elastic band off and onto his wrist so that his hair fell in fat waves around his face. I could only stare.

"It's very atmospheric." I had a strange need to defend the place.

"Dorothea Lynton believed she was done out of a fortune by the army or the government, or someone," he continued. Rivulets

52

of water were turning the pink streaks on his vest to mauve, and there were beads of water in his hair and beard. "She liked to tell anyone who would listen that she was swindled out of her possessions." He refilled the glass and handed it to me. This time I sipped at the water.

"And was she?"

"I'd say she had a few loose marbles, but you're living there. I've heard it's been gutted, hasn't it? Nothing left. I think the army patched the roof but that was about it. I can't imagine it's much fun staying in a house in ruins."

"But it could be such a lovely house when Mr. Liebermann does it up. And the grounds are —"

"Mr. Liebermann? The American who bought the place?" Victor closed a wardrobe door, tugged his vest out of his jeans, and when he saw me looking, gawping, he said, "Off duty for the afternoon." He slotted his prayer book into a space on a shelf. "My uncle used to tell me about the Christmas parties the Lyntons would have at the house every year before the Great War, for the villagers. Back when money wasn't an issue. A fir tree that reached the hall ceiling, music and dancing, as many mince pies as a man could eat. And a game of hide-and-seek for the village children. Apparently, they'd have to line up afterwards to receive a gift from Dorothea. They were probably expecting dolls or spinning tops. My uncle used to laugh when he described the expressions on their little faces as they were handed a ragged piece of tapestry, a polished stone, or a dried and pinned beetle and told it was a family heirloom." Victor shook his head. "Yes, a difficult old bird."

He walked me to the lych-gate and we shook hands once more. As he was turning away, almost as an afterthought, he said, "I hope you'll come to the service on Sunday with your friend. God knows I could do with a few new faces in the church." And before I could say that I didn't know who he meant, that like Dorothea Lynton I had no friends, he was heading across the churchyard towards a gap in the wall that led through to what must have been the vicarage garden.

The town was smaller than I had imagined: a baker's, grocer's, sweet shop, and fishmonger's, no cinema, no bookshop. The narrow pavements were full of women with baskets and children dawdling behind them, or women standing in small groups talking with ease about — I imagined — schools and shoes and the price of cabbages. What would it be like to have such a life? One that revolved around a husband and children. I didn't understand how it had happened to them; what trick of make-up or hairstyle or conversation had these women shared when they were in their late teens or early twenties that I had missed? It wasn't that I hankered after a husband or longed for children, just that these other lives seemed so alien, I couldn't imagine how they had come about.

There wasn't a tea shop in the town, but I passed the Harrow Inn, a public house which advertised sandwiches and coffee on a board outside, and realising how hungry I was, went in.

Two women stood at the entrance to the dining room, blocking the doorway. They glanced at me as I approached and then turned away without acknowledgement.

"Sandra told me she posted her letter last week," one of the women said. "We just need a few more to do the same."

The other, undoing the knot of her headscarf, tutted. "It's blazing out there." She lifted the scarf off her head and pushed up her flattened curls with the palm of her hand. A chemical smell of perming lotion came from her hair. "Christine said I should avoid direct sunlight for the first day or two. But I don't see how I can go on wearing this thing when it's so blazing out there."

"I could give you the gist of it, if you like," the first woman said, waiting for an answer from the woman with the new permanent wave. When none came, she said, "It is important."

"I heard he won't be around much longer anyway," the permanent wave woman said. "He's thinking about leaving."

"Good riddance."

I gave a small cough. The first woman glanced at me again, then turned back to her friend and said something I couldn't hear. She put her hand on her friend's arm, and the two of them bent their heads together, laughing. Friendship appeared so simple and yet so impossible.

"Excuse me?" This time they both looked at me square on, their laughter gone. "Are you waiting for a table?" I said.

"It's full," said the permed woman.

"Oh dear," I said. "I'm parched. As you were saying, it is dreadfully hot." I plucked at the front of my blouse and smiled.

The women paused and faced forward again. "I'll write a letter to the bishop tomorrow if you want," the permed woman said to her friend.

■ ■ ■ ■

I bought eggs, half a pound of bacon, butter, potatoes, and two bottles of chilled lemonade at the grocer's. I stopped by the sweet shop for a bag of Everton mints and at the fishmonger's I treated myself to a whole plaice which a boy in a bloody apron wrapped in white paper and a sheet from *The Times.* In the bakers I bought a loaf and, on a whim, three Chelsea buns, imagining popping downstairs to see if Cara and Peter would like to share them with me. Four shop people spoke to me with a *good morning* or a *thank you* as they handed over my items or change. I liked to count these things. More than seven was a good day.

I walked back the way I'd come, past the church, but I didn't see Victor. I stopped by the grave filled with fresh soil which was already turning lighter where the sun was drying it. There was no headstone yet of course — if there ever would be — nothing to say that the last of the Lyntons was lying under the ground. I was still thirsty and hungry too. Making certain nobody could see me, I drank half a bottle of lemonade and ate one of the Chelsea buns from the paper bag, although Mother used to say it was the worst of manners to eat or drink in the street. *If food is worth eating, it's worth eating properly.*

I went along the avenues of yews and limes with the sun again burning the top of my head. Beyond the house at the far end of the lake, the top of the mausoleum tower showed above the trees. I'd looked at it from the outside on my walk around the grounds, and although I had noticed that the lock was broken I hadn't gone in. When I reached the carriage turn, I put my shopping bag into the dry basin of the fountain in the shadow cast by the marble woman. I dithered over the buns and then took the bag with me, deciding I couldn't offer Peter and Cara the two that remained when there were three of us in the house. I ate another while I walked.

The mausoleum's door was ajar, the wood splintered around the lock. From an empty lobby I climbed the spiral stairs which clung to the distempered walls. At the top was a small landing, a wall ladder and a hatch that I pushed open with my shoulders and clambered through. The roof lantern was open on four sides and gave a view over the length of the lake, glittering in the sunshine and leading my eye to the bridge at the far end. Behind me was what remained of the

58

kitchen garden, brick-walled and overgrown, and another forty-five degrees took me to the house, glowing white in the afternoon sun like a boat sailing over a green sea, and set back from it, the orangery. A flash of sunlight caught the door as it opened and a figure, Cara I thought, came into sight. I couldn't make out any details or features, but I saw her perform a peculiar beckoning movement with her arm, her palm moving up and down in front of her, and it wasn't until she had repeated it for a third time that I realised she was throwing something into the air and catching it; throwing and catching.

The main room at the bottom of the tower contained three tombs: an early Lord Lynton and his first and second wives, buried either side of him, with carved stone gisants on top. At some point a fire must have been lit in the room, and one wall and the ceiling were scorched black. The recumbent lord was missing his nose and three of his fingers, broken off for relics, I assumed, by some soldier, turning the man into a leper. Worse damage had been done to the women. By the light coming through the open door I could make out that where their hearts might have been, holes had been punched into the stone. I peered into the dark cavities but couldn't see anything, and I wasn't brave enough to reach in with my hand. I said a prayer for all three and left.

When I returned to the front of the house I startled a cat, scrawny and ragged, which ran from me with something hanging from its mouth, and as I came to the fountain where I had left my shopping, I saw that the mangy thing had been at my bag. It had licked the sun-softened butter, dragged out the wrapped fish, ripping the newspaper, and taken everything except the severed head, leaving its two googly eyes staring up at me. The headline from the torn newspaper trailed in the grass: *Man Takes First Steps on the Moon.* I picked up a handful of gravel and threw it at the cat.

I spent the rest of that week walking the grounds, making a better map of the monuments: the mausoleum, the obelisk dedicated to a dead horse, the flint and shell grotto, the icehouse, and the bridge. I worked with methodical precision, enjoying the good weather and knowing I had the last days of July and the whole of August to produce my report. There were many other smaller pieces of statuary hidden in the foliage — an urn on a plinth inscribed for a concubine, the bottom half of a statue that

I suspected was Eros. Every day I went to the bridge hoping it would have changed, that a saviour might have come in the night and stripped away the plants, cleared the flotsam and jetsam from the water, and made it Palladian. I had another uneventful walk into the town. I closed my window when Peter and Cara were cooking, or I went for an evening stroll amongst the bats. The weather stayed warm and dry. I didn't meet them, my downstairs neighbours, I didn't hear or see any more arguments, and I worked hard at forgetting about the loose floorboard in my bathroom.

FOUR

The vicar — Victor, because of course I know it is him although his title is still slippery — comes once more to sit beside my bed and hold my hand, or he has always been here, waiting while I've been sleeping. Soon one of these sleeps will be my last. I will never again gaze up through the branches of a tree to see light moving between the leaves, never press hard against the bark until its pattern is imprinted on my skin. I will never again smell earth after rain, never hear the sound of water lapping against stone.

Victor asks me about regrets and whether my conscience is quiet, and then he whispers, "Tell me what really happened."

"What about the seal of the confessional?" I say, to see if I can catch him out; perhaps he has forgotten everything he learned.

"All priests have a duty to secrecy." He shifts his bottom to the edge of his chair. I would like to see if the fingers of his other hand are crossed. I know he is not everything he pretends to be.

"Even after death?" I say.

He nods, squeezes my hand. I can sense his anticipation, but it's not gossip he's asking for, only the truth. It is for my benefit that he wants to know.

"Even if it conflicts with the laws of this country?"

I once overheard them talking about me when I'd been here a year or so. Bolshie, that's what they called me, and I was pleased. The women here go one way or the other: angry and defiant, or compliant and meek. And surprisingly, considering the sort of person I was for my first thirty-nine years, I refused to be meek. A difficult old bird. Yes.

"Inviolate," Victor says, but a Nurse Assist is in the room. I will try to remember to ask him my questions another time, when we are alone.

I close my eyes. Will the last things I see be my comb, my reading glasses, my watch, the cigarette case, long empty? So few belongings, and of course this time I'll leave without any of them. Victor lets go of my hand and I am back in my attic bathroom at Lyntons.

■ ■ ■ ■

I decide to have a bath on Sunday morning, although the water that spurts from the clunking tap is brownish, and flakes of rust settle grittily at the bottom of the narrow tub. I dressed in my green skirt and jacket, and a blouse, and fashioned a hat from cardboard, covering it with a piece of yellow fabric I found in a cupboard. It smelled a little damp and the cloth had rust stains in places, but I was pleased with it — wide-brimmed with a domed crown. I wore it with pride as I walked between the trees along the avenue.

Victor greeted me at the church door. "I'm so pleased you came." He glanced over my shoulder. "You didn't bring your friend?"

"No," I said, "not today," still bemused.

I was one of the first to arrive. I always liked to be a little early — I thought it showed good manners. I dipped my head towards the altar and sat in an empty pew on the left. A family arrived and settled in a short way behind me, a boy of about seven whining and fidgeting, the mother shushing and hissing his name, *Christopher, Christopher.* An elderly couple shuffled in and sat in the pew opposite mine. I smiled at the woman and she glanced up at my hat. A few more families and other elderly people sat in the empty seats. As Victor walked along the aisle in his white surplice with his hair tied, I heard a commotion at the back: some jostling and a few loud whispers. I turned and saw Cara squeezing people along in order to make space for her at the end of a row. Her hair was untethered, dark against a long yellow dress, a spot of sunshine on the colourless church walls. I turned to face the sanctuary before she spotted me.

There were the usual prayers, a hymn I didn't know well sung to an out-of-tune organ. Victor climbed the steps to the pulpit. He'd seemed rather blunt when I'd met him in the vestry, or at least irritated by his parishioners, but now he was brooding, with long gaps between his words. I kept my head lowered while willing him to speed up, to show some enthusiasm. He mumbled about wombs and conception and moral corruption from the instant we're formed, and then drifted off into something I couldn't hear. I strained to listen; I was interested in sinners. I had always thought the Church too ready to hand out absolution, only worrying about keeping up the quota of those who achieved heaven.

There was another prayer or two and then we were straight on to Holy Communion. I didn't go up. I wanted to get a feel for the church first, to see how things were done. The line beside me was shorter than I had been used to in London, half a dozen people at most. They knelt before the altar and Victor moved along the row from left to right. "Body of Christ," he said and presented the wafer. "Blood of Christ," he said, sounding bored. A small boy moved along beside him holding out a chalice. "Body of Christ," Victor said again. "Blood of Christ," he intoned and then paused. Cara in her flowing yellow dress was before him. Victor looked down at her and then at me and I knew then she was the friend he had meant. I couldn't see her face but I could see her shoulders shaking, her head and hair bobbing, and I thought at first that she was laughing. I was shocked that she could face the altar and laugh.

"Body of Christ," Victor said. Her head went forward and although I couldn't see, I imagined her opening her mouth, sticking out her tongue ready for the wafer. The vicar moved aside to let the boy hold the chalice up to her lips. The woman kneeling to Cara's left, in a woollen skirt and jacket not unlike mine but pink instead of green, edged sideways knowing something was about to happen. I thought I heard Cara moan when the boy tipped the cup, and I realised she hadn't been laughing, she had been crying. I closed my own mouth, swallowed as though my mouth were hers. Another sob shook her, a convulsion similar to those I had seen in her bathroom, and her shoulders rounded as she coughed with her mouth shut, choked almost, and coughed again, turning her head to avoid hitting the vicar or the altar boy, turning towards the woman in the woollen suit. Cara's mouth opened and wine and wet wafer sprayed out, droplets of scarlet speckling the pink fabric, like a cut, pumping. The woman cried out, struggling to move away from Cara, pushing into the kneeling man on her other side, toppling the person beyond him. It might have been funny if Cara hadn't let out a wail and grabbed at the woman's skirt, dipping her head and pulling the fabric to her mouth, latching on and sucking at the spilled drops.

"No, no," Victor said, but he took a step back, his expression one of horror as if Cara were biting into the woman's leg and drawing blood.

The woman tugged at her skirt, yanking it

until Cara was forced to let go. Cara staggered up, her long yellow dress nearly tripping her, and turned to face the rest of us: the couple with their walking sticks waiting to receive Communion, the handful sitting in the pews. I saw Cara's stricken face, her smudged lipstick and mascara running down her cheeks. She pushed her way through, and as she passed me I put out my hand. I don't know what I would have said or done if she'd stopped because my fingers didn't touch her skin; she didn't even see me.

"Mi dispiace," I thought I heard her say as she went. "I'm sorry." The elderly couple separated to let her pass, all of us watching this exotic and fantastic creature.

I went after her, but when I reached the vestibule she was already passing through the lych-gate. On the other side of the churchyard wall a blue car was waiting. Its engine was running and I could smell the exhaust fumes as though the driver had known a quick getaway would be required. Cara got into the passenger seat, the door closed, and the car drove off.

After the service, outside the church, huddles of people formed and re-formed. I hovered for a while but the little snippets of conversation I heard included *Roman Cath-*

olic, Lyntons, and *disgusting.* Pressing my hat on my head, I set off around the church and was through the back gate when I heard my name called. Victor, still in his vestments, was standing in the grass holding a glass of water.

We went to sit on the bottom lip of one of the chest tombs in an overgrown corner, hiding from the last stragglers. "Sorry it's not tea," he said. "It's meant to be tea and biscuits after a service, isn't it? But I just can't face that lot, not today." He passed me the glass and leaned his elbows on his knees. "All the sniping about flowers and jumble sales. Besides, they were only hanging around in order to say *I told you so* for letting a Catholic come to a Church of England service . . ."

"I hope the stain will come out," I said.

". . . and spilling the blood of Christ." He sighed.

"Salt would have done the trick." I drank some water.

"Catholics, as I understand it, think the wine *is* the blood of Christ. Not just a representation."

"But you have to be quick."

"Hence all the sucking of the skirt."

"I heard too that white wine poured on top will cancel out the red."

"Your friend, Cara . . ."

"But I don't see how that would work, not really."

"She's a bit of a liability, isn't she?"

"She isn't my friend," I said. "In fact, we haven't met."

"Maybe you should keep it that way," he said, and my surprise must have shown because then he added, "Sorry. I can't say I know her, not really, but there's something . . ." He trailed off. "She came to me asking for confession."

"From a vicar in the Church of England?" I said, shocked also that he was telling me. "Although since she's Italian . . . Catholic . . ."

He stared at me with curiosity. "We can offer confession, you know, it's just we don't do it in a little booth with a curtain and a grille." He took the glass and gulped some water. I imagined sitting opposite him in the vestry and laying everything bare. Did confessing our sins appease anything? I wondered what penance he had doled out for Cara, and I slid Mother's locket, which I was still wearing around my neck, along its chain. I didn't have her earrings on because I had forgotten to retrieve the lost one after I had put back the floorboard the second time.

"Confession is open to *all* my congregation," Victor said, and I lowered my eyes. He sighed again. "I'm not confident that I helped your friend though." I didn't bother to correct him this time. "Cara would more likely benefit from a visit to the doctor than a priest."

"Is that what you told her?"

He looked at me. "No, of course not." After a moment he said, "The bishop is sure to hear about this: wasting the wine, the cost of a good woollen suit, Catholics wailing during the service. There will be more complaints." He pulled at his hair and it fell loose around his face.

"More?" I said.

"A few members of my congregation think I should be more spirited in my delivery and like to report their opinion upward." His fingers played with the elastic band and the little ball of black hairs that was knotted around it.

"Your sermon was rather . . . subdued," I said.

"Subdued, yes," he said. He drank.

We were silent for a while, regarding the church tucked around with green, and I tried to work out what he was thinking from the way he sat: a kind of resignation that everything would go wrong if it hadn't

71

already, an apathy that nothing could change for the better. Once, a couple of months ago, I would have agreed with him, but now, watching the tiny flies settle on the flat heads of yarrow that had spread amongst the graves and how its white flowers blended with the lichen that bloomed across the stones, I held the possibility that I could become anyone. The only sound was the distant purr of a lawnmower. "Such a heavenly place to be buried," I said.

"As you start your journey to a better place?" he asked, remembering our conversation in the vestry.

"You don't think so?"

He tilted his head back against the tomb and closed his eyes. "How many would you say there were?"

"I'm sorry?"

"How many people in the congregation today?"

I thought for a moment. "Thirty, thirty-five."

"Twenty-nine," he said. "I counted from the pulpit. Every Sunday there's fewer. And there's fewer marriages, christenings. Funerals, however, are on the up. I keep waiting for the call from the bishop to say that the parish isn't sustainable."

"It must be busy at Christmas and Easter

72

at least."

"Maybe," he said. He poured the rest of his water out onto the grass and stood. "I should get going. No doubt someone has something burning to say about the flowers or the next jumble sale."

"If you ever . . ." — I hesitated — ". . . want to come to Lyntons, I could show you around." I rushed the words.

"Thank you," he said. "Perhaps." He was already walking away.

I spent the rest of that Sunday reading in my room with the window open until, when I was drifting off to sleep at about three o'clock in the afternoon, I heard someone calling, "Hello! Hello? Are you at home?" It took me a moment to realise the woman's voice — an English one, upper-class — was coming from outside, and when I stuck my head out of the window, there below me was Cara. She smiled, a different face from the one in church — the lipstick gone and her eyes clear — but she was wearing the same yellow dress. She was leaning out over her windowsill at an alarming angle and twisting her head to look up, her hair falling in a wedge. "Hello," she said for a third time. We were sixteen feet apart. "Frances, isn't it? How do you do? Peter and I . . ."

73

She smiled again and glanced back into the room behind her. "Get off, Peter," she said, laughing, letting go of the sill with one arm and falling forward, but not seeming to care. My insides lurched and I almost went to lean out too, as if I could catch her before she fell. "Would you like to come for dinner this evening? I'm Cara by the way." She turned once more into the room. "Shhh," she said to the unseen Peter.

"I thought you were Italian," I said.

"Italian? No." She sounded surprised. "You'll come then?"

"That's very kind of you, but —"

"Oh, please don't say no. I've had boring old Peter and no one else for weeks. We're having *tagliatelle al limone* and I've made enough pasta to feed an army." She pronounced *tagliatelle al limone* and *pasta* like an Italian.

I'd never eaten pasta but I knew it was served in dark Soho restaurants, the kind I'd walked past but never dared enter. Red candles glowed from wine bottles on tables set for two. Mother would have said it was nasty foreign food, but I was hungry and tired of the tinned meals I was making do with.

Seeing me hesitate, Cara said, "And I want to know everything about you, since

74

you're our new neighbour."

"Thank you," I said, my stomach overriding my unease. "I'd love to."

Cara looked back into her room. "See?" she said to Peter. "I told you she'd say yes." And I wondered what they'd been saying about me, why Peter had thought I would refuse their invitation, and what I could talk about when they wanted to know everything. I had nothing I could tell.

"Good," she said to me. "Seven thirty? It's a little late for Peter but we can't let him eat at six like a workman or at four for that matter, because then it would be nursery tea and we'd have to have boiled eggs and toast." I saw Peter's hands on her waist tickling, and she screamed with delight. I didn't tell her that at four I'd always had to take in the tray with Garibaldi biscuits on a plate and a pot of tea for Mother.

I washed and put on the same skirt and blouse that I'd worn to church. It was my outfit for formal occasions: a second cousin's christening, a meeting with the editor of a journal. There weren't any mirrors in my rooms, and although I'd lost a little weight since Mother had died, I knew I was heavy, wide-hipped and big-bosomed, as she had been before she became ill. Mother though, in the years when we had lived with my father in our grand house in Notting Hill, had been tall with long legs and an elegant neck, and had carried her extra weight well. I changed out of the skirt and blouse, and instead put on Mother's evening dress, which I had brought with me. I recalled my father crouching with his arms wrapped around me while we watched her descend the sweeping stairs, holding the fabric of the dress between thumb and forefinger to keep it clear of her feet, stepping so slowly it seemed to me that she floated. The dress had a short velvet cape and a velvet belt with a velvet buckle, which nipped in her waist. I remembered how much I had wanted that dress, to own it, to put it on and to walk down the stairs in it. I ran out of my father's arms towards her, and she bent down to sweep me up and then I was squashed between them, between the velvet and the weave of my father's suit; the smell of her perfume and the feel of his moustache against my cheek as he kissed me goodbye remaining long after they had left for the evening, leaving me with the housekeeper.

Now, the dress rucked and creased itself around my stomach, and as much as I tugged the sides together, it gaped, surprised I was attempting to wear it. I removed it, smoothed the wrinkles as I laid it on my bed, and squeezed myself into Mother's underwear, which had also come with me. Her girdle dug into the pudding of my stomach and my breasts rolled over the top of her thick brassiere. I attached her black stockings to the suspenders, stretching the nylon to transparency around my thighs. It was impossible to take a full breath with everything on, but the dress's zip closed, and the hook and eye met. The underwear snagged my skin when I moved, as though Mother were following me around, and even when I was standing, a ring of fat circled my stomach in between the brassiere and the girdle, like a child's inflatable swimming ring jammed around my waist. It would have to do.

In the bathroom I put on the one Hattie Carnegie earring lying beside the talcum powder and thought about what was under my feet. I lifted the skirt of the dress and, holding on to the sink, dropped to my knees; as quietly as I could, I lifted out the board and laid it on the floor beside the gap. I couldn't resist; I looked again through the lens.

Peter, wearing his pyjamas, sat on the edge

of the bath, which shone where the water had been drained, while Cara, in her underwear, bent over him. She pressed his cheek with one hand so that he tilted his head away from her, and with the other she scraped a razor along the side of his face. After every stroke she moved back to wave her hand in the soapy water that filled the sink. He was motionless, only his eyes following her while she worked. Each of her movements, the press of her fingers on the skin of his face, the upward slice of the blade, was precise and focussed. I'd had no idea that the act of shaving could be so intimate.

I drew away and let go of the breath I hadn't known I was holding. Efficiently, busily, as if spying on my neighbours were a normal and regular occurrence, I picked up the earring, put the board back as silently as I had removed it, and raised myself up.

FIVE

At 7:28 I was ready and going down the back stairs, which circled around a rusted dumb waiter, then along a short passageway, and through a servants' door padded with green baize which divided the known from the foreign. Beyond it was the landing of the grand staircase of an imperial design with two flights of stairs that descended to a half landing, where they joined and switched back on themselves. A void soared upward here, double height past the walls of the bedrooms and attic to a glass cupola. Magnificent, as Peter had said. Every time I stood there it lifted me and at the same time emphasised my insignificance, a type of exaltation I never achieved in church. The last of the sun shone through the stained-glass panes, lighting the staircase and turning the walls, streaked with brown where the rain had got in, rosy. I had explored only a little of the interior of the house in the week since I'd arrived, scurrying down the grand staircase, anticipating that it would come out in an entrance hall, but discovering that the bottom flight ended in a dim hallway that ran north to south through the house. The unexpected layout unnerved me, as if I had been spun around without knowing it, and I'd run back up the stairs towards the light.

On the middle floor, the wide hallway leading off the top landing had an arched and coffered ceiling and was decorated with what once must have been white plaster mouldings on duck-egg-blue paintwork. The blue was all but gone, lumps of the plaster were missing, and the floor crunched with the debris. Several holes as big as heads showed the wall's lath insides. On my left there was an odd blank wall, and two closed doors on my right. I went beyond them, past an arched niche, empty now but once probably containing a statue, a muse perhaps, who had been tipped from her pedestal and smashed, the head taken home as a souvenir of war. After this there were open doors showing high-ceilinged rooms beyond, stuffed with broken army-issue beds and upended mattresses, everything piled together. Bird droppings and feathers coated it all, and through the twisted metal I caught glimpses of the drive and avenue on one side, and the parkland on the other.

Calculating the location of my attic room, together with where Cara had talked to me from her window, I went back to the first closed door. I stood there gathering courage, smoothing the skirt of my dress over the girdle, standing straighter, running my tongue over my front teeth. I took a breath and knocked. I waited, looked down at my chest and adjusted the dress again, then checked my watch, 7:32. I knocked once more, a little louder. Another couple of minutes went by in which I worried that I had got the time wrong, that she hadn't meant this evening, or that they had forgotten. I dithered, considered going back up to my rooms and pretending I had also forgotten, but started worrying they would be offended. I tapped again. At least I could say I had knocked three times.

I heard someone running, something falling over, followed by a curse, and then Peter flung open the door. He was still in his pyjamas. "Oh bloody hell," he said when he saw me, and his hands went up. "Is it that time already?"

"I'm too early," I said, heat shooting over my face. "Or another night." My words came out in their own order, nonsensical.

81

"Another night?"

"I could come another night."

"God, no," Peter said. "It has to be now. Look at it all!" He opened the door wide and put out an arm. The enormous room must have once been the salon — the space where the Lyntons would have received their guests in the original Georgian house. Now it was almost empty. The only decorations, if you could call them that, were the strips of pasta draped over half a dozen lengths of string that ran from high above the three great windows to the opposite wall. The effect was that of a laundry, ivory stockings drying for an army of thin-legged women. But it was the light which made the room beautiful. It poured through the open sashes, splashing the floor with amber oblongs, turning it to honey.

A door on the left opened, their bedroom I presumed, and Cara stuck her head out, her dark crazy hair the first thing I saw. "Frances! Two minutes! I'll be out in two minutes."

Peter plucked at his pyjamas. "We'll be with you in two ticks. Make yourself at home." He disappeared into their bedroom and I heard talking, the voices too quiet for me to make out what was being said.

I stood in the middle of the room and

looked around. I averted my eyes from the door opposite their bedroom, which stood ajar and must have led through to the bathroom. An electric stove, similar to mine, sat with its back to the wall, and next to it was an old refrigerator. A long wooden board had been placed on top of four upturned packing cases made taller with books, to create a long table, with two more packing cases and a stool tucked under it for seats. The surface was cluttered with newspapers, ashtrays, notebooks, and a typewriter, and at the "kitchen" end there was a heap of dirty dishes and a loaf of bread which had been cut straight onto the table. The floorboards were bare and there were no other chairs or sofas, no rugs or pictures on the walls. I tried not to look at the debris on the table but noted the fact that aside from the pasta there was no sign of any dinner preparation. I went to one of the windows and gazed out at the parkland and the hangers in the distance. Again, I smoothed my dress over my stomach to try to make the bulge between brassiere and girdle disappear.

Ten minutes later Peter and Cara emerged from their bedroom, apologising for their lateness, blaming each other and laughing. Cara came towards me like an old friend, her arms out wide. She hadn't changed her dress from the one she'd been wearing when she invited me to dinner and which she'd worn to church, but she'd hung three bead necklaces around her neck. Her hair was still loose, framing her face, and her feet bare, the nails still painted green. Peter was wearing a baggy untucked shirt and flared jeans. I grew hot with the thought that I'd ever imagined my floor-length dress with its velvet cape and belt, thirty years out of date, would be suitable to wear to dinner with my new neighbours.

"I'm sorry it's taken us so long to meet," Cara said. She took me by the shoulders and leaned in as if to kiss me on the lips. I stiffened but at the last minute she embraced me.

It was new and shocking in 1969, Cara's hugging. Now I know people do it all the time; I see them sometimes here in this place, when one girl is coming on shift and another leaving. Women embracing women, women embracing men, men embracing women; I wonder how they know when it's going to happen. What tiny movement, what piece of body language that I have always missed, means they are about to put their arms around each other? And do men embrace men? In this place, I have no one to embrace and no one comes to embrace me.

Cara smelled of citrus, sharp yet sweet. Her hair pressed into my face, springy and not quite as soft as it had appeared. When she released me she said, "Come and sit. It really is the most wonderful evening." She led me by the hand to a window seat and sat down. "Did you ever see sunsets like the ones at Lyntons?" In the distance, the cedars were hazy and the cows had gathered beneath them. I lowered myself onto the edge of the seat, aware of the girdle constricting my hips. I folded my arms across the fat ring that grew from my middle. Warm air carrying the smell of grass came in through the window.

"Sorry about the tin cup. We're rather short on glasses," Peter said, handing Cara and me drinks. His feet, poking out from his flared trousers, were bare.

Cara stretched out on the window seat, her back against one side of the frame, her feet up on the other. The flimsy material of the yellow dress fell down over her thighs, exposing her knees, and she didn't adjust it. "They say we're in for a hot August, and that's fine by me." Cara clinked her cup on mine.

"It's very kind of you to invite me to dinner." I hoped this might prompt one of them to say they should start cooking but Cara didn't move, and Peter, leaning on the wall beside us, took a sip of his own drink. I tried it too; I thought it might be a martini, very strong. We'd kept sherry in the cupboard at home in London, and as Mother had become more bedridden I'd sometimes taken a swig to brace myself for my nursing duties and as a kind of compensation or gift I allowed myself when I left the bedroom and retreated to the kitchen.

"We should have got you down much sooner," Peter said.

"I love the sunshine," Cara said. "To have its heat on my skin." She lengthened her neck and tipped back her head. Her voice was upper-class, English girls' school I thought, but with a trace of something else. She seemed a different Cara to the one I'd created in my head from the glimpses I'd seen. That one had been Italian, Catholic, hot-headed, quick to argue. This one was languid, sleepy, not worried about what anyone thought of her.

"Yes," I said and took another sip, trying to think of some topics of conversation. Cara began to speak just as I said, "I thought you were Italian," immediately realising I'd already told her that. I drank again to hide my face, glad the cups were large.

"I grew up in Ireland," Cara said. "Anglo-Irish parents. Peter arranged Italian lessons for me. It's such a beautiful language, don't you think? I'm not proficient, though. It's just that I can do the accent."

"And the swearing," Peter said, winking and taking a packet of cigarettes from his shirt pocket. "But —"

"But I'm not very good at normal conversation," she finished for him, smiling.

Peter pulled a cigarette from the packet with his lips, lighting it with a silver lighter.

"I can't speak any languages," I said.

"How about English?" Peter said with a smile.

"Oh, yes. English. Of course." I looked down.

Cara took the cigarette from Peter's lips. He held the packet out to me and I shook my head. "No, thank you," I said. "I don't smoke."

"It's a terrible habit," Cara said.

"I can't speak any other languages either," Peter said, covering my embarrassment. He lit another cigarette for himself and they both smoked without speaking, not seeming worried about the silence.

"Have you been here long, in England, I

87

mean?" I asked.

"We've just arrived," Cara said. "We were four and a half years in Scotland."

"Scotland?" I said at the same time as Peter said, "Well, that was after . . ."

"Yes, Scotland," Cara said.

"How lovely," I said. "Sorry. After?" I would have liked to step outside the room, knock on the door, and start again.

"Oh, you know," he said.

I didn't know; I had lost the thread of the conversation.

Peter, still leaning on the wall beside us with his cigarette in the corner of his mouth and his eyes squinting from the smoke, put his fingers into Cara's hair near her scalp and worked through the curls to the ends, teasing out the strands while she looked out of the window. They seemed so much in love. I tried to keep hold of what I'd seen in the church that morning, the shouts I'd heard coming from these rooms, my view through the judas hole of Cara's sobbing, and Victor's warning, but these impressions were overtaken by the reality of the people in front of me.

"Here we are at Lyntons," Cara said. "Sitting on this window seat, meeting our new neighbour." She raised a hand up behind her head and Peter took it, squeezed it, and let it go.

"And you as well," Cara said.

"Me too?" I asked.

"Here you are, come to survey the gardens." She twisted around to look at Peter, who had pushed himself off from the wall and was crossing the room to the kitchen area. "Isn't that what you said, Peter?"

"Sorry, yes," I said, my own voice inhibiting me like an echo on a telephone line. "I'm writing a report on the follies and other garden architecture for Mr. Liebermann."

"A report?" Peter stubbed out his half-smoked cigarette on a plate left on the table and took a battered saucepan from the fridge. "Bloody hell, I was planning on jotting down a few points about the house on a scrap of paper. You'd better not show me up." He pointed at me and filled his tin cup from the saucepan.

"Oh dear," I said. "I wouldn't want to do that. I mean —" I shifted and the stiff underwear creaked, a loud awkward noise which none of us commented on.

"Frances," Cara said. "He's teasing you." She laughed, moved her legs, and I saw a flash of snowy thigh. "Peter makes fun of everything. You'll have to get used to it." The significance of these words wasn't lost on me: she had already decided we would be seeing more of each other; they were already planning on inviting me to their rooms another time. Maybe we would be friends. Maybe this was how it was done.

Peter returned to the window with the saucepan in one hand and his cup in the other.

"Isn't that right? Always teasing," she said, smiling at him, tilting her chin upward. He bent from the waist with his arms out sideways like an actor taking a bow, keeping the cup and saucepan horizontal, and he kissed her long and full on the lips. I was transfixed by these two people. When they drew apart, Cara's eyes stayed closed as though she wanted the kiss to last for longer, but Peter stood and looked at me before I glanced into my cup, surprised to see it was empty. I thought he looked at me as a man looks at a woman, not as one might look at a daughter, or a student, or a library-card holder, or a writer of obscure historical articles, and I liked it.

"Another martini, Frances?" Peter held up the saucepan and poured some into my cup. "It won't keep until tomorrow, martini goes off very quickly."

"Really?"

Peter winked, and Cara rolled her eyes.

He sloshed martini into her cup as well. "Seriously though, I don't think Liebermann expects much, just a few words of what's what. Have you managed to get to the bridge yet?"

"I have," I said, the disappointment coming back. "Unfortunately I don't think it's anything special, although it's hard to see, there's a great deal of vegetation."

"What were you hoping for? Surely not Palladian or anything like that?"

I dipped my head, drank. "No, no," I said. "Not that. I was only hoping for something nice."

"And it's not even nice?" he said. "Oh dear."

"Well . . . I suppose it's pretty, in a bucolic way."

"There might be something about it in the library," Peter said. "I don't know exactly what's in there. I haven't examined the books in any detail."

"There's a library at Lyntons?" I said, excitedly.

"South-west corner, ground floor. It's had extensive water damage and no doubt any valuable books will have gone already, but you might find a mention of it in any that are left."

"You should take Frances on a tour of the

house," Cara said.

"If you'd like, Frances," Peter said over his shoulder, going back across the room with the saucepan.

Cara was suddenly animated. "And Frances must show us the bridge. We'd love to see it. I still haven't been to the lake. Peter could dip his toes in the water and I could make us a picnic. It's stifling up here in the middle of the day. Why don't we go tomorrow? What do you say?"

Her enthusiasm was daunting; I wanted to believe in it but an old need to protect myself from rejection clutched at me. "I'm afraid I haven't much food to contribute to a picnic," I said. "I was planning on going into town tomorrow to pick up a few things."

"I'm sure we've plenty," Peter said. "Cara seems to go there for something every other day. Costs me a fortune." He swung open the fridge to show the shelves crammed with food. The sight of it reminded me that my stomach was sloshing with alcohol and there was still no sign of dinner.

"That's decided then," she said. "Oh, look." She pointed out of the window to the terrace below us. The scrawny ginger cat was lying on the stone flags. "It's Serafina."

"That's the cat which ate my fish," I said.

"It made off with a whole plaice."

"I don't think Serafina would do something like that, she's very friendly."

Even from a distance I could see that the back of the cat's head was nearly bald.

"Don't you think it would be nice to be a cat?" Cara said. "Never having to think about cooking, or happiness, or what's going to happen tomorrow. You can come and go as you want. You don't have to answer to anyone."

I wasn't persuaded that it was that simple — there wouldn't usually be plaice lying around when you were hungry — but I made a quiet noise of agreement.

"We had a ginger cat when we were in Ireland," Cara continued. "He was Peter's really, though, not mine." I looked over at Peter, who was searching through packets of food in a box beside the stove. "Peter liked him to sleep in our bed, stretched out between us like a little furry man."

I didn't think it sounded hygienic.

"It used to irritate me, having the cat in the bed. Even though I loved him."

"Because of the fleas?" I said.

"He didn't have fleas. He was a good clean cat. I don't know why I was irritated. Because I wanted to be alone in the bed with Peter, because I couldn't love him as much as he needed to be loved, or because he was different from other cats. I would chuck him out and then he'd have this expression on his little face and I'd feel so guilty. It's all they ever want; all any of us ever wants. Look at me, look at me, love me, love me." She gave a small laugh. "Serafina! Serafina!" she called out of the window, but the cat didn't look up.

"What happened to him?"

"Who?"

"Your cat."

She paused to think about it. "One day he was there and the next he wasn't. I think he was a stray."

"A feral cat? He wasn't your pet?"

"Pet? Yes, I suppose he was our pet, but free to go when he wanted."

"You must have missed him," I said.

She turned back towards the room and in a louder voice said, "Now Frances, I want you to tell us everything."

"Everything?" I turned my head too fast and the room spun. As I took another sip of the martini — which was now delicious — I thought about drinking more slowly and wondered again when they would start dinner, and then, with another swallow, it was no longer important.

"About you," she said. "What you like doing, who your parents are, where you live, everything."

"Weren't you living in London?" Peter called from the kitchen area.

They both looked at me, waiting for my answer. "Yes," I said. "With my mother. She . . . she passed away last month." I touched the locket around my neck and Mother's brassiere dug into my skin.

"I'm sorry," Peter said. His hands rose and fell.

"I'd been caring for her for some time."

"That must have been very difficult," Cara said.

"And your father?" Peter asked.

Had anyone ever been that interested?

"He left her . . . us. When I was ten, for someone else. We haven't stayed in touch. In fact, I haven't seen him since."

Had I ever said this much about myself?

"Oh, Frances," Cara said, putting her hand on my arm. "That must have been dreadful. I know what it's like to lose both parents."

Whether from the alcohol or the sympathy, my vision blurred.

"We shouldn't have asked," she said, although it was Peter who had done the asking. She squeezed my arm. "I'm sorry."

"Yours have passed away too?" I asked her.

She shrugged and said, "Peter still has both of his, squirrelled away in Devon or Dorset." Her voice was low, whispering a secret. "I think he's embarrassed by them — their cheeks are too ruddy, or they look too much like their dogs."

I stared at her, shocked, until she laughed and I realised she was joking.

Peter, coming back to us, said, "I have to admit that when Liebermann telephoned to offer me the job and told me you would be looking over the gardens, I was expecting a man." He held out a hand in which he'd placed a small pile of peanuts. I hadn't been offered peanuts from someone else's palm before, but I took one. He held out his hand again and I took a few more.

"*Frances* and *Francis*," I said. "*E*-s or *i*-s. It happens often. There was a big muddle when I went up to Oxford, which was nearly very awkward. Luckily I ended up in the right place."

"You were at Oxford?" Peter said. "I don't suppose it was St. Hilda's, was it? Did you know a Mallory Swift?"

Before I had time to explain, Cara threw the last of her cigarette out of the window, moved her legs around me, and stood up in one fluid motion as Serafina might have uncurled from a sleep. "I should start dinner," she said. "You must be starving, Frances."

I took a gulp of my martini. "Well . . ." I laughed loudly, and looking down saw a green olive rocking against the enamel of my cup like a sunken eye, a tiny piece of pimento for a pupil.

He must have understood Cara's cue because Peter didn't ask me any more about Oxford or Mallory Swift, but took the empty place beside me on the windowsill where Cara had been sitting and leaned in towards me. He smelled of aftershave, a clean fresh smell, and I remembered how he had inclined his head while Cara shaved him. "It sounds like you've had a difficult time. You should just enjoy the summer here, with Cara and me." He reached out and touched the back of my hand with the tips of his fingers. They were on my skin for an instant, but it was as though one of the bones in my hand had been healed by Peter's touch; a bone I hadn't been aware was broken.

"I'm starting below stairs and working my way up," Peter said, turning his fork in his pasta until it caught two strands. He lifted his hand, his fork making circles in the air while he spoke, the tagliatelle remaining coiled. "It's labyrinthine down there — storeroom after storeroom, and larders, pantries, and goodness knows what else. It's all below ground, which means there's no natural light. The kitchen's there too, and acres of wine cellars." He lifted his cup. We had moved on from martinis. "Luckily I don't think Liebermann gives a damn about what's there."

"Surely the history of Lyntons is of interest to him," I said. "I thought all Americans liked English history." My hands and feet buzzed with the alcohol, and my cheeks were warm. I was enjoying the feeling.

"Only if they can make money from it." Peter poured more wine.

"He's not hoping to sell Lyntons on, is he? I thought he was planning on emigrating here, renovating the house and garden," I said.

"Liebermann? Emigrate?" Peter's mouth was full.

"Isn't that why he's employing us? To assess what's here and what needs doing before he moves in?"

"Not bloody likely." Peter waved his fork. His lips were shiny with oil. "He wants us to survey Lyntons so he can ship the interesting pieces across the Atlantic. When I say the interesting pieces, what I mean is the valuable pieces." The fork waved, conducting his words. "The fireplaces, the grand staircase, fountain, orangery, whole rooms, all going piecemeal, sold off to American collectors." He spun some more pasta around the tines of the fork. "I imagine Liebermann was hoping that the bridge would turn out to be Palladian. It'd be worth a fortune." He put the tagliatelle in his mouth and touched his lip with a knuckle where a smudge of lemon sauce gleamed. "Sorry," he said, eating. "I thought you'd realised."

Cara was dabbing with her fingertips at a patch of salt spilled on the table. "Oh Peter," she said, "now you've upset our guest with all your talk about the house." She turned to me. "Is the pasta all right for you, Frances?" She lifted her right hand over her left shoulder as though stretching, but a tiny sprinkle of the salt dropped behind her.

"It's delicious," I said, picking up my fork again, my words running together.

"I get the flour sent from a little Italian shop in London. It's impossible to buy good pasta here in the middle of nowhere."

"Isn't she a wonder?" Peter said, reaching out to squeeze her hand. "She taught herself how to cook from books."

"And Dermod," she said. "He taught me the basics. I asked at the grocer's in town whether they had pasta and they showed me tins of alphabet shapes in tomato sauce. In Glasgow, I could get anything and everything Italian. Oh, the ice cream. Do you remember the ice cream, Peter?" She put her elbows on the table. "I'm going to order a food parcel with olives, parmigiano, and flour, every month," she said. She offered me the basket with the last piece of bread in it and I took it, though it might not have been polite.

"See how much she bloody costs me," Peter said, smiling.

"Isn't it worth it for the dinners, though?"

"Is that where you were living, in Glasgow?" I said, smearing the bread in the lemon sauce left on my plate as my hosts had done.

"For a while, and then in a castle beside a loch, and before that another country house. Goodness that castle was cold, wasn't it, Peter, but at least it had chairs, something more than army beds, and it had a few glasses." She held out her tin cup. "We were meant to be renting a cottage in town but —"

"It comes down to money in the end," Peter said.

Cara put down her fork and wiped at her mouth with a tea towel that had been shoved along the table with the rest of the things to clear space for us to eat. She stood and stacked our plates.

"All the houses we've lived in have been pretty ruinous," Peter said. "Or if they were watertight and upright, they were scheduled for bulldozing anyway. It makes me want to weep when I think of what we've lost."

In their bathroom, after more wine and my first taste of grappa, which Peter had pressed upon me, I stood with my forehead against the cool wall, filling my lungs with air. Beneath my feet the floor lurched. I moved sideways from door to basin, keeping my palms in contact with the wall, knowing that if I were to let go, the ground would rise up again. I bent over the basin and turned on the cold tap, which spluttered and spat until a steady flow came out, then I cupped my hands under it and sank my head into the pool. Feeling a little better, I lowered myself to the floor and rested the back of my head against the wall, hoping I would be able to make it through Cara and Peter's sitting room and up the stairs to my own bed without making a fool of myself. And at the thought of my own rooms, I looked up. The bathroom ceiling was scooped out and the inside of the dome was painted with dark clouds, menacing and beautiful. A stormy sky scudding inside a giant teacup. Grey plumes puffed outwards in concentric circles from a black centre; something had exploded, the detonation point a central glass eye looking down on the room, on me, curving at the perimeters and staring back.

It was Cara who came to find me with my head over their toilet bowl, undigested pasta and a foul red liquid retching out of me, too sick to be embarrassed. She gathered my hair together and held it away from my face as I vomited, rubbing my back, and handed me a cold damp cloth and a glass of water when I was able to sit up. It was Cara who helped me stand and led me through their empty room — Peter must have gone to bed — back along the hallway and through the baize door, while I apologised and she told me I mustn't worry, that next time she would make me eat more, she would cook earlier. She sat me on my bed, took off my shoes, and tried to undo the dress but I flapped her away, thanked her, and told her I could manage. I wasn't so drunk that I had forgotten I was wearing Mother's underwear.

In the morning, my tongue was dry and there was a pain behind my eyes when I moved my head. Later, a noise from outside the attic door woke me, and when I was well enough to rouse myself to open it I found an envelope with *Frances* written on it in ink, the handwriting elaborate and scrolled. I kept the note that was inside, tucking it into the pocket of one of my suitcases. If someone had asked me why, I might have said that it was the first letter I'd received from a friend, but what I would have meant was that it was a letter from my first real friend.

Dear Frances,
Peter sends up his apologies, and hopes you won't hold yesterday evening against him. Please for goodness' sake, don't do anything hastily, I can imagine how much you must be hurting, just stay in bed for a while.

Yours,
Cara

I looked again in the envelope. At the bottom were two white tablets and, printed on each, the word *Aspirin*.

SIX

I swallowed the pills Cara had given me with some water and, for the first time since I was a child and ill with tonsillitis, went back to bed.

I must have slept because someone was calling me in a dream that slipped away, and when I opened my eyes the voice continued: Cara singing my name. I got out of bed and below my window her head peeped out, her smiling face looking up. She was sitting sideways on the window seat again, her feet once more pressing against the woodwork. The angle of her body and the drop below her made my insides flip over.

"Are you feeling better?" she said, cocking her head and raising her eyebrows. She had wrapped her hair in a deep-blue cloth, a high, flat turban that emphasised her cheekbones. I thought she was enchanting. A sparrow or a dove, and me a guinea fowl.

"Would you like some lunch? I've made a picnic. We were hoping you'd show us the bridge."

My thick head was taking too long to respond. "The bridge?" I said, looking down. "What time is it?"

"About two o'clock, or three. Although, I have to say, you don't look too good, Frances. We could go on our own."

"Give me ten minutes." I moved back into my room thinking about what I should put on, thinking about Mother's underwear, which could give even a game bird a waist.

"I hope you're hungry," Cara called.

I put my head and shoulders out of the window again. "Starving," I said, but she had already gone.

In the bathroom, I brushed my teeth and washed my face, and when I went back into my bedroom a mouse was lying on its side on the open windowsill. The black bead of its uppermost eye was glossy, its brown tweed coat was pristine, and there was no sign of blood or damage, but it was dead. Two or three minutes before, when I had spoken to Cara from the window, it hadn't been there, couldn't have been there — hadn't I leaned on the sill and looked down? I wondered if somehow Serafina had got in when I had collected the envelope, and I

105

checked under the bed and went into the bathroom but she wasn't there either, and all the other doors in the attic were closed. I returned to the mouse and the back of my head prickled with a horror that wasn't about the dead, sad little body, but an intimation that someone had put it there for me to find. My hand went to Mother's locket on its chain around my neck, and then I picked up a shoe and pushed the mouse off the sill. I hoped Serafina would take care of it.

I led the way past the Nissen huts, through the rhododendrons, down the steps to the lake. The water, glimpsed between tree trunks and bushes, drew us on. And when we came to it, the expanse of it, the turquoise edges and the blue sky reflecting at its centre, was splendid. I wanted to keep Peter and Cara there, admiring its beauty, but Peter said, "Where's this bridge, then?" and I took them left through the trees until we came to a gap where we could see it, draped in green, only two of its arches clear of plants. "Oh, but it's charming," he said, and I felt as though it were a drawing I was unsure of and had been persuaded to show, only to be told it was rather good. I was suddenly proud, and thought that it was in fact a sweet little bridge. "We'd need to pull back some of that undergrowth to get a proper look, but I think you might have something there."

"Really?" I said.

"Wasn't the original house built in 1740 or something?"

"1745," I said.

"We'd have to take a few measurements."

"Of course." I tried to sound matter-of-fact.

"Is that good?" Cara said, tucking in the loose ends of the turban she was still wearing.

"Well," Peter said. "Frances would have to see."

"I suppose it is a little like the Palladian bridge at Stourhead," I said. "But if it was Palladian, or something interesting, wouldn't it have been mentioned in Pevsner, or some other record?"

"Oh," Peter said. "You looked up Lyntons in Pevsner, did you?"

"Didn't you?"

"Actually, no," Peter said with an embarrassed laugh. "I suppose I should have, but Pevsner's always so negative. I prefer an element of discovery when it comes to architecture."

"Well, yes, perhaps," I said, unsure now

whether he thought the bridge was important or not, but we had reached it by then
and we went single file along the path where
I had beaten back the nettles. In the centre,
a short section of the waist-high balustrade
was clear of plants and we spread out here
to look over the lake. The sun on the water
made my eyes ache, a headache threatening.

"Do you ever think about the people who
lived here before us?" Cara said. "The
servants and the gardeners, the families?
The children who jumped into this lake
from this bridge on a day like today, just as
hot, just as still, but when the bridge was
new? What kind of people did they grow
into, I wonder. What happened to them?"

"Everyone dies, Cara," Peter said gently,
as if breaking this to her for the first time. I
thought of Dorothea Lynton buried in the
churchyard with no one except our dissatis-
fied vicar and the gravedigger to mark her
passing. And I thought of Mother, of course.

"And what then?" she said. She might
have asked him the same question a hundred times before and each time hoped for
a different answer.

"Nothing," he said, and she turned her
head from him but covered the movement
by pretending to gaze into the distance

where the lake narrowed. "Dead is dead," he continued, his voice soft, his hands open. "No heaven or hell, no ghosts. If we're lucky we might be remembered for a generation or two, and then that's it, and that's fine."

"Is that what you really believe?" Cara said, still looking away.

"You know I do. And if we're unlucky we'll make it into a history book, but even then it won't be us, it'll be a made-up version, someone else's interpretation. It can't be the full story of who we are. That's only in our own heads and in the memories of the people who have loved us." He seemed to be waiting for an answer. "Cara?" he said to prompt her.

A few months before I was ten, while I was standing in the kitchen of our Notting Hill house, Mother had said to me, "Your father believes that when we die we're put into the ground and we rot and we make grass, and then the cows come and eat it up." I was aware of my father behind me, saying nothing. There was a tension in the room between my parents, a battle I didn't understand. I wanted him to tell me what she'd said wasn't true, that he didn't believe this, because it didn't happen. "Whereas I believe," Mother continued, "if we're good we go to heaven." The vision of the cows and the grass and the bodies was too terrible. I began to cry. "What should I believe?" I said. Whether she answered, and what she said if she did, I didn't recall.

"I'm happy to be forgotten in a generation or two," I said to Cara and Peter, needing to fill the gap. "And for me it'll probably be a lot sooner." I laughed.

"Come on," Cara said, turning and, with an effort, smiling. "We should eat."

"We should swim first," Peter said.

"Swim?" I looked from one to the other. "I didn't know we were going to swim. I don't have a costume." Mother's girdle poked me.

"Frances and I will watch," Cara said. "I never really learned how to do it."

On the middle of the bridge, Peter began removing his clothes. Cara laughed. "He's not shy, is he? You're not shy, are you?"

Under his trousers he was wearing a pair of blue swimming trunks. His body was spare, narrow hips and broad at the shoulders. Tufts of light hair stuck out from his armpits, and a little covered his chest. He climbed onto the stone balustrade and stood with his feet together. I wanted to warn him that there might be something under the surface, submerged posts, sharp-toothed pike, or pieces of rusting metal;

anything could snag that skin and tear him open, but then he was gone, diving through the lilies and pondweed. For a moment, we saw his body flowing below the surface like an animal under ice.

Cara and I leaned on the warm stone and watched him surface in the middle of the lake. We shaded our eyes while he continued swimming, his head and shoulders becoming a ripple through the sky and the clouds.

"How did you two meet?" I asked.

"Oh, it was in Ireland in '63," Cara said. "I was twenty-one. It already seems such a long time ago. I can't believe it's only six years. All I dreamed of was getting away, to Italy. The Irish have always left Ireland, haven't they? For one reason or another. I got as far as Dublin once." She laughed at some memory.

"Was that a long way from where you lived?"

"A hundred miles or so. It could have been another planet. I caught the bus to Thomastown, as Cara Cal-*ace,* changed my clothes, put on some lipstick, and became Cara Cal-*ay*-chee. I'd been teaching myself Italian from my father's dictionary, but like I said last night, I can't speak it, not really. On the bus to Dublin I remember pressing my forehead up against the window and

111

watching the thin men outside the sad pubs, and the thin women with their tired faces hanging out the washing. I wasn't going to be one of them." She turned around so her back was to the lake and I did the same. I could see her, a tragic figure on the bus, dreaming of something better. I let her talk, her consonants becoming softer, increasingly Irish. I knew hers would be a more interesting story than my own.

"I'd already lined up a job for when I got to Dublin. Or at least an interview for one, at the Adelphi Cinema. I rolled over the top of my skirt, put on some more lipstick, and when the manager invited me into his cubbyhole beside the projectionist's booth, I took the cigarette he offered me. He leaned forward to light it and do you know what he said? *You're very pale for a wop.* I was delighted, I'd got away with it. I put on my best Italian accent: *Ireland, it is a very nice, but there is no sun for months. Only rain, rain, rain.*"

It was odd to hear her suddenly become so convincingly Italian, to my ears anyway.

"I got the job, behind the cloakroom counter, taking people's coats. And I rented a room in a boarding house that took in girls. They all believed I was Italian too, and it was great fun for a while, sitting around the tea table and telling them about how the new pope had a terrific way of waving, and how wonderful the weather was, and about the oranges you could pick right off the trees beside the road. All they really wanted to know about was what the Italian men were like. I just rolled my eyes and let them imagine. They worked in Brown Thomas, the department store, those girls, and the butcher's around the corner, and the accounts office of the Player Wills tobacco factory on the South Circular Road. I forget their names now, but I remember that they came up to me one by one and slipped me a packet of nylons, or a couple of pork chops, or twenty Players. They wanted me to get them tickets to see the Beatles."

"The Beatles?" I said. Even I, who knew nothing about popular music, had heard of the Beatles.

"They were playing at the Adelphi, but the tickets had sold out weeks before and I knew I wouldn't be able to get any. I took the chops and the tights and the cigarettes though and said I'd see what I could do. I made sure I was working that night, and I thought I'd sneak in the back of the auditorium before the Beatles started, but the manager's boys wouldn't let me in. I can't tell you how angry I was, sitting on the floor of the cloakroom for the whole time, smoking cigarette after cigarette. I couldn't even hear the music because of the screaming.

"I had to hand over the coats when the audience came out, but I wanted to go backstage, so I started giving out any old coat, and of course the customers started complaining, so I just swung my legs over the counter and left them to it.

"I bumped into George in one of the corridors backstage. It was a warren back there — staircases and blind corners; it was ever so easy to get lost. He was wandering around looking for the others, I suppose. I thought I'd better carry on being Italian, and we had one of those funny conversations that you have with foreigners: half mime and half made-up words, except that I was the foreigner. He pretended to play the guitar and I got out the coat-ticket stubs and said things like *cloaker-roomer.* He asked me back to his hotel for a drink, and we went and stood outside the stage door for a while, making conversation and waiting for John and Paul and Ringo. It was so cold, November 1963, I'll never forget it. George was wearing a huge fur coat and I was shivering so much he took it off and put it around my shoulders. It went right to the ground. I don't remember what we talked about, Liverpool and Rome maybe. I think we had a cigarette, and then a newspaper van came around the corner. *Evening Herald,* I think it was, and then the rest of the Beatles came running out of the stage door and all of them, including George, jumped inside the van just as a crowd of girls came running around from the front. The van drove off with them all in it and me just left on the road being run down by these girls who were screaming and shouting like you'd never believe. They knocked me right over. Holes in the knees of my stockings, palms scraped — the shock of it brought tears to my eyes. There was a reporter who helped me up, asked me a few questions, like where I worked, and took a picture. I was in the paper the next day with mascara smeared all down my face, looking a real state."

"Oh, Cara," I said, imagining the excitement, the shock of it.

"That's how my mother found out where I was. Someone must have told her my picture was in the paper and that I was working at the Adelphi, although the manager sacked me for leaving the cloakroom unattended. Apparently, someone made off with a whole load of other people's coats.

My mother sent Dermod to fetch me in the Wolseley."

"Dermod?" I asked.

"Dermod helped around the house. A kind of servant, I suppose. He'd been living with us since before I was born, feeding the chickens, you know, a bit of housework, and he did most of the cooking as well. He's a little simple, but very sweet, and he hated driving that car. He wasn't supposed to drive at all, but my mother liked the idea of someone taking her around, and you didn't have to sit a test, not then. I was surprised he'd made it to Dublin on his own. We fought on the street outside the boarding house with all the girls hanging out the windows, watching. I said I wasn't ever going home, but he started crying, bawling his eyes out. He's such a soft lump."

She paused in her story, her eyes unfocussed as she remembered.

"Anyway, I drove the Wolseley home and on the way I told him the story about meeting George Harrison. To make him laugh we rolled down the windows and shouted *cloaker-roomer* at the tractors when I overtook them and at the thin women in their thin coats who were running to bring in the washing before the rain set in. I kept the coat George gave me though —"

116

She was still talking when, from the other side of the lake, we heard a long whistle and Peter calling. I had forgotten about him. We both turned, and in the distance he appeared to be standing on the water and waving his arms above his head.

"I'll show it to you later if you like," she said. "But it's just a man's fur coat. Come on. I expect he's hungry." She lifted the picnic basket she'd brought and walked back the way we'd come. I went after her to the end of the bridge and then returned for Peter's clothes, which he had folded and left in a neat pile — his shirt and trousers, his shoes and socks. As I walked beside the lake, thinking about what she'd told me, I realised she hadn't explained how she and Peter had met, in fact she hadn't mentioned Peter at all.

Three-quarters of the way along the lakeside, near to where the tower of the mausoleum poked up through the trees, a concrete jetty jutted into the water. The remains of wooden posts ran alongside it, as if there had once been a more picturesque pontoon made of timber, something the soldiers had made more practical and uglier. At the end of it Cara was unpacking the picnic, flapping a checked tablecloth, and farther along the bank Peter was standing on the soft ground and peering between the bulrushes.

"Look," he said as I approached. "An old rowing boat. If we could drag it out, I'm sure I could repair it, a few tarpaper patches and we'll be able to go on the lake. What do you say?"

I imagined Peter rowing, Cara and me lounging together in the bow, trailing our fingers in the water. An image of Waterhouse's painting *The Lady of Shalott* came to mind.

"That would be lovely."

He looked over his shoulder. "You brought my clothes. Frances, you are a wonder." He came back to the bank and I averted my eyes from his swimming trunks and torso, keeping them on his face. Only when he held out his hands for his clothes did I realise I'd been hugging them to my chest. "I knew Cara wouldn't have remembered," he said, forcing his wet and muddy legs into his trousers and pulling his shirt over his head. The cotton stuck to his skin. "I thought I'd have to swim back to the bridge."

On the tablecloth Cara had laid out the contents of the basket: slices of buttered bread, smoked fish pâté, a salad of beans and onions, half a dozen quails' eggs, and a screw of paper filled with salt.

There was no wind that afternoon, the lake was a new penny lost in an unmown lawn, and the unseen birds that chirped and twittered in the bushes didn't disturb a twig. I lowered myself to the concrete — it is never easy for a large woman to sit on the floor, especially one wearing a girdle. She must fold her legs beneath her as a horse does, and there comes a moment where she has to let go and drop, and hope it will work out all right.

The lake puckered at the edges of the jetty and the strands of weed that grew there lifted and fell back. Peter pulled out a bottle of champagne from the water where Cara had tied it to a post, and the ripples he made spread out across the lake, slicing into the reflections of the trees.

The bottle could have been in the lake for only a few minutes but Peter declared it cold enough, popped the cork, and poured it into our three tin cups.

"To Fran, our new friend," Peter said, holding up his.

"To Fran, our new friend," Cara said, tipping hers against Peter's. They waited, their cups raised.

"To us," I said. They had persuaded me it was true. We drank.

SEVEN

In the evening as I was sitting on my bed, writing up an observation I'd made when I was standing on the bridge, there was a knock on the door to the attic.

"Can I come in?" Cara called, coming in.

I had already changed into my nightdress. I tugged it higher around my neck and put a pillow on my lap to hide my stomach. "In here," I called.

She came into the room. She was still wearing the turban. "I hope I'm not disturbing you. I didn't realise you were working." She stared at the books beside me on the bed and stacked on the floor. "I didn't get a proper look at your room when we came up last night. I thought we were living rough downstairs, but you don't even have a packing case to sit on."

"Oh, I'm managing," I said, straightening my papers.

"When Peter works, at least he can perch

at the table. Don't you get backache sitting on the bed like that?"

She bent her head to window height and looked out. She walked around the small room, and took in my open suitcases with my clothes folded inside, my hairbrush on top, a towel hanging over the peg on the back of the door, my plastic shower cap over it. I was being examined, my belongings assessed, and I was concerned she would find them lacking.

"Is your bathroom next door?" She went out into the corridor and I almost ran to follow her, convinced she must have come upstairs with suspicions about the hole in her bathroom ceiling. "You don't even have a mirror," she said, taking a glance around the room. "There might be one in another bathroom. Peter could look for you."

"Thanks," I said. "But really, I am managing." I was desperate to draw her back into the bedroom. I went and sat on the bed, hoping she would follow. She came and sat beside me and picked up my book, *Garden Architecture*. She rubbed her fingers over the gold lettering: *A Pictorial Guide for Gardens Old and New.* If she wasn't here to expose the judas hole, I wondered why she had come upstairs. To tell me she and Peter had made an embarrassing mistake? That I wasn't the right sort and we could no longer be friends?

"Do you miss your parents now they're gone?" I blurted out, wanting to delay her announcement.

She looked at me, momentarily surprised at the question. "Not really. My father died when I was born."

"Oh no," I said. "I'm terribly sorry."

"He was running up the stairs when my mother was having me. He was holding a bowl of hot water or a pile of towels or something and he tripped and cracked his head open. Died in childbirth." She made a noise, half laugh, half sigh, and I could tell she had said this story many times until now it was a joke even while she recognised its tragedy. "I used to try and work out where it happened, examining each step for a trace of his blood. Of course, there was nothing there."

"And your mother?"

"Jesus," she said, slipping into an Irish accent. "Where do I start with Mammy?" Another half-hearted laugh, and back to her English accent. "Isabel Catherine Calace. Née Gentleman. Dutch ancestors, I think. She grew up at Killaspy — the house I was born in. Met my father, Augustus James Calace, at a hunt ball. Fell in love, blah,

blah, blah. Still alive and well and living there as far as I know."

"But I thought you said you'd lost them *both*?" My mind scrabbled back to our conversation before yesterday's dinner.

"Did I?" she said. "I meant that we're estranged. I haven't seen Isabel, or heard from her, in five years. Isabel, that's how I think of her now. Anyway, I'm positive someone would write and tell me if she died, Father Creagh, or Dermod."

"You were telling me about how you met Peter, when we were on the bridge."

"Do you want to hear it? It's a long story, and aren't you on your way to bed?" She gave a teasing tug on the sleeve of my nightdress.

"Please," I said. I had been listening to Mother's stories for years. Her wonderful life before my father left, the fabulous parties she'd attended before they'd met. I was happy to listen, and I knew when someone wanted, needed, to tell me their history. With Cara it took only the tiniest bit of encouragement.

"Well, first I have to tell you about Killaspy."

"The house you were born in?"

"Yes." She put her hands up, felt for the ends of the turban, and unwound it, her hair springing free and settling into its wedge shape. She scratched at her scalp. "It's just outside a small town in County Kilkenny. South-east Ireland. It's not as big as Lyntons, not as majestic, but handsome in a run-down way. Three storeys, symmetrical, solid, a few outbuildings, a duck pond, drawing room, parlour, dining room which we never used, six bedrooms if you count the attic. Except that it would have once had double that, and stables. But in 1921, when Isabel was five, a group of men came with cans of petrol and set fire to the back of the house, and the stables caught alight. She tells this story better than me; she could remember it of course, or at least she could remember the story. No one died, no people anyway.

"Isabel was sent to the end of the drive in her nightdress, clutching her old dressing gown that she used as a comforter. Some people came from the town to help put the fire out, but not before the back half of the house and the stables were destroyed. The remaining walls were shored up and the mess was cleared away, but it was all so expensive that my grandparents had to sell off most of the land, and they couldn't afford to send Isabel to boarding school in England so she was taught by governesses

124

until, as I said, she met Augustus. And the house was left like that, and now, or at least five years ago when I was there, it was still the same."

I shuffled back on the bed until I was against the wall, the pillow again over my stomach. I wanted to hear more. Cara lay on her side across the end of the bed, her head propped up on one hand, and continued.

"Sometimes when no one was looking, I would take the house keys from the peg in the kitchen and go up to the attic. At the end of the corridor there was a door which was always kept locked and beyond it was just empty space, a drop of three storeys down to the ground. I liked to stand there, right on the edge. It was wonderfully frightening. Lots of the walls of the burnt part of the house were still upright, but all the floors had gone, and across from me I could see the fireplaces with plants growing out of their grates. The roof had gone too, and I would just stand there and let the rain fall on me.

"So, that's where I grew up. You need to know because Killaspy's the reason I met Peter. I knew something was up when Dermod and I arrived back from Dublin. The rooms smelled of polish, there were flowers in a vase on the hall table, and the dogs' beds had been dragged into the scullery, though that didn't stop them sleeping on the sofas in the drawing room. The fire had been lit — and that was usually only done when it was cold enough to be able to scratch off the ice on the insides of the windows. I knew it hadn't been lit for my homecoming.

"Isabel was in her bedroom putting on her make-up, spitting into her block of mascara and brushing it on her eyelashes. She'd trapped a bee under a glass tumbler, on her dressing table, and it was buzzing. I don't know how it was there, in November — did you know bees form a cluster in their hives in winter? — but maybe it had been woken when the fire was lit. Isabel asked whether I'd had a good journey, as if I'd been visiting relatives instead of having been away for a month without her knowing where I'd gone. I asked her what was going on and she said we were having a visitor, a Mr. Robertson. And that was Peter!"

Cara smiled at me, and I smiled back, both of us excited to have reached the point where Peter would enter the story.

"No one ever visited us," she continued. "It wasn't that sort of house or we weren't that sort of family. People didn't know what to make of us, living in Killaspy with the rain coming in, and the back half of the house burnt. The front had a beautiful yellow algae blooming across it from the water that overflowed the gutters. I rather liked it. Anyway I asked her if Mr. Robertson was coming to do the repairs. I was sitting on the end of her bed and the bee was buzzing and she looked at me in the mirror and she said, *No, he's coming to buy it.* I knew she wanted me to be sad — it was the only home either of us had ever known — but I was happy, because I thought that if it was sold there would be enough money for me to get away from Ireland and go to Italy. And I knew she knew that, so we just stared at each other and then she put her hand over the bottom of the upturned glass and the bee went quiet; it just kept walking round and round its little prison. *What does the bee have to say?* I asked her, because she would sometimes do that, question animals about things. And she didn't move, like she was listening to it, and then she said, *One mustn't believe what bees say,* and scooped it up inside the glass and let it out of the window.

"Before Peter arrived I went to see Paddy. He was our neighbour's son, and the same age as me. I suppose we had a sort of understanding. I liked him, I'd always liked him. When we left school he took over his mother's herd of Friesians. I loved those cows, and maybe I loved Paddy too. Isabel wanted me to marry him, although farmers were having a difficult time in Ireland then, but the Brownes had a nice farmhouse and cattle, and marrying Paddy would keep me near her. Anyway, I put on my father's wellington boots and went to see him. He was bringing in the cows, giving the last ones a little tickle with a stick and saying, *Go on girl, go on.*"

Cara jerked up her chin as she spoke, and I could see her there, standing in the farmyard ankle-deep in slurry, the sun going down, and Paddy, gazing at her with his green eyes.

"I hadn't seen Paddy for a month, hadn't told him where I was going, but he'd heard I was back. He said, *Did you have a grand time in Rome hobnobbing with Pope Paul VI?* Paddy liked a joke and he knew I'd only got as far as Dublin before Dermod fetched me home. I asked him if he'd missed me but he turned on the milking machine so he didn't have to answer. It was ever so loud — it wasn't possible to hear each other without shouting. We had a nice routine when I helped him in the dairy. He would go along

128

the row of cows and hang the belts over their backs and attach the milkers, and I would go after him with a bucket of warm water and rags to clean the udders, and then he would attach the teats. We were a good team. I miss those girls, they were used to me. I remember thinking that if Mr. Robertson bought Killaspy straight away, then I would be gone within the month, and I pressed my cheek against a cow's flank when Paddy wasn't looking, so I could breathe in its smell of hair and straw. I never thought they smelled bad like some people say.

"I kissed Paddy while the milking machine was pulsing away. I'd kissed him before, at the dances we went to. He used to taste of the port wine he would slip into the fruit punch which was all we were supposed to drink. But this time he tasted of milk, and I let him put his hands inside my coat and up my jumper and under my bra. I quite liked the scratch of his calluses on my skin. But that was all he did, that was as far as I let him go."

Perhaps Cara thought I looked shocked at her frankness because she added, "It's important for you to know. That's all I let him do. I said I had to leave, that we had a visitor, and he said he'd heard that my mother was selling Killaspy, and I felt I was already leaving him and the dairy and Ireland. But of course, things never work out like you expect them to, do they?

"As soon as I got home, Isabel called for me to come and meet Mr. Robertson, and even though I wanted her to sell the house and I knew I was supposed to be the good daughter, I went in with my wellington boots on and kissed her on the cheek and said, *Hello Mammy.* She hated being called Mammy, but I was cross with her for not admitting that she'd missed me, and cross with her for sending Dermod to bring me home. I was only twenty-one. She was sitting in one of the wingback chairs beside the fire, and Mr. Robertson, Peter, was sitting opposite, on the sofa. Between them was a little table we owned, with an inlaid Chinese design. One of the swallows was missing and on every other day, the hole where it had come out was filled with dust and crumbs, but I could see that Dermod had even cleaned that. The table was one of a set of three; the others had been sold off years ago. Dermod had baked a seed cake, which was usually delicious, but this time he had covered it in yellow icing and it was the most lurid thing in the room. And I could see he'd been told to put out the best china for our visitor.

"I'd expected Peter to be old, fifty or sixty at least if he was thinking of buying Killaspy. I had no idea how much it was worth, probably very little, but everything seemed to be a lot of money then. And I thought he was handsome. He is handsome, isn't he? Isabel introduced us and he half stood up to shake my hand, but then he realised he was holding a plate in one hand and having to fend off one of the dogs with the other. Suki had her nose in his crotch and wouldn't go away; she always was a devil. I didn't feel like rescuing him, so I dragged the piano stool over and took a piece of cake. I asked him what he thought of the house and he said, *Charming, charming,* in that way he does, as if he really is fifty or sixty, and I said, *It's rather bruciare though, isn't it?* I ate the cake but left the icing. I curled it up so it looked like a poisonous caterpillar crawling across my plate. Isabel rolled her eyes and explained that I was teaching myself Italian, but Peter laughed and said, *Yes, it is rather burnt,* and then he said, *Mio padre è il direttore di un'azienda agricola.* And that was when I fell in love with him, because I thought he could speak Italian and already I was imagining us flying off to Italy, and walking down the

131

plane's steps into sunshine, and thinking about the oranges we'd pick straight from the trees, and the little blond-haired children we would have.

"But then he admitted that his father wasn't really the director of an agricultural company and he only knew that one sentence in Italian. We must get him to say it to us sometime. Then Isabel went through the whole thing about my father having wanted to take us to Italy when I was born and show us all the things he loved, and how he was going to teach me Italian — although Isabel said he couldn't speak it very well either — and how he'd died before any of that could happen. *And now I'm all alone,* she said in a little voice, and she hid her left hand, which had her wedding ring on it, under her leg, and fluttered her eyelashes at Peter. I was wondering what she would say if I told him that she spat into her mascara to get her eyelashes looking so thick and dark and while I was thinking that, I realised her plans to get Peter to buy Killaspy had changed into something else.

"She was so blatant, but Peter is hopeless at noticing the effect he has on people, on women. He's such a careless flirt. He thought he was just being polite by asking

Isabel. He actually didn't notice those fluttering eyelashes, but I didn't know that then. I think she would have kept him there the whole afternoon if she could, but eventually he put his plate down and said he had to be off. I thought he was running away. Suki was whining and Isabel was trying to make Peter stay by calling for Dermod so he could make another pot of tea. While Isabel was shouting, Peter held his hand out, and when our palms touched it was as if he had transferred something to me. I don't know what, his blood, or an electrical charge, or an inked message. I was sure that if I looked at my own hand when he released it, I'd find something there. He was very friendly to Isabel, saying thank you for the tour of the house and that he'd give his decision some thought and let her know.

"It was raining when he went outside — he had a little green sports car then — and Isabel and I stood just inside, and I was terribly sad because I knew he would never buy Killaspy now or take me to Italy. Isabel had messed it all up. And then to make it even more embarrassing, she draped her coat over her head and ran out to his car, tapped on the window, and asked whether he'd like Dermod to make him something for the journey, some sandwiches or a flask of tea. Of course, he just shook his head and she had to run back to the porch. But then that blessed little green sports car wouldn't start. He tried again and again but nothing happened.

"I went out with an umbrella while he peered under the bonnet and rapped his knuckles on bits of the engine and wriggled a few of the tubes that were in there. I remember he whispered to me, *I don't know anything about cars.*

"Isabel didn't like us talking together and she shouted, *Is it broken, do you think?* so that she could join in the conversation without having to come outside and get wet. I told him that Mr. Byrne who owned the garage would be having his tea now but if I telephoned I was sure he'd come over afterwards, and Peter slammed the bonnet closed and we went inside. Dermod had refilled the teapot even though we'd all had enough tea, and then Isabel looked at her watch and said, *Mr. Byrne who owns the garage will be having his tea now, and I know that he doesn't like coming out afterwards.* I caught Peter's eye and had to look away or I would have started laughing, she was so obvious. He didn't laugh and I realised then that he had no idea what she was up to. And then she said that Dermod was plucking a chicken if Peter would like to stay to dinner, and that I could make up a bed in one of the spare rooms if he would care to stay the night and then Mr. Byrne could come out in the morning. It didn't occur to me until later when I was in my own bed, but I wondered if Isabel had done something to Peter's car so that it wouldn't start, because for as long as I could remember we only ate chicken at Easter and Christmas. There you are, that's how we met."

"But what happened then?" I said. "What about Killaspy? Did Peter buy it?" I was tired, but like a child with a bedtime story, I didn't want it to stop.

Cara looked again around my room. "You don't have a fridge." She sat up. "Peter and I have been talking," she began. "And we think you should eat with us all the time. It's silly for you to be up here in your room without a fridge and only two rings to cook on when it's no effort for me to shop and cook for one more."

"That would be far too much work," I said, knowing I was going to let her persuade me.

"We insist," she said, standing up. "Tomorrow, if it's hot like today, shall we have breakfast on the terrace?" She wasn't expecting an answer.

She bent to hug me, her strings of beads jangling between us, her hair pressed against my cheek. "I know we're going to be the best of friends." After she'd gone, her citrus smell lingered in the air and on my skin.

In the very early morning I was woken by someone flushing the toilet in my bathroom next door. There was the thumping noise of the handle being pumped several times before the cistern released its gush of water around the bowl and, as it refilled, the hollow clanking and rasping, like an old up-and-over garage door being opened. I waited for Cara or Peter to call out that the toilet downstairs was broken, although there must have been others nearer their rooms, and then I remembered Peter had told me that there were only two functioning bathrooms in the house — mine and theirs. I waited for a footstep or the sound of the bathroom door opening, but when the flushing noises stopped there was nothing. A glitch in the plumbing, I told myself, but still I got up to see.

The door to the room opposite was open and the sky behind the avenue was peach, piled with cumulus clouds. The bathroom door was shut. Had I closed it after I'd brushed my teeth? I couldn't remember. I hesitated and, feeling foolish, knocked. There was no answer, no cough or shuffling of feet to let me know the person was at their ablutions. And suddenly it seemed wrong, the corridor, the space around me, as though there was something so close behind that if I were to turn, in an attempt to see it, the thing would move with me and never be caught. I held Mother's locket for a moment, the back warm where it had lain against my skin, and then I grasped the bathroom door handle and swung the door wide until it bumped the wall. The room of course was empty, the toilet lid closed in the way that Mother had taught me.

Somewhere in the pipes under the floor, water was churning and slopping about like an upset stomach. I turned to go and saw the pillow in the bath. It was the spare pillow I sometimes used, the same pillow I had held across my lap while Cara told me her story the previous night. I hadn't noticed it gone. It had been placed at the opposite end to the taps and there was a slight indentation in the feathers as though someone had slept there, in the bath. It horrified me, its appearance, its incongruity, like a pile of human faeces in the middle of a living room carpet. I picked up the pillow by a corner. A long grey hair adhered to the cotton, and I stripped off the case in such a way that I didn't have to touch the outside. I stuffed the case behind the toilet, and as I took the pillow back to my bedroom, the shadow at my back followed close behind.

EIGHT

"Miss Jellico?" Victor is saying. "Your lunch is here. Would you like something to eat?"

I used to be able to smell the food in this place an hour in advance of its arrival, the still-pink sausages, potatoes mashed before all the water had been drained off, and baked beans in tomato sauce reduced to a paste from reheating. I would eat it all.

My gut complained and I tried to ignore it, said nothing, and my disease hid itself inside me, undetected until it was too late. And now it is too late. Victor helps me to sit up. They must be glad to have him here, helping out for free, propping me up, listening. I am lucky to have my own room, and that there was funding to build this wing for those of us who are dying. I have heard them call it *end of life,* but whatever the nomenclature, it seems one of us pops off every other day. Victor wears his vestments to gain entry, given that he isn't family and

139

I haven't asked for him, but I know he doesn't visit any other people at the end of their lives; it's my sins he wants to hear, no one else's.

He puts the plastic spoon in my hand, tries to wrap my fingers around it, but the pain in my joints is too great. Without the awful pity I see on other faces, he takes the spoon back. He must think I am much changed, transformed from the person I once was: shy and awkward, large and plain. Now I am a woman of bone and skin, the patches of pigmentation like a map of a rocky archipelago; I am obdurate and unco-operative, drifting on a sea of memory between islands of lucidity.

Ignoring the re-formed meat slices in their too-brown gravy, he chases insipid sponge pudding and vivid custard around the bowl and blows on it before he holds the spoon to my mouth. I am starting to like him more than when I knew him previously: pudding before the main course. Priest, preacher, imam, minister? I have forgotten the word.

The food tastes of sugar. I swallow. "What would you choose for your last meal?" I ask.

"This isn't your last meal, Miss Jellico. I'm certain you'll have plenty more meals."

Platitudes. I ignore them. "What would you choose?"

He blows on another spoonful of pudding. "Oh, I don't know. A nice roast dinner? Rare beef and Yorkshire pudding."

"Not a beef vegetarian, then?" I say, remembering.

"A beef vegetarian? Does such a thing exist?"

I could tell him that it once did, but instead I say, "I'm surprised you wouldn't choose bread and wine." He smiles as though he knows that I'm in on his joke. Bread and wine is the last meal I eat with Peter and Cara. No, not the last meal, just the last food in the house. Empty bottles stand around their room as if we have been having a party. On the table amongst the used glasses and dirty plates there is a woven basket and inside it, the dry end of a morning roll.

"Is there anything you want to tell me, Miss Jellico?" Victor asks. In his voice I hear the love I once ignored and it draws me back from Lyntons. "Jesus forgives all sins." He says it at volume, seemingly for someone else's benefit, and I realise one of the Care Assisters is also in the room, coming to see if I've finished my meal. I used to be a fast eater.

"And yet I am still paying for mine," I say, and he leans forward and I know he is hoping for something new, a tiny piece of bright cloth with which he can patch the hole in his knowledge, something I've never told in twenty years. Should I tell it now? He has forgotten he's holding the spoon, and a slop of custard and sponge pudding falls onto his knee and down his cassock, and he springs up.

"Bugger it," he says and grabs at the paper napkin that has been left with the food, and smears the cloth. "Damn it," he says. And I think he isn't very good at pretending to be a clergyman after all. I am full, of sponge pudding and custard, of life and death. I close my eyes and three weeks before the crust of bread and the empty bottles are in Peter and Cara's sitting room, I am walking onto the side terrace at Lyntons.

On the side terrace Peter has placed a rusty stool from the basement and three upturned packing cases, one as a table. He came up to the attic, knocking on the door at the top of the stairs, then knocking on the bedroom door to ensure I was decent, and asking whether I minded getting up and having breakfast with Cara because he had to go and meet someone. He didn't say why he didn't want Cara to be alone. Breakfast was coffee and figs picked from a tree in the kitchen garden, thick cream with gooseberry jam, and tiny sponge cakes studded with currants that I hadn't seen when I'd visited the baker's. I was hungry.

Cara, in a white embroidered blouse which was grubby around the neckline and a long skirt, was sitting on the paving stones in the shade, her back to the wall of the house. She was holding a book open on her knees and smoking a cigarette. In my mind she smiled as she let a rough farm boy touch her in a barn in Ireland, and then I chased the thought away.

"Peter's gone into town," she said, squinting up at me. "He had to make some telephone calls and post a couple of letters. He said he'd take you on a tour of the house when he gets back." I didn't tell her that he had woken me and asked me to go down to eat with her. He hadn't asked me not to say, but I liked the idea of us having the tiniest of secrets.

She flapped the book in front of her face. "Will it rain today, do you think? Everything is horribly heavy. Shall we go to the lake? There might be a breeze by the water."

I stared at the food and wondered if it would be impolite to put two of the little cakes in my mouth at once. "I ought to visit the kitchen garden," I said. "I need to add the dimensions to my plan of the estate."

"But that's work," she said. "It's too hot for work." She saw me hesitating, eyeing the food. "We could take breakfast with us. You could dip your toes in the water while we eat." She scrubbed out her cigarette on the terrace paving and got up. "Liebermann's report can wait another day."

Cara put the pot of jam and the bowl of cream in the wide pockets of her skirt, and tied the little buns and figs in the tablecloth. She poured us both a coffee from the pot — I didn't ask for milk since there didn't seem to be any on offer — and she passed me a cup to carry. I drank my lukewarm coffee while we walked through the garden. When the words *If food is worth eating, it's worth eating properly* popped into my head, I dismissed them with a private smile.

"Where will you go in September when you leave Lyntons?" I asked. We were walking through the rhododendrons. I had a daydream that they would ask me to go with them to Italy; a vision of the three of us standing on a Venetian bridge, gondolas tied up alongside the buildings, the sun catching on the water.

"Wherever the work takes Peter, I suppose."

"Maybe you'll go to Italy."

144

"No," she said. "I don't think so."

The picture in my head vanished in an instant.

"But isn't that where you've always wanted to go?"

"How about you?" she said. "Will you go back to London?"

"Oh, I don't know. Wherever the work takes me, I suppose." We laughed.

I held back a thin branch and let her go in front. "How long have you been married?" I hoped she would continue with her story. Already I was a willing audience.

She stopped and turned. "Peter and I aren't married," she said, tapping her wedding ring on the tin cup she carried. "This is just for show." And I was surprised that a secret pleasure leaped inside me, one that shocked me even as I noticed it. We carried on walking and she continued to talk. "Just like everything else, he says it'll happen one day, but he won't speak about it, Fran. He doesn't like speaking about anything important, he brushes it away. He says he wants to look after me, keep me safe, and I know he's telling the truth, that he loves me when no one else would."

"I'm sure that's not true . . ." I trailed off, embarrassed that it wasn't clear whether I thought he didn't love her, or that no one else would. We came to the lake and walked out onto the jetty. Cara dropped the food wrapped in the tablecloth and put down her coffee cup, and before I knew what she was doing, she'd pulled the ring from her finger.

"I wear it because Isabel would expect it of me, and for those small-minded people in the town, and so the vicar will let me in his stupid church. Have you noticed how much he looks like an effeminate Jesus — all that dark hair and beard?"

And while I was thinking that maybe she was right, she tossed the ring far into the lake as if she were skimming a stone.

"What?" she laughed, seeing my face. "It's all about free love now, isn't it? And anyway, Peter's married, you know. To his first wife, Mallory." And in an instant my absurd hopefulness for something I couldn't name was snatched away. Cara sat on the concrete and picked at the knot she'd tied in the tablecloth. I was still standing and she looked up at me. "I expect that's who he's gone to telephone. He pays her alimony, you know. That's where the money goes, not on the food I buy. And she's always complaining that it isn't enough. I suppose he feels guilty for leaving her. Poor old Peter. She was desperate to have children, but it didn't happen. Anyway, he thought she

146

would have made a terrible mother, so he left. And then he found me." She said her last words too lightheartedly, and gave up on the knot in the tablecloth. I sat beside her.

"Sorry, Fran. I've shocked you. I thought you'd worked it out. I did. We were in Ireland, in his car, and he said he had to go back to England and couldn't stay with me. I wrote *wife* on the misted-up window and he got very angry and rubbed it out, and said he was trying to get a divorce but that it was difficult."

"He stayed on with you and your mother when his car broke down?"

"He stayed three nights that time: Mr. Byrne had to diagnose the fault, order the part, wait for it to arrive, and fit it. Dermod arranged for Father Creagh to come around when Isabel was out. Did you know that Dermod taught me the rosary, took me to Holy Communion and confession, told me all the Catholic stories while I sat next to him at the kitchen table? Isabel knew he did it, but she pretended she didn't. She'd been brought up a Protestant, but I was allowed to pick and choose. I liked Catholicism, I still do; I know where I am with it. But at school they called me *the Protestant,* even though I learned my catechism with the rest of them. That was Paddy's name for me too.

"I had to sit opposite Father Creagh in the back parlour and listen to him saying I was ungrateful, and a worry to my mother and to God, and that good girls don't run off to Dublin. Dermod had hung up the one picture we had of Jesus for Father Creagh's visit, but it wasn't like the holy pictures my friends had in their houses — the ones where you can see flames coming out of Jesus' chest and he looks so sad and pathetic, or where he's holding his heart in his hand. The one we owned was by a Spanish painter, I've forgotten his name. Not the actual one of course, a copy. Jesus was wretchedly handsome on his cross, and looking like a real man with real blood coming from his hands and feet, and all he had on was that little white cloth tied around his waist. I sat there in the back parlour while Father Creagh talked to me, and I said, *Yes Father, sorry Father.* And all the time he was speaking I was looking up at the painting and imagining it was Peter's face instead of Jesus' and that I helped him down from the cross, and lay next to him, and the cloth, which suddenly didn't seem to be tied on anywhere, just slipped off."

She said it to shock me, and I was shocked. I was starting to learn that this

148

was what Cara did. But what I didn't know then was that each scandalous statement or action was designed to be more outrageous than the last. She laughed at the memory of it, and to hide my hot face I took the tablecloth with the food inside it and picked at the knot.

"After that I didn't spend much time in the house," she continued. "I couldn't bear seeing Isabel making eyes at Peter, and him letting her win at draughts out of some social obligation. I took my Italian-English dictionary and went up above the river to learn some new words. That's where Peter found me, under the umbrella, practicing. I think I was on the *C*s: *corsetto, corsia* . . . I'm already forgetting the words. He came under the umbrella and I taught him the meaning of *corteggiatore* even though it wasn't the next word in the dictionary. It means suitor, or lover. I wasn't sure though that he got the hint. He is the most naive man I've ever met. But we sat on the rock for an hour or more, talking about my plans to get away, about Italy, which he'd never been to, France, which he had. And then he said that the car was ready and he was leaving, and I wondered if he'd come to find me to say goodbye. We walked home in the rain, and when we got back to Killaspy he

149

tilted up the umbrella and Mr. Byrne was there, wiping his hands on an oily towel, and we realised the rain must have stopped ages ago.

"I asked him if he was going to buy the house and he said, *No, I don't think I will,* and I took that to mean he wasn't interested in me and that he would be going away and not coming back. But he only meant he wasn't going to buy the house. It's very easy to read too much into what Peter says. He went inside to pack and I couldn't bear to stand there with Isabel, so I ran across the fields to Paddy.

"He was in the barn sweeping. I can't remember what we talked about. I was thinking of Peter saying goodbye to Dermod, going out to the porch with Isabel, shaking her hand, giving her a kiss on the cheek. I wondered whether he would ask where I was so he could say goodbye to me too, or whether he wouldn't think about me at all. In the barn I let Paddy press me up against the hay bales while I imagined Peter putting the case he'd arrived with into the boot of his car and getting into the driver's seat. I thought about Isabel tapping on the car window to delay him again while Paddy rubbed himself against me. We were still dressed. I was angry with Peter; I had my eyes closed but I could see him starting his little green car, Isabel standing on the drive, and Dermod watching from the house. Paddy was groaning and his wet mouth was on my neck, and suddenly it was disgusting, he was disgusting, and I pushed him off. He shouted that I was a tease, and didn't all Protestant girls give it up? He put his hand down his trousers and adjusted himself and then picked up the broom where he had dropped it and said, *What difference does it make whether we do it now, or after we're married?*

"I ran out of the barn, around the farmhouse and through their vegetable patch at the back, and then I was on Hatchery Lane, running in my father's wellingtons, galumphing up to the Thomastown Road. The little green sports car came around the corner. I didn't think it would — in all the stories the girl is always too late, the boy has left — but there it was, coming towards me with Peter in it. His face lit up when he saw me — I knew he was pleased. He asked if I wanted a lift back to Killaspy, and I said, *No, I want to go for a drive,* and although he seemed surprised I got in and we drove off into the countryside. I told him a story about Saint Brigid and how she was fed on the milk of a white cow and that her skull is in Portugal and the Portuguese bring it buckets of water and her skull turns the water to milk. He laughed and said he'd never met anyone like me before.

"He stopped the car in the entrance to a field and I thought, Go on then, kiss me, but he just sat there, staring out at the rain while the windows steamed up. I took one of his hands and put it on my knee, on top of my woollen tights, and he said, *Oh, Cara.* And I was shaking so much that he asked if I was cold. *Will I get you the blanket from the boot?* he said, and I laughed and told him that he'd been in Ireland too long. And he looked at me and said he didn't want to leave, but then he seemed to regret saying that and he took his hand off my knee and said he had to catch his plane back to England, and then he drove me home."

The knot in the tablecloth I had been picking at came undone. "And was that when you wrote *wife* on the steamed-up window?" The little cakes had broken into twos and threes, crushed under the figs.

"That was later. When he came back." Cara took the jar of gooseberry jam from her pocket and set it on the jetty. She looked in the other, and we could both see that the pot had turned over, and the cream, clotted with its yellow crust, filled her pocket. "I think we'll get married when his divorce comes through. And we'll have lots of blond-haired children and live happily ever after."

I didn't say that she'd already told me that. Instead I said, "I think you'll make a marvellous mother." But I knew I was saying those words because they were required, not because I thought she would.

"Yes," Cara said, and then immediately, "No." She picked up a piece of sponge, dipped it in the cream in her pocket, and held it up to my mouth, waiting, until I leaned forward and took it. She selected a fig and used a fingernail to make a slit in the skin long enough to insert the tips of her thumbs and rip it open. "There was a child, you see, and I let him go."

I was surprised, shocked even. I had imagined a simple love story, albeit complicated with a first wife. But now here was a child that Cara had let go. I wasn't even sure what that meant; adoption, I supposed.

"It took me a time when we got to Scotland, to recover." She didn't look at me but turned a section of the fig inside out and ate it. "Peter thinks I still haven't. He wants me to see more doctors, specialists. But it isn't me who has the problem."

I remembered what Victor had said about

her needing a doctor rather than a priest. And as I took in all this information, I tried to make sense of who the father must be. Had I missed this piece of the story or was she coming to it? If it wasn't Paddy, then Peter, surely. But why give up the child when they were together now? I saw the wedding ring flying off into the lake. Perhaps, like the rest of us, even Cara was bound by convention.

I closed my mouth, tried to compose my expression into one of sympathy rather than shock. "Oh Cara," I said. "I'm sorry." And I was. It was a tragic story and because of it they fascinated me all the more.

"Would you believe it?" she said in a perfect Irish accent, hiding her anguish with a joke. "I was a mammy for a little while." She picked up another piece of cake the size of her thumb, dipped it into the jam, then into the cream, and fed me again.

She fumbled with her cigarettes, taking one out and lighting it, and held the packet out to me. I took one, and when she lit it I saw that her bottom lashes had collected some tears. She had forgotten I didn't smoke.

It was hot on the jetty. Cara took off her blouse and skirt, dropping them on the concrete. Underneath she was wearing a bikini, less fabric in both pieces than in Peter's swimming trunks. She lay back, making a pillow for her head with the clothes, her hair spreading out over it.

"After Father Creagh told me I was a sinner and I had imagined the painting of Jesus changing into Peter, I went into one of the outhouses in Killaspy's backyard and I took off all my clothes and lay on the concrete floor, like this." She spread out her arms. "And I waited for the rats to come."

"Oh no!" I said, shocked again. The taste of my cigarette was ashy, disgusting.

"Punishment. It was what I deserved." She said it as though it didn't bother her, and closed her eyes.

Later, I told her that I would wash her skirt for her if she liked.

"Oh, Fran," she said. "That would be grand."

As we were packing up, when she was dressed and was squashing her cigarettes into her pocket with the jam, and I was shaking out the tablecloth, she thanked me for listening, and I saw it was that easy, that was all I had to do to make a friend, she wasn't looking for answers. It was that afternoon when she told me I was beautiful, and for a summer, for a month, I chose to believe her.

NINE

In the early evening, I sat with my sketch-book and tin of paints on the low wall which ran along the edge of the terrace. I'd found a jam jar for water in one of the outbuild-ings, and I was trying to capture the cedars in the parkland beyond the ravaged garden, with the hangers rising up in the distance.

"Nice," Peter said, making me jump. He was gazing over my shoulder. "But haven't you missed something?"

We looked at the landscape. The cows stood on their own or in groups of two and three with their heads lowered, eating. We looked at my work, cow-less. I turned the page, covering the painting, although I knew that later I'd find the leaves stuck together and the picture ruined.

"I don't like cows," I said.

"Clearly."

"Their rectangular bodies, the way their heads sway. There's something about how they stare. Vacuous and yet they lumber about in a terrifying way."

"Don't let Cara hear you. She loves them."

"I know."

He sat beside me and jangled a large metal ring with a dozen old-fashioned keys hanging from it. "Would you like to see the house?"

The east elevation, the one that would have faced the Lyntons' guests as they drove up the avenue by carriage or car, was plain, sombre, sitting in its own shadow except in the early morning. It was as if the architect had been saving the best — the light, the landscape, and the portico — for those who dared to enter. The central front door was small and stained where the grouting between the pediment stones overhead had eroded and water from a leaking downpipe had dripped through. The stones seemed loose, like wide-spaced teeth, and I worried about the way Peter was shaking the door to get the key to turn. I followed him into the entrance hall, and with the door wide, a black-and-white-tiled floor was visible, an imposing fireplace, panelled walls, and above them, on three sides, a painted gallery.

Peter flicked a light switch up and down but the room remained dark. "I've been trying to get the electricity to work on the ground floor for days. A junction box has gone somewhere in the basement, but I'm damned if I can find it."

I stood in the middle of the hall amongst the shrapnel of plaster that littered the floor, and turned slowly, gazing upward.

"Do you see?" he said, looking up too, his hand gestures expansive, excited. "The gallery is trompe l'oeil on only two sides. Someone boarded up the real gallery on the third."

High up on the walls were painted handrails, pilasters, and scrolled plasterwork arches, but staring harder, I saw that on the wall facing the front door, the balustrade was real, and the gaps in between had been painted onto board to create shadows and depth, to suggest a hallway beyond.

"Why would they have done that?" I said. "The gallery would have been opposite your rooms, wouldn't it?"

"Yes, but who knows. Maybe the army boarded it up."

"They wouldn't have bothered with disguising it though, to match the trompe l'oeil."

"No," he said. "I suppose not. I don't know then. This way." He led me through to another dark room. The hollow sound of the grit under my shoes suggested it was of a considerable size, high-ceilinged, the walls distant. I heard bolts being shot back, and as Peter folded open a pair of shutters twice my height, the evening sun came in through the French doors that overlooked the terrace and the parterre.

"The blue drawing room," he announced with a flourish. It was empty apart from an enormous mirror, foxed and dirty, propped against one wall. I caught a glimpse of myself and then stood with my back to it and looked at the gap where the fireplace should have been. "Ripped it out, the bloody vandals," Peter said. He opened the next set of shutters and French doors, and the next. The dusk came inside: the smell of the day ending, the song of a blackbird. "Even the servants' bell has gone." Beside the exposed bricks a wire stuck out from a hole in the wall. We turned from it and towards the mirror at the same time, the two of us reflected there, speckled and sepia-coloured, unsmiling. I thought we held each other's gaze for a second too long before I broke away.

"It's rather out of keeping with the rest of the neoclassicism." Peter waved towards the wallpaper. "I wonder if some Lady Lynton had a thing about peacocks."

The walls were covered with chinoiserie, ragged now and bleached where the sun had rested, darker behind the door to the entrance hall and around the fireplace. Pagodas, blossoms, and birds hand-painted on silk. The peacocks were surrounded by garlands and dimpled oranges.

"But who could have done this to them?" I said, horrified.

"What do you mean, done what?"

"Someone's cut out their eyes."

"Good Lord," Peter said, looking around. "I didn't notice before. They've done it to all of them." Every one of the peacocks had been blinded, each circular eye removed with a sharp blade. We went from wall to wall, touching the disfigured birds and exclaiming at who could have been wicked enough to go to the trouble of fetching a ladder in order to cut out the eyes from the birds just below the ceiling. "Would you prefer it if we shortened the tour?" Peter said. "We could see the rest another day."

It was disturbing but I was happy to go on. He led me through an adjoining door into another empty room, and two more, opening the shutters as we went. "Music room," he said, striding across the bare floorboards. A small door hidden near the back wall opened on to a low corridor that ran under the half landing of the grand staircase, dark and cobwebby, coming out through a similar door into the dining hall, with the remains of another vaulted ceiling. In a corner he opened a cupboard and revealed the shaft of the dumb waiter.

"I read that the dining table could seat forty," I said. "Kings and princesses, film stars, apparently."

Peter went to the fireplace and gave the marble surround a tug. "It would have made my job easier if they'd looked after the place better."

"Can you imagine the amount of work needed to keep the food coming, the beds made, the fires lit?" I said.

He pressed his ear to the wall. "I think there might be a deathwatch beetle infestation. Have you heard the blighters clicking in the walls in the night? Sometimes I can't get to sleep for the noise they make."

"I found a census for Lyntons before I came here." I went to the window overlooking the drive and rubbed at a patch of glass. "Twenty-four maids, butlers, and cooks to keep the house going for a family of five. Do you think they were all crammed into the attic rooms? Martha and Edith rising first to clean the grates. Jane in the kitchen warming the milk on the range for the babies' bottles, progressing to housemaid in a few years, hoping that Stephen Hipps, second butler, would be able to save enough money to ask her to marry him."

I looked at Peter, but he shrugged, didn't seem to want to join in. He opened another door and I followed him through to the hallway and then into a study, the desk gone but with shelves still lining one wall and a metal filing cabinet in a corner with the drawers removed and stacked one on the other.

"When you first came upstairs, to the attic," I said, "you mentioned an old retainer, a nanny or a butler who had lived up there."

"Did I?" Peter said. He was picking up pieces of yellowing paper from a drawer, looking them over, and dropping them so that they floated to the floor while he took another.

"The vicar mentioned them too. Do you know who it was?"

He stopped, with one hand in the drawer. "No idea. It was just a guess because someone had bothered to put in a bathroom. Why do you ask?"

"Oh," I said. "Just curious about who was in the rooms before me. It doesn't matter."

I could see he was trying to work out if I'd found something interesting. I was never going to tell him about the hole in the floor.

He gave up on the filing cabinet drawers and we went on, sticking our heads into built-in cupboards made for housekeepers and housemaids, their shelves empty apart from dust and spiders; a smoking room, although I couldn't tell how Peter knew; and a single WC for the whole ground floor. We stopped in the billiards room, where he showed me the graffiti — bombers and bombs, swastikas and busty women carved into the window frames and the plaster. He tried to hurry me past the worst: *kill the cunts, Churchill is a stinkweed, fuck the huns up their bums.* The poor rhyme made me smile, and I didn't tell him that there had been times when I was living with Mother when I'd gone to the public lavatories in King's Cross in order to have the shock, the spark of life that jolted through me when I read what was written on the walls there. When we left the billiards room we had come almost full circle — to the library.

Here, he opened the shutters and the French doors that led to the portico and the terrace, and I thought about how we had sat just outside in the shade or the sunshine and I'd had no idea that the library was behind these doors.

Outside it was almost dark and the corners

163

of the room were gloomy. Two of the walls were lined to the ceiling with books and more lay about the floor, their spines broken and pages torn out. When a breeze came in through the open doors the pages on the floor lifted and fell with a dry rustle. A little higher than a person might have been able to reach with their arms raised was a narrow ironwork balcony that wrapped around the walls, accessed by a spiral staircase.

"Welcome to the library," Peter said. "The architecture section is up there." He nodded at the balcony. "But it isn't safe." He pointed to a section where the shelves had buckled and the books had swollen and fallen. "I think the rain must have got in before they repaired the roof. I've been up there but a lot of the screws fixing the metalwork to the walls have rusted. I'll have to try and shore it up."

"It's beautiful," I said.

I would have liked to preserve that room as it was on that date, like Satis House, with the dust and the spiders, the mildew, the water damage halted, but nothing improved, the dry rot and deathwatch beetle kept in abeyance. And Peter and I would be paused too in that room before either of us learned too much about the other, before anything happened. Later I craved neatness and

164

order, but not that evening.

"That's what Cara thinks too," Peter said.

"What?"

"I see a room which needs repairing, or ripping out and starting again." His hands demonstrated the actions. "You and Cara see antiquity and beauty. The more something's falling down, the more you bloody like it. Both of you are always looking backwards, when you should be looking forwards to the future."

"But everything we have, everything we are, is created by the past," I said, surprised at his angry tone.

"You're both too full of sentimental rubbish. Ghosts and ghouls!" He lifted his arms above his head and spread his fingers, his eyebrows raised. A joke apparition.

He put his hands on his face and rubbed it as though he were washing. "I'm sorry," he said. "That was uncalled for. I have some things on my mind."

"It's all right," I said.

"No, I'm sorry, I didn't mean it to come out like that. I had some bad news this morning."

"Is there anything I can do?"

"Not unless you happen to have a few thousand in the bank." His laugh, when it came, was desperate.

"Oh," I said. "Sorry." I thought of the wife Cara had told me about and the alimony that was eating up his finances. I wondered if he regretted leaving her.

After a moment, to break the silence, I said, "Do you really think Cara and I see ghosts?"

"I think you'd like to."

"Has Cara seen ghosts, in the house?"

"Are you kidding? She sees ghostly apparitions at every turn. People in mirrors who aren't there, children staring out of windows, Jesus' face in the clouds." He laughed. "She'll see whatever helps her get through."

We were close together, standing next to the spiral staircase in the dark. I struggled to read the expression on his face.

"Get her through what?" I said, believing I already knew the answer, but hoping he would open up to me, where he couldn't or wouldn't to Cara. Perhaps he would tell me, still really a stranger, how difficult it had been for him to give up their child. I was ready to listen and to help. I almost put out my hand.

"She's not everything she seems. You must have worked that out by now."

I hadn't worked anything out. I didn't have anyone in my room at night to discuss

the events of the day as other people did —
as Mother used to do, letting out her resent-
ments about my father while I lay in the
bed next to her trying to fall asleep, and as
I knew Peter and Cara must have done
about me.

I pulled a book from the shelves, opened
it and stared at the words, but didn't read.
"Really?" I wanted him to tell me everything
without me having to ask.

"She grew up in a house a little like this,"
he said. He sat on the spiral staircase and I
heard metal grate against metal, one of the
poles that supported the balcony shudder-
ing. "Not with a library and a billiards room
but somewhere sad and broken. Half of the
house was completely burnt away. She
didn't live above the shop in a little market
town in Dorset like me and my parents. She
was born to greater things."

I turned a page of the book. "The shop?"
I said. I wanted to know more about him,
not Cara.

"My father owned an antiques shop," he
said. "Sideboards, dining tables, silverware,
that sort of thing. He loved meeting customers, selling them something they didn't
know they wanted. I've always preferred
meeting the owners, working on a little
persuasion, a little negotiation. For me the

excitement is in finding some ratty old thing in an attic that turns out to be worth a fortune."

I remembered the trips out to the country with my father before he left us. The great houses we visited, the landscaped gardens, the antiques shops with a promise of a few interesting books. We would catch an early train from Paddington and alight at the station of some market town. If it was books he was after, I would wait while he went through the boxes the dealer had kept for him in a back room. Sometimes he would buy one book, sometimes a whole box. I didn't remember the names of the towns, but I wondered if my father and I might have rung the bell above the door to Robertson's Antiques or whatever it might have been called. We might have stepped into a shop where everything was polished and warm. My father might have chatted with the owner about provenance, and after a deal was struck, Mr. Robertson might have called upstairs for a pot of tea, and his son, a year or two younger than me, blond-haired and concentrating hard so that the cups didn't rattle on their saucers, might have brought it down to us.

"Well, I can promise you there are no treasures in the attic at Lyntons," I said to

Peter. "Unless you count a few dead mice."

"I don't think they'd go for much at auction. Although at Sotheby's we once sold a Dürer engraving of Adam and Eve. Eve had a cat curled around her feet and Adam was treading on the tail of a mouse." Peter took out his cigarettes and shook one from the packet.

I put the book back on the shelf. "Do you think . . . ? Could I?" I stretched my hand towards the packet.

Peter raised his eyebrows but said nothing, only shaking another out and lighting it for me.

"You were at Sotheby's?" I said, trying not to cough.

"For a while. I went there straight from school. I wangled a letter of introduction to the chairman. My father wasn't too happy when he found out."

"He wasn't pleased for you? Proud?"

"He wanted me to take over the shop, but God, the customers would have driven me mad. Those women in their pearls with lipstick on their teeth, and the men coming down from London hoping to pull one over on my father. Anyway, I just needed to get out of that town. Stultifying." His hands made a gripping action.

I dipped my head. He might have been

169

reading my memory of my father. "A restless young man, then?"

"I suppose. Although I think it's Cara who's been the most restless. Striving for something more."

I wanted to say, *Aren't we all*. I wanted to tell him how it had been with Mother in London during those years, the change in her, the airless rooms, the boredom that books and self-education relieved, her moaning first in criticism, later in pain, but instead I said, "You're worried about her?"

"Not exactly." His tone was serious. "I'm saying she's fragile; she hoped for one thing and ended up with another." He stood and took a step towards me. "Actually, I wanted to ask for your help. I know I can trust you, Fran."

I waited, resting one elbow on my other hand, the cigarette raised, then, self-conscious, dropping my arm to my hip, cigarette dangling. I would have said yes to anything.

"Cara sees the world differently from you and me. She might say things . . ." He paused, considering his words. "About what happened. She likes to retell, change things. It's just her way. You know the Irish, born storytellers."

"What things?" I said.

He picked up a loose page from under his shoe and blew dust from its surface. "I'm trying to encourage her to see someone again, but she's resistant."

"A doctor, you mean? And you want me to persuade her? I'm not sure —"

"No, no —" He held his hand up as if to make me wait, and in the dark room I could just make out his eyes, screwed closed. He sneezed three times, each one a bark or a cough. He sniffed and patted his pockets, and I took from my shorts a clean, folded handkerchief and held it out to him.

"Thank you." He blew his nose and put the hanky in his pocket. "I'm just asking for your help to keep an eye on her." His voice dropped. "Let me know if she says or does anything . . . silly. I can't watch her all the time."

"Silly?" I said. "Silly, in what way?"

"I don't know," he said, although I thought he did. "Anything."

I would have pressed him but we heard Cara calling. When I looked beyond the doorway, out to the garden, the sun had set and the sky was mauve.

We ate again at their makeshift table, drinking Mr. Liebermann's wine out of the tin cups and talking late into the night about the houses they had stayed in, Edinburgh, Glasgow, and the places Peter had visited. The cigarettes tasted good.

I watched Cara for the fragility Peter had mentioned and I had seen through the judas hole and in the church, but I saw none of it that evening. She was full of life and she was happy, and the glow she gave off spread over us all. I watched Peter too, to see if he spoke to me with a new intimacy, whether he regarded me differently after what we had shared in the library, and I believed he did.

TEN

Over the next few days I ate all my meals with Peter and Cara. The weather stayed warm and I avoided my attic room, which trapped the heat under the lead roof, even with the window open. I adapted to their clock, settling into a routine of rising late, taking breakfast — peaches and coffee, pastries and figs, eggs and toast — in the shade of the portico. Often, we didn't bother with the makeshift chairs and table, and sat, instead, on the steps, Cara resting against Peter's legs, the three of us smoking and contemplating the ruined lawns, the overgrown flower beds, and the trees that surrounded the lake. If we spoke it was for Cara and me to tell stories about what Lyntons would have been like when it was filled with servants, when carriages pulled up to the front door, when there had been an unimpeded view of the water.

For a day or so it seemed miraculous, that

173

they welcomed my company and that I was able to relax in theirs. I wondered why it had never been like this for me before. Had I changed? Then after a while I stopped noticing and accepted it, and was happy.

"I thought I might go and clear some of the undergrowth off the bridge," Peter said after breakfast on Thursday. He stood up so that Cara had to lean forward.

"What, now?" she said, shading her eyes and looking up at him.

"That sounds like a good idea." I stretched. "I could do with some exercise."

"Sounds like hard work," Cara said, lying back again.

"Why don't you come with us?" Peter gave her a nudge with his foot. "It'll be cooler down there. You can watch us work."

She stared at us as though she thought we were plotting something. Peter put his hand out to her and with a sigh, she let him pull her up.

We took some of the tools Peter had found and sharpened, and we were beside the Nissen huts when Cara said, "Actually, I think I'll cycle into town. We need something for lunch." She said it to Peter like a challenge, daring him to make her come with us to the bridge.

"If you're sure?" he said, while I looked

174

between them, trying to understand what they weren't saying.

"I'm sure," she said, wrapping the sacking she was carrying around my neck like a scarf. "Don't look so horrified, Fran." She smiled. "And don't worry, I'll be back in an hour or two," she said to Peter. "If not, you can send out the search party." When he didn't smile, she said, "For God's sake, I'm cycling into town." And she strode off towards the house.

When we reached the bridge Peter was enthusiastic, saying that he thought it could be Palladian, something about the span of the arches, the Italian elegance of the balusters. I wasn't convinced, and at first I pulled half-heartedly at the ivy and hacked at a few brambles as if it was a hopeless undertaking. But after a while Peter's energy and excitement enthused me too, and I began to enjoy the physical activity until it didn't matter what sort of bridge we were clearing. We worked for two or three hours, speaking only when one of us needed help or after we had uncovered a bit more. When we had packed up and were walking to the house, I glanced back. The stone was whiter where we had pulled away the plants, the arches a little more defined and elegant, and I thought that perhaps he was right, maybe we had discovered a Palladian bridge.

Cara was already home when we returned to wash our hands in their bathroom sink. As I turned on the taps I was aware of the domed ceiling and the glass eye above my head. I didn't look up. Laid out on the table in their sitting room was a trout Cara said an angler she'd cycled past had given her, a clutch of eggs bought from a farm gate, as well as cheese and bread she'd charmed from the farmer's wife, and cigarettes for us all.

We took the food, some wine, and a blanket out to the shade of the mulberry tree, a lumpen and crooked specimen that grew in the middle of where a lawn had once been — the remains of the brick paths and flower beds around the edge could still be made out, although now the grass was rough and knee-high. We ate, and Peter opened a second bottle, and when we'd finished that, we lay back and slept. When I woke, Cara was sitting up, smoking. Peter had gone into the house to itemise the contents of a basement storeroom, she said, although I thought it more plausible that he was continuing to catalogue the wine. I thought I should go upstairs and read my notes or document the grotto, but the warm afternoon, the shadow patterns of the leaves upon us, and the wine all contrived to keep me there. I let Cara continue her story without me asking.

"After Peter left Ireland, life went back to normal, more or less. Dermod doing the cooking and some cleaning, Isabel worrying about money, and me thinking I was never going to escape, and when I couldn't stand it any longer running across the fields to visit Paddy. Sometimes I let him hold my hand, but nothing more than that. The only change was that I got a job with Miss Landers, a blind woman who lived in the town. I went to her house twice a week to open her post for her, and write replies and cheques, address envelopes, and I had to read her *Woman's Way* aloud from cover to cover. It was a magazine we had in Ireland then, I haven't seen it here. And afterwards she would dictate letters to the editor commenting on the articles I'd read aloud. She was elderly and Catholic but not like any other old woman I knew. Her letters were about the benefits of sex education for girls, how contraception would help Ireland develop economically, or how unmarried mothers weren't evil. The magazine paid a guinea for each letter they published and every week Miss Landers hoped they'd print one of hers, but they never did, not then anyway.

"I must have been going to her for about three months when Peter came back. His car was on the drive one day when I got home. I nearly ran away again, because I thought that seeing him would just stir everything up. I was resigned by then to staying in Ireland. I'd stopped hoping, and sometimes life feels easier that way, doesn't it? But of course I went in, and he was sitting in the drawing room just like last time, and when I saw him sitting there smiling, I was even more sure that I loved him, and I could see from his face that he loved me too.

"He'd bought me a Christmas present — an Italian recipe book. Isabel wasn't pleased — he hadn't thought to bring her anything. He said he'd got it in an auction that he'd been to where they'd been selling off the contents of one of the big houses in County Kildare or somewhere, a couple of weeks before, and when I heard that, I couldn't believe he'd been in the country, in Ireland, all that time and hadn't come to see me. His job in those days was to go around the big houses and persuade the owners to sell their libraries or paintings. He'd go to sales to buy things he knew there was a market for, or he looked for houses and land that

178

could be developed into hotels or golf clubs. He wasn't looking for himself, but he never told Isabel that. She was still half hoping he'd buy Killaspy, or marry her."

Under the mulberry tree the shade had moved and I moved with it to see Cara better. "But he wasn't planning on ever doing that, was he?" I said.

"No, but then Peter never really makes plans. He just lets things happen. I think, though, that day in the drawing room, Isabel must have seen how we were staring at each other, because the first thing she said was something like, *You remember my daughter, Cara. She's just become engaged to Paddy Browne. Isn't that wonderful — a spring wedding?*

"I remember the colour draining out of Peter's face, because it was true, I had agreed to marry Paddy. It had felt at the time like there was no alternative. Peter stood up and shook my hand, and said, *Many congratulations, Miss Calace,* in such a dead voice I could have cried.

"There was chicken again for supper but I got Dermod to tell Isabel that I had a headache and wouldn't be down. I couldn't bear to see Peter's expression. I sat at my bedroom window and waited until I heard everyone go to bed, and then I went downstairs in my nightdress and ripped a leg off the chicken carcass that Dermod had left covered in the larder. I sat shivering on the counter and ate it in the dark, and when I'd finished it, Peter came in. I knew it was him just from his outline.

"He shut the larder door and said, *You're going to marry Paddy, are you? Or something. A farm boy.* He sounded heartbroken. *I like cows,* I said, just to annoy him. I said that Paddy wasn't a farm boy, that he would have ten head of cattle when he inherited the farm, even though inside I couldn't bear the idea that if I married him my whole future was laid out as though someone had carved my next fifty years in stone. Peter said, *You'll be a farmer's wife in rural Ireland. What happened to your dreams of Italy?* He cracked that lump of stone, a tiny gap to begin with, but enough.

"I asked whether he was offering to take me, but he didn't answer; he just moved a step closer and we kissed. That was the first time, in the larder. He said I tasted of butter and chicken. I so badly wanted us to make love, I opened my legs and sort of hooked my ankles around the backs of his knees until he was pressed into me, but he said, *Not now. Not in the larder.*"

Cara caught my eye, and she started

180

laughing, a naughty kind of laugh, and I started laughing too, until we were doubled over shaking with the thought of it, and then we fell backwards onto the blanket.

"We didn't promise each other anything," she said after we had calmed down. "Peter didn't say he would stay in Ireland, and I didn't say I'd break off my engagement to Paddy. Isabel carried on hoping that either Peter was interested in her or he was going to buy Killaspy. He was uneasy about deceiving her, but I wanted him to stay in the house, and I wanted to keep him there for as long as possible. We met every night in the larder, and went for drives in his car. I told Paddy I was busy with Miss Landers.

"It was the morning before he was due to leave, Christmas Eve, that I wrote *wife* on the misted-up passenger window. It was only a guess, but he stretched across me to rub the word out and said he didn't want to talk about it, her. Peter might be able to rattle on about all sorts of things, but there are some subjects that he just bloody clams up about — emotions and relationships and, I don't know, real life. Under that charming exterior is a buttoned-up, straight-laced, old-fashioned man. I said he could get a divorce, couldn't he, or what were we doing sitting in his car every afternoon holding hands and steaming up the windows? And he said he didn't understand how sometimes I acted like I was Catholic and then when it was convenient I was allowed to be Protestant. And I said I could do what I bloody well liked, it was my religion. And that was our first argument I suppose. We were both shouting, even though all I'd ever wanted was to touch him, you know, properly, and for him to touch me back. Once, I saw him on the landing in just a towel — he must have thought we were all out — and I spent the whole night wondering what it would be like when we slept together. I was certain we would.

"Anyway, in that tiny little car our argument became so nasty, so horrible, that I opened the door and ran off. I just ran away. It was raining, pouring down. Peter came after me, but I kept running and I heard him shout, *Where are you going?* But I kept on and without stopping I shouted back, *Italy,* although I don't think he heard.

"I didn't know where we were. On our drives Peter would come to a junction and I would call *right* or *left,* however the mood took me, until I thought we must be lost in the middle of the Irish countryside, but he always knew, he could always drive me straight home. When I got out of the car I had no idea where we were. It was winter and freezing, and although I was marching along I was wet and cold, and all of me was shaking. But I kept on going. I planned to carry on walking until I fell into a ditch, and the next day, or the next week or sometime in the future, they would find my body and then they would feel guilty: Peter, Isabel, and Paddy. It was Dermod I worried about, though: he needed someone to look out for him. I walked for an hour — it was dark by then and still raining — but eventually headlights came towards me and I saw it was the little green sports car. Peter was angry with me for running away, but mostly because he thought I might catch a chill and die, the ninny. I couldn't speak, I was so cold. He got the blanket out of the boot, sat me in the front seat, and turned the heating on full, but I was shaking, frozen to the core, and I actually thought I might die. I tried to take off my wet clothes, but because my fingers were numb and wouldn't work, Peter had to undress me, making me lift up my arms or my bottom, and then he wrapped me in the blanket and just held me. It was tricky across the handbrake and gear stick, with those bucket seats, and although I was still cold, I was sure he would make love to me then, now he'd seen me with no clothes on, now he'd undressed me, but once I'd stopped shivering he drove me home, back to Killaspy."

She let out a long sigh and turned over onto her stomach, head resting on her folded arms. "Is this too personal for you, Frances? Please say if it's too personal."

"Oh, no," I said. "I really don't mind. I mean, it's fine." It was personal. I had never considered what people might look like under their clothes, or how complicated other people's lives were when they appeared so simple and happy from the outside.

"Only, I do so love our conversations," she said.

On one of those afternoons that we spent under the mulberry tree, after we'd eaten and drunk and slept, I took Peter and Cara to the mausoleum. We climbed the tower and gazed out, but they were more interested in the tombs at the bottom. I showed them the punched-out chests of the stone wives.

"Two wives?" Cara said, inspecting their faces. We had brought candles with us, and they threw shadows on the walls that stretched and arched as we moved about the room.

"One after the other, I should think," I said. "Not both at once."

"No," she said, still looking. "Not both at once, clearly. This one seems sad. I wonder if she was the first wife or the second." She bent over the stone face and kissed its lips, pausing there for a moment. The action was somehow too private, even more personal than everything she'd told me, and I turned away, catching Peter's eye across the room. He gave a tiny shrug and his candle dimmed as he lowered his hand into the chest cavity of the other woman and peered inside, a surgeon probing a heart.

"What are you doing?" Cara cried out. "You can't do that." She went to him and pulled at his arm, but he resisted her.

"There's nothing here," he said. "It's empty."

On the way back to the house Cara fell behind, picking off grass heads and shredding them, keeping her thoughts to herself. Peter and I discussed the gisants in the tomb, deciding that the wives must have been buried with their jewellery and someone had cracked open their chests to get at it. I told him about Thomas Cure's cadaver tomb in Southwark and we chatted about Alice de la Pole's in a church in Oxfordshire, the lady shown in all her finery on top, and below as a corpse.

"We should visit her," Peter said. "Drive up there sometime. Pay our respects."

"That would be wonderful."

"It must only be a couple of hours away."

"I'd love to."

"Talking of jewellery," he started.

"How about tomorrow?" I said. "Or the day after?" I imagined an idyllic morning with Peter, poking around an old church, a light lunch, and then two hours back in the car sitting next to him.

"Cara's lost her wedding ring. I don't suppose you've seen it?"

"Her wedding ring?" I said, remembering it skimming the lake.

"She says she took it off when she was doing the washing-up in the bathroom, but I've searched everywhere. I even undid the U-bend, but it's not there."

"No," I said. "Sorry. I haven't seen it. Was it valuable?"

"Sentimental value," he said. "I suppose she'll want me to buy her another."

The following afternoon Cara and Peter invited me for a walk, and the three of us struck out across the estate, past the largest of the cedars where the cows grazed. I was pleased that this time they were gone, in another field or being milked.

Cara took Peter's hand and we talked about what we would have for dinner, if the warm weather would continue, the inconsequential things that friends talk of. When Peter let go of Cara's hand she linked her arm in mine, releasing me as we came to some barbed wire, which Peter held up for us. We went single file along a track through the middle of a meadow, which sloped uphill in the direction of the hangers, and when we got to the gate at the far end the three of us stopped, me puffing a little, still with Mother's brassiere holding me tight. Without speaking we turned to look back the way we had come. To our right, the top of the mausoleum tower showed above the trees of a small wood, while in front of us the land dipped towards the lake and the grotto, golden and green, clumps of mature trees, grass, and nettles grown tall around fallen limbs. In the distance, the white pillars of Lyntons glowed as if something were alive inside the stone, and behind it the dark wooded sweep of the hangers rose up and arched around the landscape to our backs.

While we stood catching our breath, four deer came out of the trees. They walked through the meadow just a few feet away, and when they were in front of us they stopped and turned their heads. They tilted their snouts and we were close enough to see their nostrils open and shut as they sniffed the air, but I knew it was Cara they were smelling, Cara they were observing with their dark eyes, Cara they turned their ears towards. None of us moved, and after a moment the deer walked on across the meadow, melting into the grass on the far side.

"I'd like to stay at Lyntons forever," Cara said.

I took a packet of cigarettes from my shorts pocket and knocked one out. It was ripped and the tobacco loose. I tried another but that was the same.

Peter laughed and took out his own packet. "Last one, sorry," he said, lighting it. "Even without a proper kitchen, or chairs, or glasses to drink our wine from?" he asked Cara.

"Yes, even without those things," she said. "We don't need them, not when we have all this. This perfect day."

We were silent for a time, staring out over the landscape.

"Do you think Mr. Liebermann would notice if we didn't leave?" I asked.

"We could hide under the beds if he came looking." Peter passed his cigarette to me and I thought about his lips having been on it, before I put it between mine.

"We could drape sheets over our heads and scare him away," Cara said.

"By September he'll have forgotten he bought a house in Hampshire," Peter said.

I passed the cigarette to Cara.

"Shall we go back that way, through the wood?" Cara nodded in the direction the deer had gone. The cigarette did one more round and we went down, across the meadow.

It was cooler under the trees, the ground dry and full of ferns and rabbit holes. We were a little way in when we smelled it, something musky, ripe. We wrinkled our noses at each other and carried on walking.

The fox was caught in a gin trap, its left foreleg mangled. It cowered when it saw us, shrinking and tucking in its tail. There was blood around its mouth, and I didn't want to think about what it had been doing to try to free itself. The smell was pungent, and I supposed the fox must have released its scent when it was first caught.

"I thought those traps were illegal now," I said.

Cara edged closer and the fox jumped and twisted around the metal teeth and its own leg. It began to bark, a high-pitched and panicked yapping.

"They are," Peter said, grimly.

Cara crouched. "Shhh," she said to the animal.

"Keep back," Peter said. "They have a terrible bite."

"Shhh," she repeated, and the fox lay back on the ground, its nose down and its ears cocked, watching her. The shoulder of the trapped leg was twisted at an obscene angle.

"It's too badly injured," Peter said. "Come away."

"Help me get the trap open." Cara reached her hand to the fox, which was quiet now, its breathing slowing.

"Even if we could get it open, it wouldn't survive. I've seen it before, there's nothing we can do."

"It's all right," Cara crooned, and the amber eyes watched her. She held her hand flat to the muzzle as I'd seen people do with the horses that pulled the tourist carriages in Hyde Park.

"We can't just leave it," I said, and Peter looked at me, his lips pressed tight together. I knew what he was thinking. I handed him the sample knife I still carried in a sheath attached to the belt around my Army & Navy shorts.

Peter moved in front of her and slit the

fox's throat. It didn't make a sound.

But Cara cried out, "No!" She shoved at Peter, who was still crouching, and he toppled into the ferns. I watched in horror as she pressed her hands to the fox's neck while the blood pumped once, twice between her fingers and then slowed. Her hands were red when she stood up, and for an instant I thought that somehow Peter had cut her too.

"You bastard," she said.

Peter sat up, his knees bent, looking up at her. The expression on his face was one of pity.

"I could have saved him," she whispered. They stared at each other as if daring the other to look away first.

"No," he said. "It was too late."

She turned and strode off through the little wood, and then began to run and had disappeared before Peter was even standing.

"Should we go after her?" I said.

"No. Let's leave her for a while. It'll be better." He tore off a handful of fern leaves and wiped my knife before handing it back. "Thank you. It's not every woman who carries a knife around with her, or not the ones I know."

I looked at the fox, its eyes already glassy, its muscles soft. I wasn't surprised that

191

death had changed it so fast. "Should we bury it?" I said.

"Something will come along and eat it soon."

"At least the trap has been sprung. Poor old fox." I turned away so he wouldn't see me wipe under my eyes. I wanted to continue to be that knife-carrying woman, someone more robust and capable than Cara.

We walked in silence, and when we came out from the trees we were nearer the kitchen garden than I had imagined.

"Have you been inside the model dairy yet?" I asked.

"I thought it was boarded up," Peter said.

"I prised off one of the panels. I'll show you if you'd like. I think it must have been built as another folly, it's far too small to be practical but the detail inside is extraordinary. The central room has a vaulted ceiling, it's a smaller version of the dining hall, and the ribs have clusters of carved oak leaves at the ends. It's very beautiful."

"It sounds it," he said, but I could tell he wasn't really listening.

We were beside one of the garden's high brick walls, on a track made by the farmer to move his cows in and out of the park. We reached a corner of the wall where the track divided, the entrance to the kitchen garden and the dairy to our left, the gate into the estate straight ahead. We paused at the junction, and I went to turn left, while Peter shaded his eyes and looked ahead.

"There she is," he said.

In the distance Cara was in with the cattle, which must have been returned by the farmer while we were in the wood attending to the fox, and with an unfamiliar flare of resentment, I realised Peter had been thinking about Cara all the time we had been walking.

"Do you mind?" he said.

"No, absolutely." I kept my voice cheerful. "Go, you should go to her."

And without answering or saying goodbye he climbed the gate and jogged away, calling her name. I rested my arms on the top bar and saw Cara spin round when he reached her; even from my distance I could see the angry set of her features. She raised her hand and I wondered if it would leave a bloody print on his cheek, but he caught her by the wrist and then drew her into him. She softened and he lowered his head to kiss her and she kissed him back. Then, almost as if he regretted starting something, it was Peter who pulled away first.

I cut back the way we had come and then

went left and into the mausoleum. On the chests of the women were two bouquets of wilting daisies and Scotch thistles picked from the field. I didn't know whether it was Peter or Cara who had left them there.

ELEVEN

In those evenings at Lyntons I learned about wine. I don't mean the grapes and the blends, although a little of these stuck too, but how much of it I needed to get a warm buzz in my cheeks, what the right amount was to loosen my joints and allow me to talk, and how many glasses it took for me to believe I was charming and witty. I came to know what my tipping point was, and when to cover my glass with my hand. Cara and Peter would drink until one of them fell asleep at the table. They would be drunk but never raucous or angry. The three of us talked and drank and laughed. I have never laughed as much as during the early days of that August. For the first time, I was no longer looking at a circle of backs; now I was inside the group.

I had Cara buy me more headache tablets when she cycled into town, and I worked out that if I slept long enough into the afternoon I could outsleep my hangover.

On the second Sunday in August I dragged myself out of bed and crept off to church; it was a habit I found difficult to break even when I hadn't had enough sleep. I discovered that in the early part of the morning a mist hovered in the hollows of the estate and the grass was wet with dew. There was a smell in the air of bonfires, the land already preparing for autumn. So much had changed for me since I'd last walked along the avenues of limes and yews that it seemed at least a month must have passed, while in reality, it had been only two weeks. The morning welcomed me and I felt lighter, more confident, walking with my head up, ready for anything. I sat in the same pew as before but didn't look around to count the congregation or to see whether Cara had come. I think the sermon was supposed to mark the Transfiguration of our Lord, but Victor grew quieter as he spoke and I found myself leaning forward to catch his words about shining light, halos, and how we all have the potential to be changed for the better even when life is at its worst. He didn't sound convinced or convincing. Afterwards he invited us to confess silently, and I wondered if he'd suggested this because he thought I needed it. I knelt to pray like everyone around me and I confessed my sins to myself, but I was already considering whether anyone was listening.

After the service, I headed for the back gate.

"Miss Jellico!" someone called, and I knew before I turned it would be Victor. He was sitting on the bottom lip of the same tomb that we had sat on before, this time with two glasses of water.

"One fewer person in the pews than last Sunday," he said.

"Cara didn't come," I said. "But she doesn't count. Your congregation wouldn't have let her in, would they? Or else they'd be after her blood."

"Not Christ's this time?"

We smiled at each other.

"I have met her properly now, and her . . . her husband, Peter. They're very nice. You mustn't get the wrong impression."

He made a sound in his throat as if he disagreed but couldn't bring himself to say so.

"They've been looking after me, cooking and showing me around the house."

"Is it as bad as it seems from the outside?"

"Worse. Fireplaces ripped out, the plaster crumbling; there are holes in the walls and mouldy books in the library. It's all rather sad."

"It sounds it," he said.

"And do you know? Somebody cut out every one of the peacocks' eyes from the wallpaper in the blue drawing room."

"Enucleation." He drank some water.

"Pardon me?"

"Surgical removal of the eyeball."

I shuddered. "But who would do such a thing?"

"The soldiers who were stationed there. Bored out of their minds and looking for a distraction."

"But surely you weren't there, during the war?"

"No, no. I don't mean I was at Lyntons. No. I was a medical student for most of the war."

I sipped my water, waited. A bee moved from one flower to another. I remembered the black-and-white newsreels of British doctors smiling and smoking with bandaged soldiers in hospital tents. I didn't press him.

"Can I tell you something, Miss Jellico?" Victor said after we'd been silent for a while. I didn't know what was coming, but I wasn't sure I wanted to hear it.

"About Cara?"

He turned his head and looked at me,

surprised.

"About me."

I tipped my glass but it was empty.

"I'm not certain about all of this." His outspread arm took in the graveyard, the church, the lane beyond. "My ministry. I gave up medicine before I'd finished my final year. I just couldn't . . . I thought I had a calling. I thought joining the clergy might help, I hoped I might be able to help. Now I'm not so sure."

"But haven't you already been a minister for what, twenty years?"

"Fourteen years, five months, and three days. It takes a long time to become ordained. Nearly as long as it does to train to be a doctor."

"Fourteen years is still quite a time to decide it's not for you."

"You think that if someone's been one thing for so long, they can't become something else? You weren't listening to my sermon." He gave a mirthless laugh.

"No, I was. Of course we can all change, but I just don't think you should be hasty."

"Really?"

He made me uncomfortable, looking at me as if he could see right inside. I covered my disquiet with blandness: "But I'm sure you must do a lot for your parishioners. A

199

town needs its priest."

"Does it? I keep hoping the congregation numbers will fall so low that the decision will be taken out of my hands."

"Wouldn't you just get moved somewhere else?"

"I can't help them," he said. "I couldn't help with medicine and I can't help with faith. And the trouble is they want too much help, too much forgiveness. Sometimes it's like they're each taking a little bit of me, inch by inch, cell by cell, until poof!" He lifted a hand, brought his fingers together, and in a gesture of throwing something away spread them wide. "And what's left will float off. Sometimes, Miss Jellico, I hate them and their neediness. Isn't that terrible? When the telephone rings or I hear the knocker on the rectory's front door, my heart sinks and all I want to do is hide. Like this — hiding from my congregation in my own churchyard. They want forgiveness, but who am I to say that all will be well?"

The shouting woke me. I lay in my bed and listened, Cara's voice and then Peter's. I couldn't make out the words. I tried to get back to sleep but objects were being thrown or knocked off a table, a door crashed, and footsteps thundered through the house.

Cara was on the terrace yelling in Italian up at Peter. I got out of bed, wrapped a blanket around me, and sat on the floor with my back to the wall beside the window. If I could hear them, I may as well listen. I wasn't certain though that if they went into the bathroom I would have the willpower not to pull up the floorboard and watch them through the judas hole.

"Please can we not go through all this again," Peter called from inside the house.

"You've never believed me," Cara shouted up to him.

"Come back to bed." Peter sounded tired.

"You think it was Paddy, don't you? You've always thought it was Paddy."

"It doesn't matter what I think."

"No, it doesn't."

"But you understand it's not possible," Peter said down to her. I could tell he was trying to hold his patience. "It's just something your mind made up without you realising it."

This seemed to enrage her even more and she roared: "What about Mary? How do you explain that?" I wondered who Mary was.

"Bloody hell, it's a story," Peter shouted, finally driven to anger. "It's made up. None of it is true."

Cara must have stormed off then; there

201

was only Peter calling her name, and after that the closing of the window and his footsteps going through the house. I went back to bed and heard nothing more.

The orangery, positioned at right angles to the house, was its smaller glass cousin. Its portico's six columns were thinner and less ornate, and the outside steps down to what had once been a formal garden — a parterre with box hedges gone wild and lost gravel paths — were narrower and shorter. In the library of the British Museum I'd read that the orangery was the first glasshouse to collect rainwater from the roof and channel it down the insides of the internal pillars to water the plants.

Peter hadn't included it in his tour, and the door was kept locked, so all I'd managed to do was to peer through the green-stained windows at the broken floor tiles and the rusting iron benches; and I had seen the orange tree. It dominated the orangery; bushy and unkempt, it reached out fifteen feet until its branches pressed against the glass and cracked the panes. Its trunk was six inches in diameter and I guessed it was thirty years old, maybe fifty.

I sat on the terrace wall and sketched the building's eight arched windows, the Doric columns, and the double glass doors. I should have measured it and noted the number of broken panes, which sections were rusted beyond repair and would need replacing, producing an architectural drawing instead of something that tried to capture the essence of the building, the light and shade, the history. But I had stopped doing any proper work on Mr. Liebermann's report. I no longer cared or thought much about it. Sometimes I sketched a building for pleasure, but Cara and Peter's indolence had rubbed off on me, and most of the time I didn't even bother to do that.

"Peter's asleep," Cara said, coming up behind me. "Did you know he sleeps with the house keys under his pillow? I think he's worried I'll escape."

I didn't point out that we were in the garden, all the external doors were unlocked, and there was nothing to stop her cycling off down the avenue. It was three in the afternoon.

"But look!" She brought the ring of keys from behind her back and jangled them. "I was so quiet. I pulled them out bit by bit and managed not to wake him." She sat beside me, her legs dangling over the wall like mine, and looked across my arm at my drawing.

"It's beautiful," she said.

I held the pad away from me and looked from it to the orangery and back again. "Not bad, I suppose."

She offered me a cigarette. Mine were always crushed; a running joke between us all.

"Peter's thinking about getting a camera so he doesn't have to do any drawings. But they're expensive." She rubbed her fingers and thumb together.

"And then there's getting the film developed," I said. We leaned back, our faces tilted up to the sun, and puffed on our cigarettes.

"He's always worrying about money," she said. "How much *this* costs, how much *that* costs." With each *this* and *that* she waved her cigarette in the air. "He's always complaining about the amount of work he does and how we don't have any money. He says I spend it all on food. But he likes to eat the dinners."

She must have forgotten that she'd already told me this.

"And here we are squatting at Lyntons rather than staying at the Harrow in town, or renting a nice little cottage." She inhaled long and deep, gearing up for another argument. Such a short time before, when we'd stood at the top of the meadow, she had said how she never wanted to leave. "But I know what he spends his money on. His wife!" She said the last word with a sneer and kicked her bare heels against the bricks of the retaining wall.

"I'm sure he spends as much on you as he's able."

She didn't answer, perhaps hadn't thought much of my reply, but after a while she said, "I'm worried, Fran, that Peter will go back."

"Back where?"

"Back to her. To Mallory. One day he'll wake up and realise she can give him things I can't."

"I'm sure that won't happen."

"Do you think he loves me? Would he do anything for me?"

I waited for a beat, for a moment, and forced myself not to look around and up to their bedroom window. "Of course. And, of course he loves you," I said.

"Yes," she said. "I think he does. One day we'll get married and I'll have another baby. Two babies! Three!" She laughed. Ahead of us the parkland shimmered. The cows were under the cedar again.

"It must have been hard giving up a child for adoption, for you and for Peter," I said, angling for more information. "Was it a girl or a boy?"

She narrowed her eyes.

"I understand if you don't want to talk about it," I continued, gripping the wall, waiting for an outburst.

"No, I'll tell you," she said. "If you really want to know." And she threw the rest of her cigarette into the garden below. "I can't remember what I told you last time. Where did I get to?"

"You'd just had a row with Peter in his little green car and run away, and he had found you and taken you back to Killaspy." I was still too coy to mention the undressing.

"You have been listening hard," she said, smiling, and then continued with her story.

"I think it was a little while after Peter left that second time that I spent two or three days in bed feeling sick. Christmas came and went. Isabel never liked to be around people who were ill; she let Dermod look after me like she always had. I suppose when she was a child they would have had a nursery maid or a nanny, before the governess. I don't blame her, it was how she was raised. Dermod brought me a glass of 7 Up — that's what we drank when we were ill. He would heat it first to get rid of the gas and bring it upstairs with a boiled egg or a slice of toast. But I couldn't eat anything. He asked me whether my visitor had arrived and I thought he meant that Peter was downstairs, and I almost jumped out of bed even though I was about to be sick. I must have looked a state. But then I realised he meant my period, and I also realised that it hadn't arrived, and I was sure it should have. Isabel worked it out too when I looked peaky at breakfast and all I wanted to do was sleep. We didn't have a conversation. She just pursed her lips and suggested we bring the wedding forward a couple of months, and what could I do? I went along with that plan too.

"I couldn't talk to her about it, so I went to see Father Creagh, but he didn't have any answers. He said it was blasphemous, what I was suggesting, and gave me the usual Hail Marys. When I was feeling better I went back to work for Miss Landers, writing her letters and reading her the magazine, and then I would go home, straight up to my room to cry. I thought about ending it then but I couldn't have done it to the baby. I thought about running away of course, but in the end I decided all I could do was marry Paddy.

"One afternoon in January, Peter was waiting for me in his car outside Miss

Landers's cottage. He told me he'd asked Mallory for a divorce. I said he was too late and I was marrying Paddy. He wanted me to get in the passenger seat for us to talk or at least for him to drive me home, but I wouldn't, and so he drove behind me all the way back to Killaspy as though his car was the hearse and I was the undertaker.

"He came in when we reached the house, I couldn't stop him. Isabel had given up on him by then, but she was polite — she asked if he'd like tea and called for Dermod. The three of us stood in the drawing room making conversation. I'd never been so unhappy in my whole life. Isabel mentioned that the wedding had been brought forward. She was grumbling about the expense and why it should be up to the bride's family to pay for everything. Peter didn't get it at first, why the wedding was happening sooner, and Isabel was too polite to say, but her eyes kept flicking to my stomach until I just came out and said that I was pregnant, and Isabel sat in her chair as if she hadn't already realised, and Peter was furious. *Do you love him?* he said, meaning Paddy. I didn't want to have the conversation — I didn't think it was going to get me anywhere. I'd spent weeks going through my options, and it seemed to me there was only one. It wasn't as simple as saying whether I loved Paddy or not. But Peter took my lack of an answer as a no and he held out his hand and said, *Well, come away with me then.*"

Abruptly, Cara picked up the ring of keys she'd placed by her side and stood. "Would you like to see the orangery now?" she asked.

"Wait," I said. "I don't understand. Was Paddy the father?" I stumbled to my feet but Cara was already halfway along the terrace.

"Oh, Frances!" The annoyance in her voice was clear. "Of course not!" she called over her shoulder, bringing the first act to an end, letting the curtains close and making me wait for the second half.

Inside the orangery the air was thick and scented — vegetation, soil, and overripe fruit. Leaves pressed around me, a sticky sap catching on my skin and clothes as I ducked under branches to a clearer spot in the middle of the room where Cara was waiting. She wouldn't look at me and seemed irritated, like a tour guide whose tourists ask pointless questions and won't keep up.

Small grey mounds lay on the floor in various states of decay, and I saw they were

209

oranges, and I realised that for years the tree must have been fruiting and dropping them on the stone paving, nature hoping some of them would seed. I flapped my hand in front of my face to keep away the tiny flies and wasps which buzzed around the rotting fruit. There were no orange tree saplings in the orangery; the main tree had been taking all the water and light. But other plants were growing: bindweed snaked across the floor, and the whole of the back wall, which must have been built of brick, once whitewashed and covered with trellis, was pasted with the great hairy trunks of ivy, and almost completely obscured. Many of the iron seats around the sides of the room had rusted away, and there were gaps in the stone pavers where an underfloor heating system must have once supplied warmth.

"Be careful," I said to Cara. "Your feet!" Under my shoes splinters of glass crunched where several broken windows in the roof had fallen inwards. "Do you think you should get your shoes?"

"I'm fine," Cara said, stepping forward as if nothing could hurt her.

"How did the tree survive without anyone to tend it?" I said, hoping to engage her in ordinary conversation and take her mind off the row that I was sure was brewing.

She jerked her head up to where the guttering had collapsed and hung inside the building. "It found a way," she said. "Everything will find a way to survive if it can."

"I suppose the rain must come in and water it," I said. "And look, there are still some ripe oranges on the tree." I pointed and she followed the line of my finger to three globes, their skins dimpled and almost misshapen. "It's a bitter orange tree. *Citrus aurantium.*"

"I tried one a little while ago," she said. "They don't taste very nice."

"Old and a bit dried up, I expect. They would have been ready for picking months ago. If you could get any juice out, you'd have to add lots of sugar. I think they're mostly used for marmalade."

"I found something else in here yesterday. Not oranges. Do you want to see?" She still sounded moody.

"Oh, yes please." Whereas I sounded as though I were trying to distract a child who threatened a tantrum.

She took me to a corner of the back wall, farthest from the orange tree. Here the ivy hung in loops and strands from the ceiling. Cara pushed it out of the way.

"Look," she said.

"What?" I saw a section of the back wall where the trunks crisscrossed each other, full of cobwebs and old leaves that had been caught before they fell.

"Look harder," she said.

Behind the ivy, I saw the frame of a wooden door. I plucked at the green leaves and ripped off the softer twigs until more of it was exposed: the metal plate of a keyhole, a bottom hinge. Together we tore at the plant until above the door a hand-painted sign was revealed: *The Museum.*

TWELVE

After Cara and I uncovered the sign and the keyhole, she tried all the keys from the set she had taken from under Peter's pillow but none of them fitted. I was relieved, although I would have found it hard to articulate exactly why. If something had remained hidden behind that door for enough years for ivy to grow that thick across it, I was uneasy about opening it now. But Cara was excited and she ran off to wake Peter. When she was gone I put my eye to the keyhole, the action as unnerving as putting my eye to the judas hole in my bathroom floor. I braced myself for what I might see, but whatever was on the other side didn't show itself. There was only darkness.

Peter and Cara returned with a saw and another set of keys that was kept in the basement kitchen. None of these unlocked the door either, and so he sawed through the stems of the ivy, some as thick as a wrist, and then they ripped them off in a frenzy, laughing while long strings snapped away from the wood and surrounding brick.

"I'm not sure about this," I said, but neither of them stopped.

Peter spent some time poking bits of wire into the keyhole while Cara watched. Of course, I could have gone and done something else, but if they were going to open it I needed to see what was behind it myself and be reassured that my fear, which I couldn't name, was irrational.

After ten minutes on his knees Peter stood and kicked the door, and I thought perhaps that was it. But he went off without speaking and returned with a sledgehammer.

He stood sideways to the Museum's door and steadied himself, his feet wide, his legs tensed.

I looked over at Cara. A leaf had fallen onto her shoulder where the neck of her dress gaped open. As I went to brush it off, the leaf opened its serrated wings and the butterfly showed its red and black markings. I watched its jointed legs cling to Cara's skin, making minute movements for balance, and I became aware of its insect nature: its waving antennae, its hairy thorax, the pulsating abdomen, and its compound eye recording a thousand instances of me. It uncurled its proboscis from its mouthparts and tasted Cara's skin.

Peter swung the sledgehammer, and the butterfly, caught in an updraught from the movement, lifted straight off from Cara's shoulder, legs flailing and abdomen quivering like a pupa.

"I don't know about this," I said as Peter took aim.

"Frances?" Cara said, her hand on my arm.

"Keep back," Peter said, although we hadn't moved.

"We could write to Mr. Liebermann about the key," I said.

"Frances?" Cara repeated.

"Or send him a telegram. Cara could go into town on her bicycle. Couldn't you, Cara?"

"Will you listen for a second?" Her hand gripped my arm through my blouse, pinching my skin. I tried to shake her off. It was Peter's attention I wanted.

"Stop!" I called out.

"Wait," Cara said. "You haven't understood, about my story, the things I was telling you outside on the wall." Her voice was low. Peter grunted while he swung the sledgehammer behind him and let its own weight carry itself forward. It hit the door just below the lock. Flakes of paint and dead leaves fell around us. In another corner, a tinkle of breaking glass.

"Please!" I said. "I don't think we should." I moved towards him, but I didn't step between the hammer and the door. I wasn't brave enough for that.

"Fran," Cara said. And I turned, took note of her urgency. "You haven't been listening properly." She could see I didn't know what she meant. "About the baby," she said. She was whispering although there was no need, Peter wasn't paying us any attention.

"What?" I said, trying to take in her words.

"You asked me if Paddy was the father."

It took me a moment to get back to the story she had been telling, and when I did, I glanced at Peter, remembering what she had said about him undressing her in the car after she'd run away in the rain.

"No," she said. "I didn't sleep with Peter either. The baby didn't have a father."

"What do you mean?" I said, one eye on the Museum door. "Didn't have a father?"

"There wasn't a father," she said. "I was a virgin."

I laughed, embarrassed, wondering if this was another joke I wasn't getting.

"You have to believe me." She was insistent, making me look at her, focus on her words. "We're friends, aren't we? And that's what friends do, don't they? Listen and believe?"

I was going to say that what she was talking about made no sense and she must be mistaken, but Peter swung at the door again with the sledgehammer, and this time it gave way with a crunch of metal and breaking wood.

"What did you do?" Victor asks.

I am tired. I want him to go away. I have had enough of them all.

"We opened the Museum." I hope it will shut him up.

"But afterwards, what happened then?"

He is persistent, I will give him that. And I know he wants what he thinks is right. I should try to be kinder.

"I read a research paper once about guilt and weight," I say, and stop. He raises his eyebrows, waiting for me to continue. I relent and fly down from my difficult-old-bird perch. "That guilt is a heavy weight to carry?"

"A burden?" he says.

"Exactly."

Good man.

The participants — American and Canadian students — were asked whether they had the sensation of being physically heavier after thinking about their unethical acts. It's no surprise to me that they did. I am heavier than when I first met Victor, even though if I were put on the scales I would be lighter; these days I have the bones of a sparrow, the beaky face too; all I am missing are the feathers. But I am a different woman from that almost-forty-year-old at Lyntons; she might have been heavyset but she was faint-hearted, easily led. I know now that we do all have the ability to transform ourselves.

But I can see Victor hasn't heard me or I haven't spoken the words aloud because he has picked up his book, and now my eyes fall shut. Best let hidden things remain hidden, I should have said. Sleeping dogs and all that. If I were then the woman I am now, I would have shouted and stood between the sledgehammer and the door that day, when Peter opened the Museum.

When Peter opened the Museum, Cara let go of my arm.

"Wait," I said. "What?" I reached out to hold her back and ask her what she meant, but she shook me off and went forward, and I, so as not to be left behind, followed. At first only the greenish light coming through the orangery door illuminated the room, showing grey and shadowed mountainous shapes, higher than our heads. We stopped and stared. A breath came against my face: a warm gust of air with nothing to blow it, like the strange breezes that surge down the escalators and through the tunnels of the London Underground even when no train is coming. It had a smell of the old days: lavender oil, carbolic soap, furniture polish.

The odour it left behind was stale, dusty, with a tang of chemical, of things preserved in formaldehyde. Cara was the first to tug off a sheet, dust rising in the dim light, to reveal not mountains of earth and rock or anything created by nature, but furniture: dining tables, side tables, desks, and chairs, stacked one on the other. Whoever had put it there had been in a hurry. Headboards and paintings, sofas and lamps, statues and a chiffonier all pressed together — everything, I realised, the Lynton family had loved and valued and decided was worth hiding when the house was requisitioned. The room and its contents must have lain forgotten and undiscovered for almost thirty years.

The walls were brick and windowless, but Peter found a pole to open the louvres in the roof and let in more murky green through a skylight.

Cara inched along a narrow pathway between the towering pieces of furniture and the cabinets placed against the walls. I followed. One contained hundreds of pieces of carved ivory — puzzle balls and dragons; another, small fossils — ammonites and trilobites; while in a third, tiny heads lay in rows, their eyelids sewn closed, their skin wizened and brown, and their hair long. Cara opened the cabinet and removed a head — an oversized walnut in her palm — and exclaimed at the lifelike features, until Peter, squeezing past us, said that it was real. She shuddered as she replaced it.

"What did you mean?" I whispered. "It isn't possible to have a baby without . . ." I was prudish, didn't know what word I should use.

"Isn't it?" she mocked. "I thought even the Church of England believed in the virgin birth?"

"But that's different. You and Peter . . . Maybe you're mistaken," I finished lamely.

"How is it different? I hadn't had sex."

She opened the lid of a tiny box inlaid with ivory or mother-of-pearl and a waltz played. Inside was a ring, black with gold symbols around the edge and a dull diamond set in the middle. She slipped it onto the finger where her wedding band had sat, and tilted her hand one way and the other. "Look at this." She held it up to me. "Isn't it amazing?" I couldn't look at the ring; I could only stare at her, trying to work out what kind of woman she was. A liar or a saint?

"Oh Fran, I'm sorry," she said, when she saw my face. She closed the box and the music stopped. "I just need you to believe me. Peter won't let me talk about it. Or what happened afterwards. It's as if the baby never existed. You know what he's like."

"What have you two found?" Peter was back, excited. "Isn't it incredible?"

I let them move on together, opening more cabinets and drawers.

I unlatched the doors to a cupboard and saw shelves of medical jars filled with yellow-tinged liquid. Samples preserved and labelled: *Bos taurus, Prionus, Buprestis.* I picked up each one and examined it without taking in what I was looking at, trying to understand how what Cara had told me might be possible. Perhaps there was another man she hadn't mentioned. *Homo,* the next label said, and I caught a glimpse of soft creamy flesh pressed against the glass before I shoved it back and pushed the cupboard doors closed.

Peter and Cara were pulling out Chinese vases from packing cases stuffed with straw, a sculpture of a man I recognised as Hercules holding three apples behind his back, a quantity of curved swords. Glass domes stood on top of the cabinets, filled with stuffed animals: hundreds of tiny birds motionless and yet flying in terror from an eagle which forever hovered above them. None of them would be caught, and yet they were already dead. There were squirrels and fish, a pair of exotic lizards with their frilled neck plates raised and their mouths open mid-hiss. An adult grizzly bear reared up on its hind legs with its canines exposed. I patted it as I went past. "It's all right, boy," I whispered. "We won't disturb you for long." On and on, the room was filled with a collector's trophies and a family's possessions. I opened a small leather case to find pots of dried-up cream and a silver-backed hairbrush with strands of long grey hair still entangled in the bristles. I shut it quickly.

Peter whistled. "This is worth a pretty penny," he said. He held a sculpture of a cat sitting upright on a wooden base, its tail curled around its paws and its ears back. He weighed it in his hands. "Bronze. Egyptian, could be Twenty-Sixth Dynasty."

"Mr. Liebermann will be delighted," I

said, making my way towards him. Cara was at the other end of the room.

Peter looked at me. "Surely you wouldn't want all of this to be shipped over to America? I thought you were against that? And besides, none of this is on the inventory, Fran. Not on mine. And, I believe, not on yours either." He put the cat on a chest of drawers and it observed us, imperious.

That might have been the moment I could have said none of it belonged to us, that it belonged to Mr. Liebermann or the heirs of Dorothea Lynton if Victor could trace them, but I said nothing.

At my feet was a flat case. I crouched and opened it so I wouldn't have to see Peter's face and acquiesce in what he was thinking, as though by avoiding his eye I could avoid complicity. The inside was covered with purple velvet and indented, holding the separated pieces of what might have been a musical instrument. It smelled of wood and resin. I lifted out one of the sections — a black tube. I wasn't paying attention, didn't register that it wasn't part of a clarinet or an oboe. I was wondering how I could ask Peter about what Cara had told me.

He took the object from my hands. "A telescope," he said, just as I blanched. "How marvellous." He expanded the three tubes and focussed the eyepiece on the end of the room where Cara was opening drawers inside a large wardrobe. "Excellent." It wasn't clear whether he was referring to Cara or the quality of the instrument. "Here." He held it out.

"No . . . thanks." I didn't want to put my eye to the lens in front of Peter, fearing that in some way the action might reveal how I gazed on him and Cara through a similar tube.

"Go on. It's exceptionally well made."

"I can't close one eye," I said. "I can't wink."

"Really? How curious."

He moved behind me and his hand came up to cover my left eye. I took the telescope and held it to my right, recognising the familiar feel of the cold metal. Together we stood in an awkward backwards embrace and I had no choice but to look through the lens.

"Now turn it to focus," he said.

"Like this?" I said, twisting it, knowing of course how it worked, until Cara's beautiful face, shaped into a Gothic pointed arch by her hair, sharpened within the circle. Peter knelt again in front of the case. "Look," he said, and I lowered myself beside him. I could hear the beat of blood in my ears, feel a blush rising from my throat. We were hidden behind a sofa, our heads close enough for me to smell his aftershave, hear the grate of his afternoon bristles as he rubbed his hand across his cheek. He slotted the telescope back into its space and I went to shut the lid. "Wait," he said. "There's one missing." His fingers went to an empty hole. "Was it here when you opened it?" He searched around the floor as if I had dropped it. "The smallest."

"It might have been. I'm not certain." I stood up too fast and my head spun. There wasn't enough air in the room. I couldn't tell him that I knew where it was.

"The set's of no value if one's missing." He scouted around the floor again. "Damn." He looked up as I swayed. "Fran, are you all right?" He stood and took my elbow but I pulled away. Cara had stopped rummaging through the drawers and was looking at us. The room was darkening at the edges.

"Fran?" he repeated.

"I'm sorry," I said. "I just need some air."

I stumbled my way out of the Museum and ran through the orangery without knowing where I was going. The original structure of the garden was still visible from the top windows of the house, but at ground level the towering and unruly box hedging, ten or twelve feet high, obscured the pattern. I dipped my head and shoved my way forward, burrowing between the stems and leaves of the box until they closed behind me. I pushed through them, moving against a tide, and when they thinned I emerged on the other side to the secret centre: a circular pond. I heard Peter call my name from the terrace but I huddled under the hedge, worried he would go into the house and search for me upstairs. Had I replaced the floorboard in the bathroom? Of course I had. But now I imagined him stepping across my bathroom floor and noticing it was loose. He lifted up the board and saw the missing telescope. But what if I *hadn't* put the board back, should I go upstairs and check? Would I make it there before him? I stood up, undecided. Again, I heard Peter call my name, and again I pressed myself into the stalks of the box hedge and didn't move until several silent minutes had passed, and then I pushed my way back through the foliage.

I ran into the house, up the grand staircase, and through the baize door. There was no one in my bathroom and of course the board was still in place. I pulled the bathroom door shut and grabbed my handbag from my bedroom. One floor down, I crept along Cara and Peter's hallway and pressed my ear to their door; there was no sound. I went into their sitting room, found a pen and a scrap of paper, and left them a note on their makeshift table:

Gone to London. Not sure when I'll be back.

THIRTEEN

I caught a bus going north-west from Waterloo and got off at Dollis Hill. I could have used the Underground, but Mother and I had usually taken the bus in London once we could no longer afford taxis. If there was an accident, she said, she wanted to be able to see her head rolling away instead of having to scrabble around for it in the dark.

I had been gone for only two weeks but already London seemed foreign, or else it was I who was the foreigner.

I stood outside 24 Forrest Road in the creeping dusk and considered the two women who had shared the upstairs rooms for almost thirty years. My mother had been brought up with certain expectations — a couple of servants, a nice house, a loving husband, a child or two. She had believed she would have all of this when she became engaged to Luther Jellico, a distant and wealthier cousin. But Luther delayed the wedding for two years, and then longer, making her wait until he had returned from Gallipoli. When I was ten, the marriage ended; the entertaining in the grand house in Notting Hill, the tailor-made clothes, the fine dinners, all of them over. My father moved me and Mother to a few rooms in north London.

Mother used to call the place we lived in *an apartment,* but 24 Forrest Road hadn't been properly converted. We shared the front door with our downstairs neighbour, Mrs. Lee, as well as the boiler and the plumbing. A bath with a lid, which doubled as a table, stood in the kitchen. Filling it used a boiler's worth of hot water, as Mrs. Lee liked to shout up the stairs. Mother and I had shared the bedroom and the bed at the front of the house since the second bedroom was full of furniture and clothes that she had brought with us from Notting Hill.

I walked up the path and peeped through the letter box, but all I could see was a slice of the bannister and the light coming in through Mrs. Lee's kitchen window. I had been hoping for a feeling of homecoming or nostalgia, but I could have been peering into a stranger's house, and I knew I no longer belonged there.

I caught the bus back into town, staring at the families in the lit windows of the houses — a man reading a newspaper with his slippers on, a child kneeling on a sofa with her nose pressed to the glass, waiting for her father to come home from work, a young woman on an upright chair, the light from a television flickering over her face. Ordinary lives.

When I got off the bus in Fitzrovia I walked until I came across a small hotel that appeared suitable: probably not expensive but with recently washed net curtains, three steps up to the front door which were free of street dust, the exterior nothing like the boarding house I had stayed in before I'd left London after Mother died.

The landlady seemed pleasant. She showed me a room on the first floor, around a corner and along a floral-carpeted hallway lit at the end by an arched window. She held the bedroom door open to show me the single bed pressed into a corner, the wardrobe too narrow for a rail and hangers. When she said the price, I said that would be fine, and then she told me I had to stay two nights because it was August, and again I said that would be fine and yes, I would like dinner in the dining room on both nights and breakfast on both mornings. She demonstrated the corridor light switch, pressing in a button which a timer released tick by tick until it popped and the light was extinguished, and she showed me the bathroom, back towards the staircase. All of it neat and clean.

When I went downstairs, the dining room at the front of the house was empty, although I had heard people coming and going through the front door and up the stairs. The food was poor but I ate all three courses: a liver pâté that crumbled on the knife, a bland chicken fricassee, and a bowl of ice cream with a wafer that was soft. I pictured Cara cooking dinner at Lyntons and then the two of them, without me, sitting on the portico steps in the dark with some wine in the tin cups, talking about the Museum and everything they had found. I had already convinced myself that there was nothing to link me to the missing telescope, that there was no more reason now for them to know it was under the floor than there had been previously. And I had also resolved to rip it out as soon as I returned. I imagined them lighting their cigarettes and discussing what to do about the things in the Museum. Surely Cara would have convinced Peter to telegraph Mr. Liebermann. When I focussed again on my dismal surroundings, I was engulfed by homesickness and I left the dining room in a hurry. Upstairs I undressed and hung my clothes on the pegs inside the wardrobe, then placed my shoes heel to toe in the gap between the bed and the wall. Other guests returned and I heard snatches of conversation, but I must have been tired because I slept right through until breakfast was almost over and all I saw were the empty cups and dirty plates of the guests who had eaten before me.

I recognised the woman behind the desk of the British Museum Library. I smiled when I showed her my pass and said, "How are you today?" hoping she would greet me by name. She nodded her head to let me through, and I could tell she didn't remember me. I walked on to the circular reading room.

I gazed up at the beautiful domed roof as I'd seen tourists do, trying to be excited by the thought of all the books as I used to be, all the heads bowed in study, hoping to find comfort in the familiar throat-clearings and sniffs. The desks were laid out like the spokes of a wheel, each stretching from the central hub to the shelves at the circumference. My usual spoke pointed to three o'clock, where I would sit in the penultimate chair. The light was on over my blotter, a man hunched over my desk. I found an empty chair near the entrance where the outside noise and a draught leaked in.

On the customary forms I requested in pencil the same books I'd studied after I'd received the first letter from Mr. Liebermann. I thought I might have missed some mention of the bridge or its architect. While I was waiting, I enquired about back issues of Irish newspapers. I told myself I was simply curious about Cara's story, it wasn't that I was checking. The man at the desk told me they were stored at a different location — Colindale, but that it was closed for maintenance. With his help I was able to confirm that the Beatles had played in Dublin in November 1963, but I didn't get to see the picture of a young Cara with mascara running down her cheeks.

When my books arrived there was nothing I had missed, no architect mentioned that I hadn't made a note of and already cross-referenced. But in one book I examined more closely a photograph of Lyntons that I had passed over last time: a woman in Edwardian dress sat at a small iron table under the portico where Cara, Peter, and I ate our breakfasts. A dog lay on her lap and her face wore that sullen expression shared by all people in early photographs as they sit still for the camera. On the table was a cup and saucer and teapot. The picture was black-and-white of course, and I couldn't quite make out the pattern on the china. I wondered if the woman was Dorothea.

I opened another book and pretended to read, at the same time placing my handbag on my lap and slipping the first book into its open mouth. It wouldn't close, and the top of the book poked out, but I picked up the bag and walked away from my desk. I wanted a hand to land on my shoulder as confirmation that I had been seen, that I existed, but I wasn't noticed, no one stopped me.

That evening, I was the only guest in the hotel dining room when the soup was served, but as I began to eat at my small table set for one, a couple arrived, noisy and apologetic, making jokes with the landlady, who let them sit at the table in the window although it had been laid for four. The woman was blowsy, big-chested, with a ring on every finger, while the man was slight, with sunken cheeks and hooded eyes.

"Have you just arrived?" the woman said, and it took me a moment, soup spoon halted at my mouth, to realise she was talking to me.

"Just visiting," I said, putting my face back down to my bowl.

"Are you going to be staying long?" she asked. "It's a pleasant little hotel, isn't it, George?"

"Very pleasant," he said.

"Quiet and yet convenient. There are lots of things to see right outside the front door. We could direct you to some if you'd like."

"I'm only staying one more night," I said. "But thank you."

"Sometimes it's difficult for ladies," the woman said. "Travelling alone."

The man looked at the woman too long and I thought there must be another meaning hidden in what she was saying that I wasn't able to comprehend.

"I'm quite happy in my own company," I said.

"It can be lonely spending time on your own. I would know."

The man didn't meet her eye.

The landlady brought in their soup on a tray and put the bowls in front of them.

"Joanna," the woman said. "Your other dinner guest is going to join us at our table. It's not right for a lady to be eating alone."

"What a nice idea," Joanna said, coming over.

"No, no," I said, holding on to my spoon. "Really, I'm fine."

Joanna put my bowl on her tray and carried it to their table. I had no choice but to follow, bringing my spoon with me.

"Lillian." The woman held out her hand. "And this is George."

We shook. "Frances," I said, reluctantly.

"What room are you in?" Lillian asked.

"Number ten."

"Do you hear that, George?" Lillian's bosom leaned across her soup. "Right opposite yours."

While I was trying to work out what their relationship was if they weren't husband and wife as I had assumed, George said under his breath, "Excellent." He finished his soup, and Joanna, who must have been hovering in the corridor, came to the table. George smiled and I saw how his gums had withdrawn from his teeth such a distance that they could at any second have come loose and dropped into his empty bowl with a clatter. Was it too late to change hotels?

We chewed through some dry chops while Lillian told me about St. Paul's and the National Gallery, and how I must be certain to see *Venus and Mars*.

"Love conquers war," George said in a bored voice and without looking up.

I got through the rest of the evening by imagining Peter and Cara on the terrace smoking and watching the bats fly in and out of the mulberry tree.

I managed to escape the table before dessert was served. In the hallway Joanna told me I would be charged for the pudding even though I hadn't eaten it.

When I reached my bedroom, I thought I might have a cigarette, but it seemed pointless without Peter and Cara to smoke one with me. I used the bathroom before Lillian and George or any other guests came upstairs. I scrubbed at my teeth with my fingertip and splashed cold water on my face, patting it dry with three squares of toilet paper.

The bed was soft compared to the camp bed I had become used to at Lyntons, and the sheets clean. I lay under the top one and stared at the ceiling. The thin curtains in front of the window which overlooked the road let in a sickly yellow from a street light. I got out of bed and pulled them open. I'd forgotten how glaring London was at night and longed for the wooded darkness of the hangers. I opened the window to get some air, tugged the curtains closed, and went back to bed. There were noises in the street, high heels and boots going past, a man talking too loudly, a woman giggling, something clacking along the pavement that I couldn't identify, and later, the distant shouts of a drunken youth. I tried to ignore them. Occasionally inside the hotel a door closed or the toilet flushed, or a *goodnight* was called, though I couldn't work out who was speaking. Water gurgled through the pipes and outside a squeak started up, followed by a clunk. I imagined a man with a wooden leg walking past.

At two in the morning I needed the lavatory. I tried to sleep, to ignore my nagging bladder. At two thirty I dressed and pressed my ear to the adjoining wall, listening for bedsprings, and then at the door for footsteps, but I heard nothing, no one. I went into the corridor and pressed the button for the light. The glare made me wince, but the corridor was empty and I hurried around the corner to the bathroom, the button ticking away my allotted time until I reached the security of the light cord. I stared up at the ceiling while I was sitting on the toilet trying to make my body offer up enough for me to last through to the morning. There was no central light point, no ceiling rose with a hidden hole for anyone in a bedroom on the floor above to look through and see me.

Outside the bathroom I pressed the switch. When I was around the corner the overhead bulb went out just as I saw someone there at the end of the corridor, standing so that the light coming through the far window shone on his shoulders. It was George. The white dressing gown he was wearing hung from his bony frame and was untied, open at the front.

I could see what he wanted. He was waiting for an invitation, a nod of understanding, and there was a perverse part of me — my need for penance, a payment for using the little lens under my floor and for everything else — which rose like indigestion and made me want to say *yes, yes, yes,* and hold my door open and invite George to step inside. He smiled, and I saw again those horrific teeth and I went into my room alone and locked the door. I stayed awake for the rest of the night, lying fully dressed on top of my bed with a shoe in my hand, the heel facing towards the door. I left before breakfast to catch the train and the bus back to Lyntons.

"How does God know who is responsible for a crime?" I think I ask the man standing beside my bed. "If a person steals some food, for example, is he, the thief, the guilty one? Or is it his parents for not teaching him right from wrong? Or society for not helping when he has no money and is starving?" The man beside my bed is clean-shaven and wearing trousers and a jacket; the dog collar has gone. "What if it seems to be one person, but it is actually another?"

He is holding a clipboard, and I strain my neck to see what it says because it is the one from the end of my bed and I want to know if they write an estimated time of death. An ETD, I think, and I laugh.

I wait for him to say something like, *God is all-seeing.* That would be his easy answer.

"Still got your sense of humour then, Mrs. Jelli-co?" the man says, and I see he is the doctor not the vicar, and from the voice, I hear that he is a she. It is easy to make assumptions. It is what helped get me here in the first place. The window is open and I close my eyes, listening to the sound of traffic on the main road, like waves on a stony shore.

The bus sighs and huffs when I alight outside the town near Lyntons. The late-afternoon shadows are long, and midges dance between them.

I went along the same track I had walked at the end of July, this time carrying only my handbag with the stolen book inside, and I stopped in the place recommended by Mr. Liebermann. I had become desperate to return home — the word I had used for Lyntons in my head when I was in London — impatient with the delays in my connections, frustrated by the circuitous route the bus had taken through the villages of Hampshire. But looking at the house now, I was as panicked as when I had left. No longer about the judas hole, but from an idea that my life was out of my control, a dread that anything could happen and I couldn't stop it. I considered turning around and walking back along the track, taking a room at the Harrow Inn, and catching another bus in the morning. But where to? As I dithered, Cara walked out onto the portico with Peter following. He stood close behind her and I remembered what it had been like to have him close enough behind me to feel his breath on the back of my neck when we'd stood together in the Museum. Cara looked over to where I waited, and I heard her exclamation and my name carry across the fields.

I would have preferred a more subdued return, one where I could have gone up to my rooms and readjusted, but Peter came to collect me in the car, raising the dust along the avenue. When he reached me, he got out and took both my hands in his as though I had been away for a month.

"I'm really glad you're back," he said, not letting go, shaking my hands up and down, and seeming so pleased that I blushed. "Cara was as excited as a child when she saw you. Come on. Get in." He carried on talking about the Museum and Lyntons, and when we were in the car he started the engine but immediately turned it off.

"You must be wondering . . ." He stared straight ahead, his hands on the steering wheel. He struggled for the words. "Look, if that's why you went, it's all right. I understand."

A pulse beat in my throat. Had they discovered the judas hole after all? Could one of them, lying in the bath, have seen the tiny circle in the middle of their ceiling and called the other? Could a ladder have been brought up from the basement and the hole investigated?

"Sorry?" I said.

"Cara told me that she spoke to you just before we opened the Museum."

"Oh, yes." A surge of relief went through me.

"As I said when we talked in the library,

she enjoys making things up. She's a fantasist."

It didn't sound like a word Peter would have used to describe her, and I thought perhaps he had got it from one of the doctors he'd mentioned.

"The harmless kind," he added.

"She made it up? About the baby?"

"Yes," he said, and then, "No, not all of it."

A thrush landed on the railings beside my open window. I waited for it to sing but it cocked its head and flew off before Peter spoke.

"There was a child. Finn."

"She didn't tell me his name."

Peter gripped the wheel. Each word he spoke was deliberate, slow, as if he were dragging them out from deep inside. "She told you I wasn't the father?"

"She said there wasn't a father at all." I put my hand on his shirtsleeve.

"I loved him like he was mine. Mallory — my wife, Cara must have told you I was married? Am married. Mallory and I didn't . . . couldn't . . . have children, you see, something I always regretted. To have a little one running around, they bring a place to life, don't they? But Mallory had got used to it being just the two of us; it was easy, comfortable. Perhaps too comfortable? We bought a house in Surrey, where she still lives. I think she'd accepted how it was between us — companions, best friends, I suppose. I'm not sure what kind of mother she would have made anyway. She's just not that sort, if you know what I mean."

I nodded, imagining a society woman, interested in cocktail parties and bridge evenings.

"I didn't intend to fall in love again, with Cara. There was something about her then, in Ireland. I tried to keep away, but in the end it was impossible. I couldn't stop thinking about her. And I know it doesn't excuse what I did, leaving my wife, but what happened with Cara was unexpected. I wasn't looking for someone else, someone else with a child."

Perhaps he felt he'd said enough, or he needed to keep some things back, because he closed his eyes for a moment or two and when he opened them he said, "Cara has a few odd ideas. She's confused. We have to be gentle with her. We have to watch her." He sat up straighter and looked at me.

"You don't mean that she could hurt herself?"

"She keeps reminding me of this deal, a pact we made, a long time ago. But she doesn't have it in her to hurt anyone, whatever she might say. We just have to be careful."

"What pact?"

"Oh, it doesn't matter. It was one of those things that couples say to each other. A promise, you know." I didn't know, but I could tell he wanted to close down the conversation. "She thinks she needs to suffer. To pay for it."

"For letting Finn go, you mean?" I was careful to use the same words as Cara had when we'd sat on the jetty. Peter gave the slightest of nods, bare acknowledgement.

"And the father?"

"A farm boy in Ireland."

"But she —" I started. "She was so convincing, so definite that they didn't . . . hadn't . . ." I couldn't say the words *had sex* to Peter, and *made love* was too romantic for the fumbles up against the hay bales Cara had described.

"We all know what Cara says!" He lifted his hands from the steering wheel and smacked it with his palms. My hand flew off his arm and lay on my lap, fingertips upwards, abandoned like a beetle turned over and left on its back. "She says it to everyone who will listen: you, probably the last Catholic priest in Scotland, and that vicar down the road. She got pregnant. She had sex in a barn or a cowshed, or I don't know where. And I don't know why she can't admit it and neither do any of the doctors I've taken her to. She's never going to be content with being unremarkable. It's the bloody Church and her blasted religion. Religions! All sensible human beings know it isn't possible."

"Yes, of course," I said. "Poor Cara." Just as Cara had almost convinced me that it was true, now it was Peter's turn, and I could see that I had been foolish. Of course the baby had a father, and it must have been Paddy.

Peter rested his forehead on the top of the steering wheel and sighed.

"I'm sorry." His voice was muffled. "None of this is your problem, Franny. I'm sorry if we drove you away."

Inside, secretly, I glowed at him using *Franny.* "Don't worry. It wasn't anything Cara said. I just had to go for a while, clear my head. And I wanted to visit the library in London to see if I could turn up more about the bridge."

He wound down his window and a breeze that smelled of harvests blew across us. "You couldn't find anything in the library here? I never fixed the balcony, did I? I hope you were safe, going up."

"I was perfectly safe," I said. "But I didn't find anything."

I had gone to the library at Lyntons one afternoon when he and Cara were sleeping off lunch and a few bottles of wine. When I opened the door, a hare was sitting in the middle of the room, on the pages of the books that no one had bothered to clear up. The doors to the terrace were open but the hare didn't turn and run. Barrel-chested and big-footed, it stared me down malevolently, until, still holding on to the door handle, I had stepped back into the hallway and closed the door.

Peter looked at me. "We missed you. I missed you," he said, and I was aware of my lungs and my liver and my heart. He took my hand from where it rested on my knee and squeezed my fingers, and I was certain he must also feel the blood pulsing in my body. "We've got used to having you around. There's something about you being here that tempers me and Cara, a soothing influence."

I laughed, feeling self-conscious. "It was only a couple of nights."

He laughed too and the moment was gone. "Of course." He let go of my hand and started the car. He put it in gear and negotiated a three-point turn. "Did you have a nice time in London?" he asked. "Catching up with old friends, I suppose? You must tell me if you have any restaurant recommendations for the next time I'm up in town, I'm sure you know lots of places."

When we were almost back at the house he said, "Cara and I are so excited. We have some surprises for you."

As we were approaching the gates, I craned my head and looked up at Lyntons through the windscreen. The east facade was as austere as ever. At the attic window, in the room opposite my bedroom, someone was staring out: a pale oval, the eyes, mouth, and nose barely visible, not clearly a woman or a man.

"Is that Cara in the attic?" I said, and Peter slowed the car so he could also look up. My fingers touched Mother's locket around my throat, the cold metal heart.

"Where? There she is." One of the windows on the floor below mine was raised and she stuck out her head.

Peter stopped the car in front of the fountain.

"Frances! You're back!" Cara called.

We got out. "But someone was up there, up at the window," I said to Peter. "Is there anyone else in the house?"

"It must have been a trick of the light. There's no one else here."

"Hurry up!" Cara called. Peter waved, and, too late since she had already ducked back inside, I waved as well. I tried to look up at the attic, but I was too close to the house to see into the top windows.

We went through the front door, and inside there was the usual damp chill despite the warm evening, and the usual crumbs of plaster debris under my feet. Peter led the way up the grand staircase.

"What is it?" I said. "What's the surprise?" I didn't really want to know. I wanted to carry on to the attic and see if anything had been touched, whether the pillow was back in the bath, or another mouse lying on the windowsill, but from the top landing we went along the hallway to their rooms.

"You have to close your eyes," Peter said when we were outside their door.

"Why?" I said. "What is it?"

"Come on, Franny, don't be a spoilsport."

I shut my eyes, one hand reaching, my fingers spread. Peter's arm went around my waist and I was aware of his body, tense with excitement. I heard and felt him open their sitting room door, and he steered me forward.

FOURTEEN

I store up questions for Victor, for when he returns. He will return. What does he know about *shinjū*? Does he believe in ghosts? Does he think there is ever any justification for killing another? Isn't it always wrong, always a sin that must be paid for? How much have I changed? Would he recognise me if he saw me in the street — if I had the strength in my muscles to walk, of course?

Do our actions betray our nature?

I had seen her somewhere before but didn't know her name, couldn't place her: glasses, big jaw with an underbite, lipstick she must have gone to the chemist for and chosen specially for the occasion. Her face niggled like an unreachable itch in the middle of my back.

"Anne Bunting," the woman replied to the question of her name.

One of the men at the wooden desks with

their notes and files and books laid in front of them asked her what her profession was.

"Librarian." She rolled her lips together, smearing the lipstick.

"Do you recognise this book?"

Anne Bunting held it with confidence and familiarity, as a sculptor holds a chisel and mallet. She turned it over, read the spine, studied the cover, and opened it. "Yes," she said. "It's one of ours."

I recognised it too: *English Country Houses, Volume III,* and then I recognised her. Anne Bunting glared at me across the courtroom and I couldn't help myself, I blushed. I had never stolen a library book before then; other things later, but never a library book.

"One that shouldn't be removed from the library?" the man asked.

"None of our books are to be removed from the library. They must be viewed in the reading room." Anne Bunting touched the corner of her mouth with the tip of a finger, concerned her lipstick had smudged.

Another of the men — they were all men and none of them had ever held a chisel and a mallet — stood and said, "Your Lordship" — or was it *Your Majesty*? — "I fail to see the relevance of this line of questioning."

251

His Lordship Majesty raised an eyebrow at the man who was putting the questions to Anne Bunting, who in turn pretended to be surprised. It was a charade, the law.

"To provide evidence of character," the man who was asking the questions of Anne Bunting said. "To provide evidence of Miss Jellico's poor character."

I'd never had a birthday party, surprise or otherwise. Never played charades or been led into the middle of a room blindfolded for friends and family to jump out. Mother had taken me and another girl to the zoo for my eleventh birthday, and although we'd had nothing to say to each other, when her birthday came around she invited me to her party out of social obligation. The terror and humiliation of that afternoon remained with me for many years: my old-fashioned dress, the present I'd given unwrapped in a frenzy and cast aside, the rules of blind man's buff that I didn't understand, the girls I understood less. And somehow worse, the kindness of the girl's mother when I cried.

Now in the sitting room, Cara was behind me and I heard her laughing, felt her fingers cover my eyes, smelled her lemony scent, and was anxious that I wouldn't understand the surprise, wouldn't get the joke. She let go, moved away, and I opened my eyes.

The three tall windows facing the parkland were pushed upward as always, and Cara was standing in front of me, smiling. But everything else was different, as though I had walked into another house, the wrong room, slid through a mirror into an alternative reflection.

The previously empty space was now full. A silver candelabra sat in the middle of a circular mahogany table. The makeshift one with the wooden plank had been moved to the edge for use as a kitchen counter, and the packing-crate seats were gone, replaced by four upholstered chairs. Places were set for dinner: china plates with a crest of three oranges and blue-and-gold rims, cutlery and cruet, crystal glasses, a decanter filled with wine, and folded linen napkins. More candles sat on side tables beside a chaise longue upholstered in burgundy velvet, worn and frayed, low armchairs arranged beside it. I stepped onto a Turkish rug.

Cara and Peter were silent while I looked around and took it in, two children waiting for praise for tidying their room.

"Where did it all come from?" I said stupidly.

Cara picked up a fallen petal that lay on a

side table. I recognised one of the Chinese vases they'd unpacked, now filled with dog roses from the garden. A few drops of water lay on the polished wood.

"The Museum, of course," she said, and I saw she was still wearing the ring from the musical jewellery box.

Peter came from the kitchen area carrying a silver tray with three cocktail glasses, each with an olive at the bottom and filled with what I assumed was martini.

A painting of a woman with a rosebud mouth and wearing a tall grey wig had been hung on the wall above the chaise longue. A silk dress billowed around her and she sat in a landscape like a photographer's back-drop — the colours too muted, the view too flawless.

"Is that a Reynolds?" I said. Peter was behind me with the tray.

"I believe it is," he said, proud of his own good taste.

Cara lifted a glass and held it out to me, but I moved to a desk that had been placed against the wall. It was small, with a curved back, long tapered legs, and three tiny draw-ers.

"Is this French?"

"1890s, I think," Peter said. "Isn't it

beautiful? Perfect condition. Absolutely no worm."

I sat on the chair in front of it. A silver fountain pen had been placed there on top of a blotting pad, next to a pile of visiting cards embossed with the same design as on the dinner service. The chair was on castors and groaned as it took my weight. The rounded arms were smoothed by the grease from the hundreds, thousands of times they had been touched. I opened one of the little drawers — the miniature handles made for a woman with more delicate fingers than mine. There was nothing inside. I picked up the pen, removed its lid, and pressed the nib on one of the visiting cards. No ink came out. What might I have written if I hadn't already been a little in love with Cara and Peter, if I hadn't spent two days in London with my memories, and the previous night hiding in my hotel room from the man in the white dressing gown?

Mr. Liebermann, we have broken into the Museum and Peter and Cara are using your things as if they are their own.

Or, *Dear Dorothea Lynton, we have found your lost possessions. Come and save us from ourselves.*

Could I have stopped everything then and told them to put it back? Would it have made a difference? I looked at Cara and, behind her, Peter, saw their faces waiting for my approval. Had anyone sought that from me before? A drop of condensation from the outside of Cara's cocktail glass fell to the rug.

"The ink bottle was dry," Cara said. "But we can buy some more." She came over, took the pen from my hand, and replaced the lid. "Please say you're not angry."

"I'm not angry," I said. I looked at Peter. "It's beautiful." An expression passed across his face which I thought then might have been love, but was likely only relief.

Cara gave me my glass, and just as we had when our martinis had come in tin cups, we chinked them together. They began talking at once, showing me what they had discovered: a floor-standing globe in a wooden frame, a virginal that unfolded ingeniously from a side table, a marble bust of Julius Caesar, paperweights and letter openers, samplers and a sewing basket, a cigar box and a Chinese cabinet, a Syrian backgammon set inlaid with fruitwood, photographs in silver frames of shooting parties and people at wedding breakfasts, infants and horses, all of them surely dead.

Peter poured more martinis and we sat on the window seats and smoked while Cara cooked — an early dinner for once — and we ate at the table using the heavy silver knives and forks, a different set for each course, and dabbed our lips with the napkins, each corner embroidered with the initials DML. And Peter poured and poured the decanted wine. We ate lemon sole with a caper butter sauce, tiny pink lamb cutlets, and lemon syllabub. It was the first dinner I'd eaten with them where Peter made no comment about the extravagance and cost of the food. We talked about the ownership of the Museum's contents in a roundabout way. I told them what Victor had said, that after the army left, the house had sat empty, apart from a month or so when Dorothea Lynton had moved back in. They told me how they had struggled up the stairs with the larger pieces, how they had worked for two days and a night to make it ready. And how they had been sure I would return home soon. That was the word they used too: *home.*

"There's something else," Cara said when we were drinking coffee, and she took me by the hand and led me into their bedroom. Over my shoulder I saw Peter light another cigarette and settle himself against a cushion that had been placed on the window seat.

Once, soon after I had found the judas hole in my bathroom floor, I went into the attic room on the other side of my bedroom and pulled on the floorboards to see if any more were loose. Now, as I stood in the room I had been hoping to also spy on, the memory made me hot with shame. Peter and Cara's army-issue beds, which they had often complained about, had been replaced by a high double bed. Clothes were flung over the scrolled wooden boards at either end, and lay in heaps on top of the covers and around the floor.

"I don't know how you managed to do all of this in such a short time," I said.

"Everything aches." Cara flopped back onto the unmade bed amongst the clothes and blankets.

I sat on the edge beside her and looked around. It was the worst of all the rooms in the house. Most of the ceiling plaster had fallen, exposing the laths, and the paper hung in moulding strips from the walls. A huge tiled chimney breast dominated the space with an ornate overmantel carved and dark, made darker by a stain that leaped from the chimney hole and spread over the wood and tiles, that might once have been green but were now mostly black.

"I think there must have been a chimney

fire and a leak from the attic," Cara said, seeing me looking. "I like to think one put the other out."

She stood on the bed, picked up a bamboo pole which was resting on the side of the headboard, and leaned with it towards the central window — one of three, just as in their sitting room. Hanging from a nail in the top of the frame was a length of string tied around the base of a wine glass — we had been drinking from the same glasses at dinner. Peter had admired his in front of the candlelight and said they were Regency and could be worth as much as ten pounds each.

"Watch this," Cara said. She nudged the glass with the cane. As it turned, the diamond facets caught the very last of the evening sun and spinning spots of light moved over the tattered walls and across her face.

She sat with her back to the headboard, her legs crossed, and picked something from the pile of clothes. Flapping it in front of her, a dress unfolded — a long blue skirt with a high bodice and short puffed sleeves.

"What do you think?" She flapped it once more to straighten it. "Here," she said and tossed it to me. "You should try it on."

"Is it yours?" I held it in front of me. "I'm

259

sure it won't fit."

"I found them in the Museum, silly. In the big press that was in the corner. Look at it all." She pulled more things from the pile: gloves, stockings, silk and lace tumbling about the bed. "And fans too." She opened one with a flick of her wrist and waved it in front of her, then she jumped off the bed, throwing the fan behind her and taking the dress from my hands. She made me stand and held the dress up to me, against my skirt and blouse, Mother's underwear beneath them holding me firm. She put her head on one side. "I'll wear this one and we'll find you another."

She burrowed into the pile, while I stood, wondering how I could escape the embarrassment of changing in front of her. She tugged out a heavy robe, embroidered with exotic birds and plants on a cream background. The sleeve openings were long, and the lapel wide. "This," she said. "This would be perfect." She stopped jumping around and stood in front of me. We looked at each other as she undid the top button of my blouse and the next. I didn't watch her fingers while she undressed me because I might have stopped her. She pulled the blouse out from my skirt and took it off my shoulders. She unzipped my skirt and lowered it for me to step out of. Each item of clothing she folded and put on the bed. I was wearing Mother's brassiere, and the girdle with the suspender attachments. My stockings hung from the clasps in swags, stretched from overuse. Behind me she unhooked my brassiere and took the straps from my shoulders and then came to face me again, and I let her take it off my arms. I didn't resist or protest. There was nothing erotic about the undressing or Cara's gaze, which was only curious, uncritical. She looked at my breasts where they rested on the ring of flesh above the girdle, my nipples pointing to the floor. She undid the zips on the sides of the girdle, inching it down, one side and then the other, the satin and the interior seams sticking to my skin, the stockings coming with it. My waist was scored with a red horizontal line where I had been held in for so long. I let it out, all the overflowing abundance of my body, the undulations and the rolls, the flab and the stretch marks, the bits Mother would tut about and pinch. I stepped out of it all and threw it away.

"It's 1969," Cara said. "You should be free."

I trembled as she leaned in towards me. If she had kissed me then I would have kissed her back although the thought had never been in my head. I could smell red wine and coffee on her breath, her face an inch or two from mine. She lifted up the locket that I kept around my neck. "This is pretty."

"It was my mother's."

She opened it. Inside was a tiny photograph of a laughing girl with ringlets and dimples. "You were a beautiful child and you are a beautiful woman."

"Yes," I said, my fingers curling into my palms. I didn't tell her that the picture had come with the locket when Mother had bought it. The photograph of a model daughter she'd never bothered to change for one of me.

Cara closed the locket, picked up the robe, and put it around me, finding a wide sash and tying it about my waist. She turned her back to take off her own clothes and put on the blue dress. It was torn around the bottom, the fabric darker in the creases and with tiny rips around the waist, which was high up under Cara's breasts.

When she was pinning my hair into a twist on the back of my head, I asked her if she'd been up to my room in the attic.

"Oh Fran! How did you know?" She took a hairgrip from between her lips. "It was meant to be a surprise. We got you a new bed too and a rug. You'll have to pretend to Peter that you know nothing about it or he'll be terribly disappointed." She tucked the grip into my hair, then turned my head to examine me from the front. "Beautiful."

"I saw you up there when I was in the car with Peter."

"When you were in the car? I wasn't up there then. We got your room ready last night in case you came back."

"But I saw you at the window."

"At the window? I know, I called to you and waved, remember? From one of the bedrooms on this floor." She nodded her head at the bedroom door that led to the hallway, to indicate the room opposite. "I had to squeeze past all that old army junk to get to the window. We ought to chuck it out and put in some furniture from the Museum, make the whole house nice." She was talking too much. "We could have friends to stay and a house party. Peter could choose the wine and I'd do the cooking, and you, you could entertain our guests." She stopped and stared at me and my pulse thudded. "What did you see?" she asked.

"Just a face, a shape. I thought it was you."

"But it wasn't me. Was it an adult's face?"

"Yes, an adult's."

I remembered what Peter had said about her seeing children's faces at windows. Was she thinking of the child? She searched through her make-up bag and I stared at the top of her head, willing her to look up and tell me, but when she did she smiled, a wide, normal smile. "Some lipstick, I think. Mouth open," she said.

"Peter told me your child's name was Finn."

"Mouth open," she repeated, and put the lipstick on me.

FIFTEEN

"I told Peter it wasn't Paddy's baby, that there wasn't a father," Cara said, putting the lid back on the lipstick. We were sitting on the middle window seat in her bedroom, below the spinning wine glass. With the last of the sun, the revolving dabs of light had gone from the walls. "He knew it couldn't be his, nothing had happened in the front seat of his car or in the larder, apart from some kissing." Now, as I listened to Cara, she seemed so credible, her story once again convincing despite its outlandishness.

"We were in Killaspy's drawing room with Isabel. I had to tell him there wasn't a father: it wouldn't have been right to accept his offer and go away with him without him knowing. He stood there saying nothing, in shock I suppose. It was Isabel who slapped me and started crying and saying not only did she have a hussy for a daughter but a liar too. She shouted about why couldn't I have kept my legs closed for a few more months until I was married to Paddy, that it wouldn't have been long to wait, would it? But no, I couldn't and now I had brought shame on her family name, shame on her. I remember Peter flinching at the slap and at her words, but I held the sting against my cheek with my hand and dared myself to smile just to annoy her some more. Dermod had come in with the tea and I could see from the look on his face that he'd heard everything. He slammed down the tray and ran out, and I couldn't believe that for all his stories of the mysteries and miracles while I'd sat next to him at the kitchen table, he'd react like that. No one believed me. That's why it's so important, Fran, that you do."

She bent forward and put her arms around me, my chin caught against her shoulder, my arms awkwardly pinned so I could only raise my hands to pat her waist. She must have taken that as confirmatory because as she drew away, she continued. "I didn't know where Dermod had gone. I looked for him in all his usual places — the broken tractor, the henhouse, under his bed, but I never got to say goodbye. I wrote him a note and I left another for him to take to Paddy, apologising and trying to explain.

"Peter was much calmer than Isabel. I packed a bag and we got into his car and drove away. I couldn't believe I was really leaving. We stopped for dinner in a hotel in Cork, and he took my hand over half a grapefruit and said he didn't care who the father was, we were going to be together and that was all that mattered. I tried to tell him again that it wasn't Paddy, it wasn't anyone, but he put a finger on my lips.

"He took me to a little house he'd rented on the west coast. It was nothing like Killaspy, two rooms and an outdoor privy, but it didn't matter. He bought me that cheap wedding ring — the one I threw in the lake — so I would seem respectable. We had two weeks — a kind of honeymoon I suppose — before he had to go back to work. He borrowed a couple of bicycles and we freewheeled down the boreens to the sea. We sat freezing on the bench outside O'Dowd's the grocer's and held hands. He bought wild oysters and I showed him how to shuck them and swallow them whole. We didn't talk about the baby. The only time it was mentioned, apart from at the dinner in Cork, was on our first night in the little house, when he said he'd heard it wasn't good for a mother-to-be to make love, it might damage things, and he didn't want to

267

hurt me or it.

"After two weeks he went off in his little green sports car to bid at auctions, and to inspect other big houses. I was worried he would meet another daughter, a different Irish girl who wasn't having a baby. He gave me housekeeping money and I borrowed more Italian cookery books from the mobile library. I wrote off to a shop in Dublin for parmigiano and pasta, and salami and jars of antipasti, and sent them a postal order. And I daydreamed about going to Italy with Peter and sitting on a terrace, just the two of us in the sunshine, walking through some gardens and orange groves, and picking the fruit straight from the trees. Then I would suddenly remember I was having a baby.

"I went through Peter's belongings when he was away. There wasn't much — he'd left almost everything in England. That was another thing we didn't discuss — England or Mallory."

Cara closed the window and we continued to sit face-to-face while she talked, and I tried to imagine her in a little whitewashed Irish cottage with the sea only a field or two away.

"But I found a photograph of her. I discovered half a dozen photographs in the inside pocket of his summer jacket. I remember a splendid but dilapidated house with an ancient man in a flat cap standing on the doorstep. I thought it must be his father, but it wasn't. There was another of a close-up of a wooden mouse carved into a bannister, and another of a room with a grand piano. I thought the surface of that one was disintegrating, and I tried to wipe it with a tea cloth before I realised it was the room's plasterwork that was crumbling and sprinkling dust over the furniture and the floor, a kind of icing sugar. Just like this place, like Lyntons. Beautiful on the surface, but look a little closer and everything is decaying, rotting, falling apart.

"The last photo was of Mallory — he'd written her name, and the year, 1961, on the back. I was furious that he'd brought it with him. But she was nothing I'd imagined. I was expecting someone tall and elegant, you know, with a cigarette in a cigarette holder, sophisticated, bored. But she was a dumpling of a woman, short and almost round. I couldn't believe it. I was going to rip the picture up but instead I tipped out the flour from the flour tin, put the photo at the bottom, and poured the flour back on top. I don't know why; so I could look at her as often as I needed, I suppose.

"The Italian food I ordered didn't arrive

that first time. When Peter came back after a week or so, I'd spent all the money, and there was only one hard-boiled egg in the whole house. He was so angry. Then I dropped it by accident, our one bit of food, and he trod on it when we were arguing. You can't be trusted with money, and you can't keep house, or something like that. I have to admit that I did hide the washing-up I hadn't done under the bed when I saw his car arriving. We've always argued about money. He says I spend too much but he's always worrying about it. He won't admit it, but I know he's paying the mortgage on their house where Mallory still lives. He feels guilty about leaving her. He says she won't agree to a divorce, but I'm not convinced he's even asked her." She stretched her arms, rolled her head. "Anyway, you don't want to hear all this," she said.

"I do," I said. "Please."

"You really are so sweet, dear Fran." She smiled and then frowned, remembering. "It was a terrible row. I accused him of all sorts of things, of not believing me when I said there was no father, of not wanting the baby, of not wanting me. I shouted at him, *Going back to your wife, are you? Your tubby little wife, who I know you'll be happy to make love to.* That stopped him, and just before he trod on the egg he said in his serious voice, *That is not what this is about.* And he went off to O'Dowd's for his tea. He wouldn't talk about it. Peter's so reserved, so English, it's infuriating.

"He came back later with a loaf of bread, a pat of butter, and some jam. He made me a pot of tea to have in bed — I was always in bed in that house, it was freezing and damp — and fed me little pieces of bread and butter from his hand. When he got in beside me he said he was tired and needed to sleep. In the morning he said he'd been to see an Italian woman someone had told him about and had arranged lessons for me.

"When I got bigger he became excited about the baby, *our* baby, he called it, as though we'd made it together. Most of the time I didn't think too much about the fact that it didn't have a father. It isn't possible to live in a state of amazement and disbelief for very long. Sometimes when Peter was away I went to Mass and confession in the local town. I could never bring myself to tell the priest I was a virgin. I knew he'd peer through the grille and see I was pregnant. I told Mrs. Sheehy though — the woman who taught me Italian. She was the only one to say that it must be a miracle. I remember her touching my stomach with

271

the tips of her fingers and then pulling them away as if they'd been burnt. I knew what she was thinking, because I was thinking it too. She never said it aloud though: that I could have been carrying the son of God, or that it was, you know, the Second Coming."

Cara laughed, and I laughed with her because it was the thing to do, although I was embarrassed, shocked that anyone could really think such a thing, let alone say it.

"Mrs. Sheehy was such a nice woman. She arranged for me to have her nephew Jonathan's old pram and baby clothes. He was twenty-three and leaving for England.

"When my due date came closer I waited for a parcel from Isabel, a matinee jacket or a baby's knitted hat or something, or a card from Dermod, just with his name would have been enough. Anyway, nothing arrived."

Cara looked out of her bedroom window and I watched her reflection, indistinct but luminous. The moon shone above her head and her shadowed eyes stared back at me. I was spellbound.

In the sitting room, the dark corners and the soft light from the candles hid the worn patches on the chaise longue, the holes in the rug, and the scratch on one of the side tables.

"My goodness," Peter said. "Look at you both."

He took Cara by the hand and lifted his arm for her to turn under it. She held her skirt and curtsied.

"And Franny," he said. He let go of Cara and she stood watching, smiling as though I were her creation, her debutante, and she were showing me off for the first time. "Charming, charming." He took my hand and bowed over it.

He opened a bottle of champagne and we toasted each other and the clothes, and later we toasted the Reynolds lady, the dinner service, the desk, and ourselves again. Cara lay on the chaise longue, her head resting on an embroidered cushion, her eyes closed. Peter took her tipping glass out of her hands and brought another coffee to where I sat on the window seat.

"I should go upstairs," I said. "Let you get to bed."

"Finish your coffee first." He nudged me over and sat beside me. We watched Cara, sleeping.

"She's beautiful in that dress," I said.

"As you are in yours."

"Oh, I don't know. It's a dressing gown really."

"Well, it suits you."

"There are so many beautiful things in the Museum. You don't think it matters, us borrowing them?"

"Of course not. Better that they're used and worn and admired, than rotting away in a locked room."

"We can always return them when we've finished, I suppose," I said, my fingers tracing the embroidery on the fabric.

A candle guttered and went out. It was late.

"You must carry on wearing it. It's wonderful to see you happy. It's good for you, anyone can tell that. And there are lots more clothes in the Museum to try, funny pantaloons, and hats and furs, all sorts."

"My aunt — my mother's sister — had a fur stole," I said, taking a swig of my coffee.

"One of those scarves?"

We were whispering, aware of Cara sleeping a few feet from us.

"Yes, fox fur," I said. "When I was ten, I came home early from school and it was draped over the bannister. I was reaching out to touch it when my aunt came down the stairs. My father was following her."

274

Peter raised his eyebrows, didn't comment.

"My aunt said I could stroke her fox-fur stole and touch the pointed face and paws if I didn't say anything to my mother."

I turned to sit sideways on the window seat, bringing up my feet and tucking the dressing gown underneath them.

"And did you?" Peter asked. "Touch it?"

"No." I tipped up my coffee cup, drank. "But I should have, or at least I shouldn't have told Mother what I'd seen. The next day I was sent to my grandparents' house in Dorset. The war had started and everyone thought London would be bombed straight away, do you remember? I believed I was being evacuated like my school friends. But a few months later my mother came to collect me and take me back to London. My father had moved my mother and me to four rooms in a house in Dollis Hill, sold our family home, and moved in with my aunt. I never spoke to either of them again, and my mother never really recovered. I think she'd always known about the affair, but she loved her younger sister a great deal, and now when I think about it there must have been more going on, more history between the three of them than I ever found out. Anyway, she blamed me, for bringing it

275

into the open, for forcing my father to act, and I had to live with that."

"Oh Franny," Peter said.

But I hadn't finished. Now I had started I couldn't stop. He was a good listener, like me.

"A couple of years ago my aunt died in a road traffic accident," I continued. "She left me the stole in her will. I told the solicitor I didn't want it but it arrived all the same. I'm not sure what she was trying to say by leaving it to me — thanking me perhaps for the fact that she was able to be with my father, the love of her life, for twenty-seven years? I don't know. The skin had become brittle and much of the fur had fallen out. It was quite disgusting. One night I took it to the end of the garden that belonged to the apartment beneath ours and buried it. Sometimes it's better not to tell. Don't you think?"

"Better to lie?"

"Or just say nothing and deal with the reparation by oneself."

"I don't know." He put his hand on my knee. "Some things might be too much for a person to carry alone."

"A trouble shared is a trouble halved? That old cliché?" I said.

We both looked out of the window. The

sky was a dark purple, not quite black, and the moon was reflecting off the glass roof of the orangery where the leaves pressed to get out. Peter's expression was a blur, unreadable.

"I have to go to bed," I said, aware of the weight of his hand through the fabric of the dressing gown. I wondered if he knew it was there and, if he did, what he meant by it. I stood up.

He stood too. "I'll come with you." He picked up a candelabra which still had a few candles alight. "There was one more surprise Cara wanted to show you," he said. "But I think we should let her sleep."

"Another surprise?" I tried to sound excited, as Cara had asked me to.

We went along the hallway without switching on the lights, Peter leading the way through the baize door and up the spiral staircase. It was only then that I remembered the face at the window and that I had not been upstairs since I'd returned from London, although I was less certain now about whether I hadn't mistaken the floors after all.

The door at the top was ajar. As Peter pushed it open, I hesitated, apprehensive, nervous of our own shadows dancing about us.

"You don't still think you saw someone up here, do you?" Peter asked.

"No." I shook my head. "No, probably not." There was an odour though, similar to the one I had smelled when I'd first arrived and had taken up the bathroom carpet. The smell of the mattress I'd shared with Mother, before the men came to take it away, together with the other things of no value.

In my bedroom Peter held the candelabra aloft. My old army bed had gone and in its place was a wooden single bed, high off the ground, beside it a matching chest of drawers with a lamp on top. He went across the room and switched it on, and I saw the rug Cara had mentioned.

He put a hand on one of the carved bedposts. "Edwardian, I think."

"Oh Peter," I said. "It's incredible. Thank you."

"I'm afraid the mattresses weren't up to much but hopefully better than the one you had before."

I sat down. "It'll be lovely to sleep here in a proper bed." I wanted to say something that would keep him in the room longer, words to demonstrate that I understood him.

"And see." He gave an exaggerated turn.

"No one else here. Just the two of us."

"Of course. I'm sure it was only Cara on the floor below that I saw."

"Would you like me to check the other rooms?"

Was he lingering? I wondered. Finding an excuse to stay with me longer? Perhaps, I thought, he had come upstairs with another purpose. After all, he hadn't needed to escort me, and not by candlelight.

I thought about the toilet flushing in the middle of the night, the pillow in the bath, and worried that he would think me a terrified middle-aged woman frightened of her own shadow. "No, no," I said. "I'm fine." Inside I was saying, *Yes, yes, stay.*

"I should probably start locking the doors downstairs at night. We don't want people getting in, not now." He was thinking of the things we'd found in the Museum and how much they were worth.

"Yes," I said. "I'm sure you're right." In my mind I saw the man Cara had described, excited to become a father, cycling to the sea with her, feeding her pieces of bread and butter. A romantic. I wanted him to confide in me.

"Well," he said. "I'm glad you like the room. Do let me know if there's anything else you need."

"It's perfect."

"I should let you try out your new bed." I followed him along the dark corridor towards the spiral staircase, reading significance into the fact that he hadn't put the lights on. I was right behind him when he stopped dead, and almost fell into him as he caught my arm. I was ready then, lifting up my head.

"Damn," he said. "I forgot to get you a desk."

He flicked on the overhead lights.

"Oh," I said. "A desk. Yes. A desk would be lovely."

He didn't kiss me. Of course he didn't kiss me.

Sixteen

In the empty attic room next to mine someone was shaking out damp linen: tablecloths or monogrammed napkins; items small enough for one person to hold by the corners and flap. The noise infiltrated my dream, and when I woke with a start of terror I lay in my new bed in the dark and listened to the sound come again. I thought of the face at the window and now I was certain it had been there, and whoever it was had gone into the room next door. I felt for my watch and held it up to my eyes: too dark to see.

I had explored all of the rooms on the attic floor soon after I'd arrived, walked their echoing emptiness, pushed away the threads of old cobwebs and crouched to look out of the tiny windows. The ones facing west had the same vista as mine: a high view of the parkland with the hangers looming in the distance.

The air was thick under the ceiling as if the lead on the roof stored each sunny day and at night pressed it down on me. I tried distraction, remembering the conversation from when Peter had led me upstairs — upstairs to this room! — had he really said *there's no one here but the two of us?* I was almost dropping off to sleep when the noise came once more and I listened, stiff with fright, imagining the face with no eyes or mouth or nose. Now, the person in the room next door was female, elderly, joints knobbed, hair thin, a crazy woman doing the laundry in the middle of the night. I heard her climb onto the windowsill, rattling at the sash and the loose glass, saw her clawing at the frame with fingernails as horned and sallow as the rinds of old cheese.

I couldn't stay in bed, just listening and imagining, and so with a willpower I hadn't known I possessed, I flung back my sheet and stepped out of bed. The noise stopped. In the corridor, I pressed an ear against the door to the adjoining room. Silence. I considered going to get Peter, but only a few hours ago I had told him I wasn't afraid. I thought about going back to bed but knew if the sound started again I wouldn't have the courage to return. Mother's locket lay against my chest and I touched it without thinking, and then I opened the door.

In front of the smashed window a blackbird lay on the floor, its head crooked, its uppermost eye already dulled, but the yellow rings around it, and its beak, shining. When I held the bird in the cup of my hands it was still warm.

"I told her I was sorry," I think I say to Victor.

The brown Nurse Assister is pressing her warm fingers over the cold slow blood in my veins and counting.

"Don't stay too long, Chaplain," she says. "Mrs. Jelli-co needs to sleep."

"Chaplain!" I say. That's the word for him in this place, not *vicar*.

"What is it, Miss Jellico?" Victor's breath is on my face and smells of peppermints. Did he think this morning he would be visiting the dying and that he would have to get close? Does he keep a packet of them in the pocket of his cassock? Do cassocks have pockets? I observe him and see that his dog collar is wonky, as if he put it on in a hurry.

"Miss Jellico?" he says, reminding me.

"Sorry," I say again. "I told her I was sorry."

"Told who?" Victor asks.

I am walking through the cows and she

283

makes them part for me, like Moses and the Israelites. I have never liked cows and they have never liked me. I am not afraid of dying. The chaplain is beside me. "Cara Calace?" he says.

I have never liked cows.

"She looked like she was sleeping," I say. "So peaceful."

"What did you do, Miss Jellico? We were friends once, remember? You can tell me."

"I did it," I say.

In the morning, I got up before Cara and Peter, and put on the dressing gown, for the first time not bothering with Mother's underwear. I found a shovel in the outbuilding where I had discovered the jam jars, and I buried the blackbird between the roots of the mulberry tree. I searched in the stables and other buildings for a suitable piece of wood to nail over the broken window but couldn't find one, so I went down to the basement. The door at the bottom of the spiral staircase caught on the flagstones and I had to shove it hard. It opened with a rusty complaint. I felt around until my fingers touched a light switch, and when I turned it on a chain of bulbs flickered into life one by one along a corridor, a spine that ran the length of the basement from north to south, echoing the ones on the two floors above. Peter hadn't taken me to the basement on our tour; possibly he had decided it wasn't worth it, or he wanted to keep the amount of wine he'd discovered a secret. He'd told me that the footprint of the basement was the same as the house, but with maybe thirty rooms: cupboards and stores, larders and alcoves, as well as the old kitchen. And I'd told him that when Lyntons was first built the basement had been the ground floor with windows onto the garden, but in the early 1800s the house had been remodelled and the earth piled up around the outside to create the western terrace and the portico, and in effect entombing the servants.

I hurried along the corridor, which smelled damp, more so than the rest of the house, and in some of the rooms that I put my head into there was an earthy waft of fungus.

While the rooms above ground were mostly empty, this floor had been used as a graveyard for the broken things: three-legged chairs, brushes without bristles, buckets with holes. It unsettled me, the dirty mutilated clutter, the lack of natural light. I worked fast, opening doors and turning on lights, making mice and spiders run for cover. At the far end, I came across a storeroom containing old tins of paint and offcuts of wood stacked against the wall, and searched through them until I found a piece that I thought would do.

Peter's tools were in what must have been the butler's or housekeeper's room, with a small fire grate and a black kettle sitting on a grill. There was a bed in there too, pulled down from a wooden box where it could be pushed upright when not in use. When I went farther into the room I saw that the bed had been made up with a fresh pillowcase, sheets turned down under a wool blanket, and the corners tucked in. Peter's tools were laid out on an old chest and beside them was the sledgehammer he had used to get into the Museum. I took a small-headed hammer and a handful of nails. I was pleased I'd got everything without bothering Peter.

I heard the staircase door open at the far end of the corridor, the sound it had made when I'd shoved against it: the scrape of it against the floor and the noise of the hinges, although I couldn't remember whether I'd closed it.

"Peter?" I called. "It's Frances. I hope you don't mind, but I'm borrowing your hammer." I tightened the sash around the waist of my dressing gown.

There was no reply, although I could hear his footsteps approaching on the stone floor.

"Cara?" I called, apprehensive now.

I went into the corridor and looked both ways but there was no one there. I called for them again but heard nothing. The shadow at my back returned, grey air pressing up against me, and I spun around to catch it. *Wrongdoing.* The word came into my head as if someone had spoken it aloud. "Hello?" I said, but my voice sounded hollow, and I ran then, along the corridor — the locket around my neck bouncing — out of the staircase door, and up into the daylight.

We ate lunch: figs and cheese and bread. Cara was wearing the same blue dress she had chosen the night before. Peter went to make coffee. I could see him from where we lounged on the steps of the orangery, passing from one window to the next, picking up wine glasses and cups we had drunk from and left on the new furniture, white rings burnt onto the polished surfaces.

"Peter said he went up to the attic with you last night," Cara said, licking her fingers. She leaned back and closed her eyes. The remark sounded innocent, but I wasn't certain.

"To show me your surprise," I said. "My new bed and the rug."

"You like it?"

"Oh, yes. Thank you."

"I thought we were both going to surprise you. I thought that's what we agreed."

"You were fast asleep on the chaise longue."

"And you didn't think to wake me?" She pushed her hair out of her face.

"You seemed tired, after all the hard work you'd done for me."

"So, you both went upstairs?"

I tried to anticipate what Peter might have told her.

"Yes," I said. "Just for Peter to show me the bed and the rug, and the bedside table. I pretended to be surprised, I thought *that* was what we'd agreed?"

She sat upright but paused, weighing up my tiny act of defiance. "I'm pleased you like it," she said. "I was just disappointed not to see your face when you went into your room."

We were silent for a few moments, letting the air settle between us. I could see Peter in their bathroom now, probably filling the kettle.

"When was the baby born?" I asked, feeling that her story was safer ground. I was beginning to understand that Cara and I both had our roles to play in the telling of her chronicle. Primarily I was the listener, her audience of one. And she needed an audience, even if it was only me sitting in the stalls with my mouth open for most of the performance. Her story would have been simply memory and imagination without me to hear it; undiscovered and unaired, like a book without a reader. My second role was from the wings: the prompter.

"Summer 1964," she said. "He was late, by my calculation."

"Your calculation?" I said, not understanding.

"Yes," she said. "Counting forward from when I'd had that conversation with Father Creagh in the back parlour, and seen Jesus get down from the painting. You remember?"

"Jesus in the painting?" I said, shocked again.

"Yes, Frances. Keep up." She sounded irritated, and so I fell silent, letting her continue.

"Peter drove me to the hospital in Cork. I wouldn't let him come in with me in case he had to go upstairs and tripped and died."

"Like your father?"

"I think he sat in the car or paced the corridors. I was frightened of the labour — the pain, the unknown, I suppose — but mostly about what I was going to deliver. If the child had no human father, what kind of creature was it going to be? I had no idea. I remember those final nights before the contractions started, I dreamed of shepherds and halos, and cows. All of it muddled and making no sense. He was just a boy though, with the right number of legs and arms and toes. He didn't look like anyone I knew, not even me. Pale skin with the fairest down, eyebrows and eyelashes that were almost white. But the hair on his head was a kind of yellowy-orange apricot, and when he opened his eyes his pupils were huge like when you wake a cat from a sleep.

"I loved him but he didn't feel like he was mine. I didn't understand how he came to be made, but Peter called him his son from the very beginning. I might have fed him and changed his nappy, but he was always Peter's. Sometimes I would forget about him, and he was so silent, hardly ever cried, and when I picked him up and held him, there was an expression on his face that I couldn't work out, as though there were thoughts going on in there that no baby should be able to think. Maybe all mothers believe the same things about their children. I don't know. Like their child is special. But Finn *was* different. Peter would bring him into bed with us in the middle of the night even when he wasn't crying, and I would wake to find him stretched out between us, sleeping.

"My plan was still to make it to Italy and the sunshine. I was tired of Ireland and the rain. When I went to O'Dowd's for the messages, the people in the village were friendly but they knew everyone's business. You had to be a relation, however distant, to fit in. But it all went wrong. There was a moment when . . ."

She paused. She was looking over my shoulder, and when I glanced back, Peter was coming out with the coffee through the French doors onto the terrace.

"A moment when, when I let Finn go. I should have held on to him. I should have held on." She was whispering and speaking fast. She sat up straight. "Coffee? Great!" she said to Peter. I imagined someone, an Irish nun perhaps, her face stern above her wimple, taking the child out of Cara's arms. Tears on Cara's face as she struggled with her conscience.

Peter had brought down a plate of Cara's home-made Garibaldi biscuits with the coffee. I hadn't told her that they weren't Italian despite the name. They had been Mother's favourite, but I could no longer bear the thought of eating one. Cara and I drank our coffee and she showed me the ring from the Museum that she was still wearing. It was a mourning ring. The symbols around the outside were tiny skulls and the paste diamond had a hidden hinge; when she opened it a curl of hair was revealed behind glass. She took it off and made me read the inscription: *Eliza Sutton, 6th June 1830, aged 17 years.*

"Her new wedding ring," Peter said without smiling.

The sky had turned dark and several large drops of warm rain fell and we scooped everything up in the tablecloth laid out for the food, but the rain stopped before we got inside. The three of us sat under the orangery portico, our backs against the closed doors.

"I went down to the basement for the first time this morning," I said.

"I don't like it down there," Cara said. "I can't help but imagine all the servants never seeing daylight."

"I thought I heard one of you come in. Were either of you down there?"

"In the basement?" Cara said, frowning.

"Not me." She looked at Peter.

"Cara," Peter said, "I was upstairs with you all morning. What were you doing in the basement?" he said to me.

"Neither of you were there?"

"No," Cara said. "And you heard some-one?"

"I needed a piece of board for the window. A blackbird got into the room next to mine last night."

Cara sat up straighter. "A blackbird? Is it all right?"

"It was flapping and crashing around the room. It gave me such a fright."

"Did it sing?" She put her cup on the stone beside her.

"Sing? No, it wasn't singing. It was flap-ping — the poor thing must have been desperate to escape. The glass in the window was smashed."

"Peter," she said, something understood between them, excluding me.

"It doesn't mean anything." Peter had his eyes shut; he seemed tired.

"What doesn't it mean?" I looked from one to the other.

"Peter!" she repeated. "The bird was in the house."

"The bird was in the house?" I said, wor-ried again about the face at the window, the footsteps in the basement, the pillow in the bath. My fingers went to the locket and I pulled the chain over my bottom lip.

Cara stood, knocking her cup, one from the blue-and-gold set with the crest of the three oranges. It teetered and Peter reached out to grab it, but the cup tipped and broke against the stone.

"Jesus Christ, Cara. That was a complete dinner service. It's not going to be worth much now with a teacup missing."

"But the bird!" She was leaning over him and speaking through her teeth.

He stood up, put his arm around her waist, and tried to press her to him, but she pushed him off. Peter had his hands out as if he were trying to catch her, a bird herself, too fast for him.

"Shhh," Peter said, but she was laughing madly and flinging her hands up to her wild hair and then down, and running a little way towards the house, and back to us. I wondered if I should slap her, or go and fetch a doctor on the bicycle; she was hysterical, but still it seemed to be a performance, stagey, and overdone.

"Come inside." Peter caught her around the shoulders. "Come and lie down. It was only a bird."

"Sorry," I said, not knowing what I was

apologising for.

"It's nothing. She'll be fine."

"It's not nothing," Cara shrieked.

"I buried it," I said. "Under the mulberry tree. Was that the right thing to do?"

"It died?" she said and sagged, and Peter held her under the arms.

"Come and lie down," he repeated.

"Can I help?" I said, but they were already going off towards the open French doors, Cara's feet almost dragging along the paving.

I picked up the pieces of the broken teacup and, not knowing what else to do, waited under the portico. Through their open bedroom window, I could just make out Cara sitting on the bed with her head in her hands and Peter kneeling in front of her. She let him lift off her dress and she put her hands around the back of his neck, her arms extended. I watched him extricate himself, pull back the bedcover, and tuck her in.

SEVENTEEN

Later, Peter came and found me in the old rose garden. I was avoiding going back into the house. It seemed threatening now, the empty rooms and dusty spaces sinister, when so recently I had thought it beautiful. I couldn't help but believe it was playing tricks on me, trying to send me mad or drive me away.

"Let's go out to dinner," Peter said. "Cara's sleeping." I glanced up to their bedroom. "I'm sure she'll be fine."

I went up the grand staircase, and just before I turned through the baize door into the servants' quarters, I saw for the first time that the niche a little way down the hallway now had a marble statue in it, gleaming white in the gloom: a naked young man, not even a fig leaf to cover him. I went closer and saw that he was shiny from where thousands of fingers must have touched him as they had gone past. In one hand he held a bunch of grapes, while the other, raised as if in a toast to himself, held a chalice: Bacchus. And then I realised that he wasn't marble but plaster, and when I rapped on a thigh with my knuckles he was hollow.

Upstairs in the attic, I opened all the doors, checking that no one was behind them, and I hurried out of the embroidered dressing gown into a man's long silk robe with a lavender-and-grey stripe. Underneath it I put on three pleated skirt petticoats with a belt around the middle to keep everything in place. I twisted my hair up behind my head, and put one of the fans in a black evening bag, which I hung over my wrist. I didn't even stop to look in the mirror that had appeared in my bathroom.

Peter drove us into town and parked outside the Harrow. It wouldn't have been my first choice after what had happened when I tried to go there for tea, but I didn't have anywhere else to suggest. Peter was greeted by name and the front-of-house manager gave me a little bow of his head. I might have got out my fan and waved it in front of my face, except he quickly showed us into a panelled dining room with thick patterned carpets, and everything hushed and glittering. The place mats had pictures of hunting scenes and the curtains were red damask. Dull accountants and solicitors in suits sat at dark wood tables with their sedated wives and demure teenage daughters. I imagined tipping their plates into their laps, disturbing the peace. Did they have no idea that Peter had asked me to go to dinner with him — Peter! I tried to calm my nerves.

"Shall we have steak?" Peter asked when we were sitting opposite each other and I was staring at my menu reading the first line over and over. He scanned the wine list. "A bottle of the Volnay," he said to the waiter, who also gave a neat little bow. Before he left, Peter had added two double gin and tonics for while we were waiting. I couldn't see the price of the wine but Peter said, "I'm due a little windfall. No expense spared tonight."

When the waiter returned with the bottle and uncorked it, Peter said, "I think the lady should taste it." The waiter raised his eyebrows but poured a small amount into my glass and I swirled it, sniffed it, and rolled it over my tongue as Peter had shown me. I was too distracted to notice how it smelled or tasted but I nodded and the wine was poured.

We started with pâté and Melba toast, a tiny gherkin sliced and splayed on the side of each plate. My nervousness made me hungry. Peter leaned closer to talk about the contents of the Museum, how amazing it was that the room hadn't been discovered by the army when it was right under their noses for years. He poured some more wine and lit our cigarettes. A corner of my Melba toast shot off the side of my plate and under the table, and I drank to hide my embarrassment. I told him about a house I had heard of in the South of France that had been left untouched for a hundred years, the owners dead, the heirs unknown, and its treasures only recently discovered.

"Was it history you studied at Oxford?" Peter asked.

"At St. Hugh's, yes."

"You wouldn't have come across Mallory, then? She was at St. Hilda's."

"What did she read?"

"Classics. We met at Sotheby's. Ridiculous that she had a degree and had to take a secretarial role, while I left school with a certificate in English and walked straight into a good job."

I almost told him how I'd been at Oxford for less than a year, that at the end of my third term Mother had become ill and I'd had to go home to care for her. That time she recovered, but I didn't return to university. "I don't recall the name," I said.

"She was a bit of a bluestocking. Isn't that the term? The absolute opposite to Cara. I was attracted to Mallory's mind, and with Cara it was all about . . . I don't know." He looked as though he wished he hadn't started the sentence. "I fancied her, I suppose.

"But anyway, I do regret not going to university," he continued. "Learning for the sake of learning. I was in such a hurry — to start earning money, to go to London, to get on. It might have been good to have some time, for study and for fun. Mallory tells me . . . told me, all sorts of stories about the things she got up to." He sounded wistful.

"Are you still in touch with her?"

"No, not really. I hoped for a while that we could be friends but it was too difficult. I miss it though, our friendship. All my fault of course. But anyway, what was your time like at Oxford? Plenty of high jinks I imagine?" Just then the steaks arrived and our conversation was interrupted. A waitress in a black-and-white uniform spooned out carrots, runner beans, and soft cauliflower cheese from aluminium dishes. As we sliced into our meat and the blood ran under the vegetables, Peter said, "It's such a shame that Cara's a vegetarian."

"A vegetarian?" I said. "But she's always cooking us chicken and fish." My serrated knife was sawing.

"A beef vegetarian." He chewed on a piece of meat. His teeth were perfectly straight. "And veal. She won't let it in the house. You must have noticed."

I wasn't certain if he wanted me to ridicule her or sympathise. "Our housekeeper used to make a lovely stew with shin of beef when we lived with my father," I said and drank some wine to chase the meat. Its familiar warmth and confidence travelled my veins.

"I expect Cara would refuse even that," he said.

"Does she believe cows are sacred?"

"She certainly loves them."

He smiled and we looked at each other for longer than was necessary, until I had to glance away. I crushed a boiled potato into the bloody liquid pooled on my plate.

"Don't worry," he said and reached a hand towards mine — the one which held my knife.

"Oh, I'm not that worried," I said at the same time as he said, "Cara will be fine in the house on her own." I hadn't been thinking whether Cara was all right. I put down my knife, ready for him to take my hand in

301

his, but he picked up his own knife and fork and continued eating. "She'll be fast asleep, I'm sure," he said, getting back to his meal.

I finished off my wine and topped up both of our glasses. We ate without speaking until I said, "I'm sorry about the blackbird. I shouldn't have mentioned it."

"You did the right thing, burying it. And anyway, you weren't to know."

"What was it all about?"

"One of Cara's Irish superstitions. If she knocks over a chair she makes the sign of the cross, if the first lamb of spring is black she'll have bad luck, and if she has itchy palms she's going to come into some money." Peter scratched at his hand with the handle of his knife and we laughed. A woman at the next table turned to stare, and I could tell she was thinking what a handsome couple we made and how wonderful it must be to find love later in life.

"And a blackbird?"

"I'm not sure I quite understand, myself. She was gabbling when I took her up to bed. A bird in a room is meant to be a premonition of someone's impending death," he said. "It's all muddled in Cara's head: Catholicism and Protestantism mixed in with Irish superstition. If the bird sings it's meant to mean one thing and if it's shrill it's another."

"And what if it doesn't make any noise at all? Just flaps about and dies?"

"Then you become a very resourceful woman and go and find a shovel and bury the damn thing."

We leaned towards each other and laughed again.

"And then a piece of board, a hammer, and some nails," I said. "I hope you didn't mind me using them."

"Not at all."

"I saw the bed when I was in the basement," I said, and although his head was down and he was concentrating on his food, for two breaths his jaw stopped working. "If you need to talk to someone, you know I'm
—"

"Yes, thank you." He cut me off and caught the waiter's attention.

"I'm sorry," I said, thinking he was going to ask for the bill and take me home, but he ordered another bottle of Volnay, and when it arrived we didn't bother to taste it.

"And you weren't down there, this morning?"

"Down there?"

"In the basement?"

"What did you say you heard? Footsteps?"

"Yes, coming towards me down that central corridor."

"It's just the house shifting about," he said, offering me a cigarette.

"Shifting?"

"You know, settling, its outsides changing with the temperature and its insides dealing with us living in it. Anyway, it wasn't me or Cara and there's no one else in the house."

"How can you be sure?"

"Because that would be ridiculous. We would have seen them by now, wouldn't we? Not just shapes at the windows and footsteps in the corridor."

I drew on my cigarette.

"Look," he said. "Logic says it's creaks and rumbles, or . . ." He seemed to change his mind about what he was going to say, and looked around for the waitress with the dessert trolley.

"Or what?" I said.

"Or else it's all in your head."

I drank some more wine, smarting as though I'd been chastised. It made me determined to be less frightened. He was right, logic was the thing to drive away the demons.

We changed the subject, talking about our fellow diners, inventing stories for them, finding everything funny. The waitress came pushing the dessert trolley.

"What would you recommend?" Peter smiled at her.

"Me?" she said. "I don't know." It looked as though she'd never been asked the question before, wasn't required to speak to the customers.

"Don't tell me you don't sneak a slice of that cheesecake when no one's looking?"

A blush rose in her cheeks and I tried to keep in mind how Cara had described Peter as a careless flirt.

We both had sherry trifle. Peter tipped the last of the second bottle of wine into my glass and paid the bill. The room was dark except for his handsome face, lit by the candle between us.

I stood and swayed into him, and he caught me by the elbow, jogging the table, and one of the empty glasses fell but didn't break. A solicitor's wife nearby tutted, and Peter and I looked at each other and giggled. We stumbled our way out of the Harrow Inn to the car. Most of the drive home was a blur of the town's high street and dark hedgerows, apart from when the car swerved onto the verge and back into the road. "Oops," Peter said, as I fell against him and he pushed me upright. Everything was hilarious.

When we got to the house, I was convinced the car was going to hit the fountain.

"Mind the Canova!" I shouted, laughing and bumping into the door while he swung the car around.

"Didn't you know, it's a bloody fake!" he spluttered, slamming on the brakes.

"Counterfeit Canova."

"Phoney Canoney."

We thought we were so witty.

We went in through the front door — unlocked — and helped each other up the grand staircase, me tripping on the ends of the robe, shushing each other. I thought about inviting him upstairs for coffee and then remembered I didn't have any coffee or even a kettle.

On the top landing outside the door to the spiral staircase we stood together and I tilted my chin up to him, ready.

"Franny," he started. "I think . . ." He met my eye, and put his hand on the top of my arm for the length of time it took me to blink once, twice. I was certain he was telling me that he would like to, but he couldn't, shouldn't.

". . . I think I should see how Cara is," he finished.

"Of course," I said, taking a step back, reaching out for the baize door behind me with my hands. "Of course." I liked that we were both behaving honourably, in opposition to our desire.

He went along the hallway towards their rooms. I willed him to look back one time, and my blood rushed as he stopped and turned. I had no doubts that his expression was one of longing and self-denial.

"You should wear that gown more often," he said. "It suits you. You mustn't worry that everyone was staring. Who cares what anyone else thinks?"

It was as if he had slapped me. I hadn't noticed anyone staring, not at how I looked.

"Well," he said. "Goodnight, Franny."

He went farther down the hallway and I watched him. After he had gone inside and closed the door, I turned and stumbled up the spiral staircase, holding my knuckles to the rough wall as I went, oblivious to the pain.

In the night, I woke to the same sound in the room next to mine: someone shaking out damp linen and clawing at the window frame. I thought about the board I had nailed across the broken window, wondered whether it had come loose, but was also certain that it hadn't. I lay there remembering Mother, the way that in death her flesh had shrunk away from her body, giving the appearance that her fingernails and hair had grown. I took the pillow from under my head and pressed it over my ears and face, breathing in the smell of unwashed linen. It is not possible to suffocate oneself.

The next morning, I slept in, rising at midday to drink three glasses of water and take two headache tablets before going back to bed. The noise I had heard in the room next door seemed improbable. Later, when I woke properly and the afternoon outside shimmered, I lay in bed piecing together the evening, remembering with disappointment that Peter had said the fountain was not a Canova. I told myself that I had misinterpreted what he had said about my robe, he liked the clothes I was wearing, that was what mattered. And I remembered how he had looked at me, the touch of his fingers on the top of my arm when we stood together on the landing, and how he would have kissed me if he were free.

Still, when I got up I put on the old dressing gown and not the clothes I had worn the previous evening. Down in the blue drawing room, I touched the disfigured peacocks and then jumped at a hunched figure reflected in the mirror: its beaky face and clawed hands reminded me of Mother on her deathbed. But this person uncurled and stood up; it was Peter. He had a tape measure in one hand and a clipboard in the other; a pencil stub was tucked behind his ear. He was actually working.

"Hello you," he said, smiling.

I looked at my hands and saw they were shaking.

"Are you all right? Sorry about last night, bit too much to drink." Peter looked down too. "What did you do?" He took hold of my hand and examined my knuckles, grazed from where I had rubbed them against the wall. I pulled my hand from his. I wanted him to know without me having to tell him.

The door opened and Cara came in wearing a new dress, a green silk that floated over her hips to the floor. The back of it was open and swooped to her waist, her shoulder blades sticking out like the stumps of wings. Ostrich feathers, dyed green, had been stitched around the top edge. "What do you think?" she said as she began to turn in the centre of the room. The mirror reflected back the flecks of green fuzz which came loose and fell around her. "I found another wardrobe full of clothes."

"It's beautiful," I said. She was beautiful, but now I could see she knew it. Peter and I watched her turning and humming and smiling at herself.

"I think the birds are still getting in," I whispered to Peter so Cara wouldn't hear.

"In the attic?" His eyes were fixed on her. I couldn't tell whether it was love there or hate.

"Could you take a look?"

"Of course," he said, winding in his tape measure.

Cara stopped spinning. "Did you hear the blackbird in the middle of the night?" she asked, lifting the green silk in her hands and letting it fall. The moths had got to it and eaten the bottom to lace. "It was singing in the mulberry tree."

"Are you superstitious?" I ask Victor.

"How are you, Miss Jellico?" He bends towards me.

"Are you superstitious?" This time I must have said it aloud, because he answers.

"Black cats and rabbits' feet?"

"That sort of thing," I say, and he leans in farther to listen. "White cows and butterflies, field mice and hares. I saw a hare once in the library at Lyntons." Victor tenses, hopeful for a net that he can use to save me. A child's net on a stick that he can thrust into the rushing water where I spin and turn in the eddies. He would scoop me out if he could. But there's nothing now that will stop me flowing downstream with the current. Soon I'll reach the falls and be swept over the brink, and that will be the end of me. "They are supposed to be shape-shifters," I say. "Women in disguise. Cara kept a piece of hare's fur under her bed. She told me it would make her more desirable to Peter and bring him potency."

"And did it?" he says.

"No."

"She was jealous of you, wasn't she?" he asks after a short gap. He wants to keep the conversation going.

"Do you believe in the virgin birth?" I ask in return.

"I do," he says, almost offended. He is a good actor. "To deny it would mean that Christ was merely human, and yet we know he was not. He is the Son of God. The incarnation is one of the cornerstones of my faith."

I see there is a Nursing Person in the room. He is always more zealous when someone could be listening.

"Cara talked to you about that too?" He whispers this, still trying to winkle out the truth.

"Did you know," I say, "that right into the nineteenth century the Irish believed that the female hare didn't need a male to conceive?"

Victor raises his eyebrows.

"Parthenogenesis," I think I say.

But Victor is fading and the hare is back in the library. It's crying, a kind of strangled wail, the sound they make when in distress.

"Shhh, Mrs. Jelli-co," the Nurser says.

I am holding the neck of a champagne bottle; the bottom half has been broken off, jagged. The hare stretches up on its hind legs to start boxing, but it grows taller, its amber eyes sinking back in its head, its fur turning to skin and its forelegs becoming arms, until Cara is standing before me, a wound in the side of her head, wide and bloody. My bottle drips onto the pages of books.

Every day Cara cycled into town for food. Peter saw her off without comment but if she was gone for a long time, more than a couple of hours, he would lean on one of the gateposts, smoking and watching the avenue for the dust which her bicycle wheels spun out. I don't know what he would have done if she hadn't come back. We ate well and we drank almost to excess, and we ransacked the Museum for items we needed or others we liked the look of. We used copper saucepans, bone-china crockery, and crystal glasses, and when they were dirty we went and got more, stacking the unwashed against the walls and under the table.

A week or so after Peter and I had been to dinner, I clutched an open bottle of champagne, my thumb over the top but the bubbles spilling, as I ran down through the trees to the lake, following Cara and Peter, laughing and shouting. The fun I never got to have in my twenties. The moon was out and shining silver on the water.

On the jetty we pulled off our clothes — dresses and dressing gowns, trousers and a top hat — hopping and laughing, and I caught glimpses of pale skin, white limbs, of Cara's small breasts and Peter's bouncing penis as he ran to the edge and flung himself forwards, and we followed him, screaming at the cold. I didn't once stop to think about those times Cara had refused to swim, had said that she couldn't.

We rose up shouting and splashing and laughing. The water was black and the shapes of our bodies tangled with the shadows made by the weeds and the bulrushes which crowded in from the bank like slender spectators. My kicking feet touched soft mud and recoiled, while above the surface it was hard to tell the heads and the hands and shoulders from the movements of the water. Minutes must have passed before we missed her. How is it possible for three to so easily become two?

"Cara!" we shouted, Peter and I. "Stop joking."

Did Peter dive and find a branch that might have been a pale wrist or grab at a handful of grassy fronds which could have been hair, dragging her from underneath, or was she floating on the surface? I was never certain. Only that next, Cara was sprawled on the bank and us beside her with the smell of pond around us, waterweed stuck to her legs, and her feet and ankles muddy as if we had uprooted her, a white lily laid out in the moonlight. Peter pushed with his hands in the middle of her chest, once, twice, I heard him counting, crouching over her. Her stomach and the triangle of dark hair between her legs lifted each time Peter pressed and I saw, just before Cara coughed herself back into life, the silver streaks across her abdomen like a starburst reaching out from her groin. I'd never had a child, had never carried one, but I knew what the marks were. I had washed Mother's often enough.

Mother used to say her stretch marks were my fault, that I had ruined her body, and if it hadn't been for me she would have been unscarred and tight like her childless sister, and my father wouldn't have strayed. After Mother became ill again, every Sunday evening I had to move the crockery from the lid of the kitchen bath. I stacked it on the floor under the window, laying out two tea towels to go beneath the plates, cups, and bowls, ensuring they didn't touch the floor. I removed the coloured flannels which we kept in the bath and turned on the taps, testing the temperature with an elbow and then going into the bedroom to undress Mother. When I had helped her into the water, I washed her with the flannels while she lay back and directed me. I was tender with her, but each time she had a specific order and colour for the particular areas of her body: her armpits, her breasts, her private parts, though I never learned them; they were never the same.

Peter carried Cara up to the house, her body loose but alive. He had pulled his trousers on and I had tugged my damp arms into my dressing gown, seemingly even in an emergency the two of us required decency, while Cara remained naked. I ran a bath for her, and he lowered her, dumb and staring, into it, and knelt by her side. I sat

315

on the toilet seat, unsure of what Cara had intended. It came to me that if she hadn't wanted to be rescued she wouldn't have tried to drown herself when we were with her, and I speculated whether it would have been possible to stage the episode for dramatic effect. A means of telling Peter and me to turn our gaze away from each other and back to her. Could she have been holding her breath in the lake and pretending to spit out water when Peter had pumped her chest? I didn't know. But I wanted to comfort Peter just as he was comforting Cara, to tell him that everything would be all right if he would only let me help.

"What can I do?" I said.

"We'll be fine," Peter replied.

The three of us sat in silence for a few minutes until I became uneasily aware of Cara's nakedness and their stillness. Neither of them had looked at me. I picked scallops of mud from under my fingernails. "Should I get a glass of brandy?" I said.

"You should go to bed," Peter said. "We'll manage."

I stood up. I didn't want to leave, to be excluded. "I'm going to get some brandy." I wanted to be helpful.

"Please," he said. "Just go to bed."

I couldn't resist looking when I went up

to my rooms, so quick to forget the promise I'd made to myself in London. I had never removed the telescope from under the floor. I lifted the board and looked at Cara in the bath, her face still turned to the wall, and I looked at Peter leaning over the rim, tenderly picking the weed from her hair.

EIGHTEEN

In the morning, Peter woke me, knocking on my door, averting his gaze and apologising when I opened it, and saying he had to go out and would I mind keeping an eye on Cara. He didn't say what I should do if she tried something similar, he didn't mention the previous night, but of course I said yes. It was a responsibility, but I still wanted to help him.

I stood at my bathroom window brushing my teeth, bending to watch Cara drag a stepladder across the terrace. I hurried, thinking I should go down to stop her. I went to the sink to spit and rinse, and when I returned to the window the ladder was under the orange tree and she was already on the top step. I leaned out farther to see what she was doing. The sun sent flashes of light through the warped glass of the orangery as she stretched up into the leaves. She teetered and my body jolted and my arms flew out anticipating her fall as though I could have caught her from my window. I went to call to her, but then worried the noise would startle her, and I knew that if I ran downstairs I wouldn't reach her in time. Her arm was above her head, flailing; I didn't want to watch but couldn't drag my eyes away. She must have caught a leaf and pulled down a branch, was probably thinking about an orange vinaigrette, or a bitter orange syrup to go with a sweet sponge pudding, though I knew the fruit probably wouldn't be edible. The oranges fell and she came down the stepladder to safety.

I went downstairs, composing what I would have said to Peter if she had fallen, what possible kind of apology I could have made for not keeping her safe. When I went out onto the terrace, Cara was sitting on the orangery steps eating an apple. I didn't see any oranges.

"It's just you and me today," she said, her mouth full. "Peter had to go to London."

"When will he be back?" I asked.

She shrugged. "He has to see a man about a dog." She took a bite of her apple and tapped the side of her nose. I sat beside her, stretching out my legs. She tossed the apple core and it bounced down the steps and settled under the box hedge.

"I expect you want breakfast," she said. "There are some of yesterday's pastries upstairs."

When I went to their room to make coffee and get the paper bag which Cara had said was on top of the fridge, three bitter oranges lay in a china bowl in the middle of the table, and I saw that the Reynolds painting — if that's what it was — had gone from the wall above the chaise longue, and a sword in a silver curved scabbard was hanging in its place.

"I was thinking about going to the obelisk," I said. "I thought I'd do a painting there." I had eaten three pastries and the inside of my mouth was coated with a buttery film. We were drinking coffee and smoking. "Want to come?" I needed a distraction, an activity to use up the time until Peter came back and I could hand Cara over.

She stubbed out her cigarette. "All right."

We went to the lake, over the bridge — our work at pulling back the undergrowth had halted after one day — and along the opposite bank. The obelisk was uphill from the grotto. Once, it must have been visible from almost everywhere in the park including the house, but a grove of beech and the occasional fir had grown up around it and now they were higher than its pinnacle. I'd read that a double-headed lead figure of Janus had once perched on the very top, but it was no longer there. We went through one of the three openings onto a small stone platform with a curved seat set along the back wall. Behind it was an inscription:

Here lies buried a horse, the property of Alexander Lynton that in the month of September 1804 leaped into a chalk pit twenty-five feet deep afoxhunting with his master on his back. In October 1805 he won the Hunters Plate on Worthy Down ridden by his owner being entered in the name of Beware Chalk Pit.

I realised I had forgotten my paints, but anyway, the trees crowded the entrance and there was no view. Cara read the inscription and we sat on the stone seat staring out at the trunks.

"Peter told you not to leave me on my own when he was gone, didn't he?"

I looked at her, then looked away.

"It's fine. I know he's worried about me doing something silly, as he puts it. But I never would, not without him."

I was uncomfortable with her talking about wanting to kill herself even in such oblique terms. Naively, I believed that talking about it would make her more likely to want to do it. I might not be thinking about food, but if someone mentioned dinner, I was hungry. Wasn't that how suicide worked too?

"I sometimes think though," she continued, "that it would be the ultimate penance. Death. A few Hail Marys aren't always quite enough." She gave a sour laugh.

"But you have so much to —"

"Live for?" she said, finishing my sentence, which had sounded like a platitude before it was out of my mouth. "It's the past that worries me more," she said. "The things that happened when we left Ireland."

"The past?" I said, hoping once again to change the subject and get her back onto her Irish story.

"You want to hear the rest of it?" She didn't wait for an answer. "When Finn was three months old we packed up the house on the west coast. We handed the bicycles back, and we gave away almost everything else. We took as much as we could fit in four suitcases. I gave the pram away too, I was sorry to see that go. Even while we were packing the cases into the car, I thought we were about to drive to the airport near Cork and catch a plane to Italy. Peter didn't tell me anything about our travel plans and I didn't think to ask. It seems idiotic now, but we'd — I'd — been thinking about it for so long that I just assumed that was where we were heading. Finn and I slept in the car — it was early in the morning when we left, dark, and it wasn't until it got lighter through Peter's side window that I realised we were going north. We had a terrible row, Finn was crying, and I was shouting at Peter to stop and let me out on the side of the road, but he wouldn't. The bastard just kept on driving north.

"He sold the car at a garage a little way south of Galway. I went into a grocer's while he haggled about the price, and I bought a packet of disposable nappies, a copy of *Woman's Way,* and a bag of oranges even though I knew they'd probably be dry inside and we didn't have enough money for any of it. The garage owner drove us to the port in his van as part of the deal. I still thought we were going to Italy, although I realised by then it wouldn't be by plane.

"It was really misty when we got there, to the port. I kept waiting for it to clear, so I could see the cruise ship, and when I glimpsed it, through the mist, it wasn't a cruise ship at all but some rusty old transportation boat. Cows were being boarded

— hoisted up in a sling and swung over into an opening in the hold. The mist was so thick that when they were lifted up they disappeared into it until all we could see were their hooves over our heads.

"We were given a tiny cabin with bunk beds and I was sitting there, bent over on the bottom one trying to feed Finn, when Peter told me the boat didn't go to Italy. We were going to Scotland because that's where he had the offer of work. He said he was sorry that he'd misled me but he knew if he'd told me before, I wouldn't have gone with him. And he was bloody right. All the time it was about the work and the money, and Mallory, I knew it was. By then I didn't care, I was tired and I just wanted to leave Ireland."

Sitting there, listening to Cara, I thought about my aunt, who had been in a similar position — living with a married man who still supported his wife. Did my aunt resent the money my father paid to Mother, the rent on the apartment in Dollis Hill? I had never thought of it that way before. Cara continued to talk while my thoughts wandered, until I heard her say, "The boat sank when we'd been going for about five hours."

And I gasped.

"I was resting with Finn," she went on,

not looking at me. "Reading the copy of *Woman's Way* that I'd bought. Miss Landers had finally had a letter published. I remember thinking that I must congratulate her next time I went to her house, and then I remembered that I no longer lived in that town and had no idea what she was doing — it could be that she'd hired a different girl to read the magazine to her and write the letters, and they'd be celebrating together.

"It was the noise of the cows that I noticed first: the sounds they were making changed, became higher, panicky. Maybe they caused the boat to sink somehow or something went wrong with the engine, we never found out. Peter wasn't in the cabin — he'd gone up to speak to the captain, to look at the controls, or something. I'd been happy for him to leave me with Finn, I didn't want to see him or talk to him. The boat began to list and everything loose slid about, and the porthole in our cabin went below the level of the water. Finn stayed asleep, arms outstretched, on the bed. He was a good sleeper. And then the boat fell the other way, but I managed to grab him before he slipped off the bed, I had him tight in one arm and I opened the cabin door with the other. I yelled for Peter but there was so much noise. I'd just gone into the corridor when the boat heeled right over and the lights went out and the emergency ones came on.

"People were shouting and the cows were making a terrible sound. Finn must have been crying but I don't remember. I was quite calm — I knew I had to get out and find Peter. I was inching my way along the wall of the corridor, my head and shoulders bent over because it was so narrow, but the door to the neighbouring cabin had swung open, and the inside was just a deep hole, a kind of a well with dark water sloshing about and a jumble of whatever had been loose piled together at the bottom. I knew if I fell in, there was no way we would be able to get out. There was a lip to the doorways — a rim about as wide as my heels — and I had to slide along it, holding on to Finn, who was wriggling and twisting.

"I don't know how I made it up the stairway, but I did. On the next deck there was more shouting and chaos, a couple of sailors had one side of the lifeboat free but the other had jammed. A man yelled at me in a language I didn't understand, and I was scrabbling around, grabbing on to doorways and handles and calling for Peter. It was almost dark, everything was wet, waves were rushing up over the hull, the engine screaming. It was like I was at the centre of a storm, people shouting instructions that I had no time to act on before they were pulled away, someone falling past me, glass smashing. The noise of the cows was awful. For years afterwards it would come into my dreams and wake me, and I'd have to go to the bedroom window to check for water. They sounded like children crying, human children.

"I found Peter in the stern, holding on to a railing, just clinging on. When he saw me he was desperate. He let go and grabbed hold of me. You wouldn't think it now, would you, someone so confident in the water, but he was terrified. I was trying to keep hold of him and keep hold of Finn, and then we were pitched into the sea — the boat tipped, or a wave came, and I was upside down. I didn't know where Peter went but I had the baby. His hair was floating and I could see him clearly, every pearly fingernail, each downy hair on his round cheeks, the flecks of slate in his blue eyes.

"There was everything with us under the water: all the bits of the boat that were unattached. And for what seemed like ages I couldn't see Peter. We'd let go of each other when we fell in. Finn and I were low down:

I could see shapes above me, barrels, bits of the boat, cows even. And then Peter got hold of my ankle and he wouldn't let go, he was hanging on and pulling us down. And so I released Finn. I just opened my arms and released him. I tried to send him upward. I thought that someone, a sailor, would find him and pluck him out. But Peter and I made it to the surface in the end and Finn was gone. I never saw him."

"You mean he drowned?" I said, shocked. I had been waiting for the part when they were rescued, expecting a sad epilogue where Finn would be given up for adoption.

"Yes," she said. "He died. Afterwards, when we were in Scotland, just the two of us, we made a pact, Peter and I. We swore that whatever happened we would be together, always; neither one of us would ever be left alone."

I didn't ask her to explain. I didn't want to know. We were both silent, looking at the trees. She lay sideways on the stone bench, curled her legs, and put her head in my lap. A robin was singing somewhere in the trees, the sweetest song, and I put my hand on her head.

When she spoke again she said, "Do you believe in heaven and hell?" When I didn't reply, she turned her head to look up at me and said, "I know you believe in God, Fran. I saw you in church that time when I coughed out the wine." She smiled but it was strained.

"I think I used to."

"But not any more?"

"I'm not sure."

"Peter doesn't believe in any of it. He won't even talk about it with me, says he's had enough of my Catholic mumbo jumbo. Father Creagh told me I'd go to hell for believing my baby was the second Christ, and that Finn would too. But in Miss Landers's letter, the one that *Woman's Way* printed and she got the guinea for, she said that hell was a cruel invention put about by the Church to scare us, keep us under control, and that it didn't exist."

"Perhaps she was right."

"But where's the proof?" Cara cried, sitting up.

"Where's the proof for any of it?" I said. "It's what you believe."

"But I need to know," she whispered, "whether these places exist."

"You will one day; we all will."

"No, Fran. I can't wait any longer." She took my arm. "I need to know now."

She stared at me until the hairs rose on

my skin and I thought Peter was right, we do need to watch her, she shouldn't be left alone.

We walked through the woods, the ground dense and spongy where leaves and needles had lain rotting and undisturbed for years. The path had all but disappeared and the hillside was steep. I led the way, digging my heels in and holding up the dressing gown to make sure I didn't trip. I was thinking about Peter being terrified under the water, clinging on to Cara and losing his child, or at least one he regarded as his own.

"I know you don't really believe me," Cara said, close behind. "About Finn not having a father." I stopped and as she careered into me, I swung around to face her, both of us almost losing our balance. We caught hold of each other, an odd embrace, like old friends. Her hands grasped my elbows, keeping me upright, and the bony chambers inside my ears knew that if she were to release me I would go tumbling backwards down the hillside, bouncing off the trees until I reached the lake. "I do, Cara, I do," I said. Her intensity frightened me.

"Peter and I don't make love." She whispered the words into my ear.

"Oh . . . perhaps —"

"No," she said, cutting me off. "We haven't ever made love." She steadied me on the sloping ground and let me go. We each took a step back. I didn't want to hear what she had to say. "He can't get a . . . you know . . . an erection. We've tried or rather I've tried lots of times but he always says he's too tired, or too busy. I know they're excuses to avoid embarrassment, disappointment." She sat down heavily. "I've always thought he couldn't do it with Mallory either, maybe not with anyone."

Associating Peter with these things was shocking and at the same time exciting.

"I won't leave him though," Cara said. "Not after everything that's happened. He takes care of me. Who else would look after me or forgive me, in the way Peter does? Anyway, where would I go?"

"You could go back to Ireland." My words came out more spiteful than I had intended, but she didn't seem to notice. She was lost in her own thoughts.

"Ireland? I'd rather die than return to Ireland."

"Come on," I said. "Let's get back to the house."

But she carried on sitting. "I've been thinking though," she continued, "that maybe Peter *had* been able to do it with

331

Mallory and there's something wrong with me, something he doesn't like. I thought for a while that it was because she'd had an education, been to university and I hadn't, but Peter despises university."

"No he doesn't," I said. "He'd liked to have gone if he'd had the chance."

"How would you know?"

"He told me."

She made a pfff noise but I could see she was disconcerted. "And then I remembered how Mallory looked in that photograph I found," Cara went on. "She was as fat as you and I was thinking whether it would be possible to become your size. How much more would I need to eat every day?"

I nearly fell again, dumbfounded by her words. Her face was composed, and I couldn't work out if what she was saying was designed to hurt or whether she was simply artless, an innocent. I remembered the evening she had undressed me, and how I had thought she'd meant it when she said I was beautiful, and all the time she'd been examining and assessing me. Did she think I would be flattered? Cara carried on.

"Voluptuous, that's the word Peter used. Maybe he'd be able to make love to me if I was voluptuous. But then, it made no difference when I was pregnant." She paused, thinking, while my surprise turned to anger. "That's one thing we have in common, you and I — both of us virgins." She laughed and I took a step back, a foot sliding. I had never slapped anyone before, could I do it now? "Do you think it's something I could get used to eventually, never making love? You're nearly forty, aren't you? Is it something I'd be able to live with, not having Peter desire me like that?"

I stared at her.

"Because, well, you haven't, have you? Ever had sex?"

"What?" I said, my brain lagging behind her words.

"Don't be like that, Fran. I just want to know."

I pushed her then, on the shoulder, just a shove but it surprised her and she fell back. I might have picked up a rock if there had been one in the wood and hit her with it, such was the fierce fury that flared in me, but instead I turned and went down the hillside at a clip, tripping and sliding until the ground levelled off and I reached the lake. I didn't hear her call after me, I no longer cared what she did. I went across the weir and followed the path past the mausoleum, stomping through the little wood where the fox had been but taking a different path.

I walked off my anger and thought how odd it was that the three of us had come together to live at Lyntons, and maybe all of us virgins. Because Cara had been correct in her assumption about me. Perhaps I wore my virginity like a flag hoisted above my head, out of my line of sight but there for everyone else to see. It wasn't something I'd been bothered about in the past. I was studious in my teenage years, working on getting into Oxford. I made friends with a couple of other academic girls at university and I spent some enjoyable hours with Hamish, a young man with only one arm, studying with him and going for walks beside the river, always making sure I was on his right should he have wished to take my hand. But I never thought about it going further than that. I didn't stay in contact with him or the girls after I left Oxford.

What Cara had said about Peter's physical issues didn't worry me. Up until that point, in the same way that I'd thought about Hamish, I'd always considered our connection — mine and Peter's — to be based on intellectual respect. Now though, by just mentioning that she and Peter hadn't consummated their relationship, Cara had planted in me a seed of emotional and physical longing. An idea that there could be something for the two of us beyond this summer. And the fact that things weren't working out between Peter and Cara, conversely, gave me even more reason to think it would be different for us.

Beyond the gate where Cara, Peter, and I had stopped at the top of the meadow, I joined a sunken track, six feet or more below ground level. The trees met overhead and formed a dim holloway, which went uphill towards the woods that clung to the line of narrow hangers. Pieces of rock stuck out from the earthen sides where spring floods must have flowed off the fields and down the path, back the way I had come.

As wide as a cart, it was a route made by and for humans; the earth rubbed smooth by feet and, later, wheels. I trudged uphill as the path switched and rose. At the top, it curved around a scarp, the run of a potter's nail in a clay pot, formed as it turned on the wheel. I stopped to let my heart slow and to gaze through a gap in the trees. Below me, the land fell away, the bank of green reaching the very edge of Lyntons, its white-grey roofs glowing. The light also caught the glass of the toy-sized orangery, flashing back. I couldn't see it but I knew that just behind the glasshouse, subsumed by the garden, was the Museum.

After a minute or two I followed the path into the trees. It seemed well used, the edges free of plants, the loose stones pushed to the banks.

Five hundred yards on, the route stopped; an abrupt dead end of ferns and bramble, with no space for a vehicle to turn, no tracks to show that any had tried. While I stood there in the middle of the wood, my own movements now silent and my breath held, I realised I could hear nothing. There was no wind in the canopy, no scrabbles in the undergrowth, no birds singing. I looked back the way I had come: the path snaked around a corner I couldn't remember walking past, and I tried to reassure myself that the way always appears different when one turned to go back.

I must have stood there for three or four minutes, dread fixing me to the ground like the trees that spread their roots down through the soil. I listened, as though I might have been able to hear those roots worming towards me. I ran the locket back and forth on its chain around my neck. And then there was a pinch in my side, a nip in the flesh of my waist, and two more in the same place, twists of the skin between fingers. A pain I knew, and the panic of it set me off into the trees, the dressing gown catching on sharp twigs, and low branches flicking into my face. My foot caught on a loop of bramble and I flew forwards, my hands stopping my head from smacking into the ground, but immediately I was up and running headlong without looking behind, slipping and sliding down as the hill became steeper, through the ferns with the bushes scraping and tugging at my hair. It was a wych elm that saved me; I fell against its mossy trunk where it clung to the brink of a drop, my toes kicking lumps of chalk over the lip. They bounced and tumbled downwards into dark green.

I stopped at the gate to the park. If the cows had been grazing, I would have gone the long way around rather than walk across the open land, but the field was empty and I climbed the gate. When I reached the large cedar in the middle I looked up through the layered branches, stark against the blue of the sky. The contrast was painful and I closed my eyes. I thought again about the things Cara had told me. Perhaps it had all been for effect, perhaps she did need a doctor as Victor and Peter suggested. And then I wondered whether Victor believed that the Bible's virgin birth was possible and how much Cara had told him about Finn's conception and the boat, and about how the child had drowned. My burst of anger had dissipated, and the terror I'd experienced on the hanger had gone, all drained away. When I opened my eyes, the cattle were lumbering towards me.

I moved back and stood in a cowpat, my foot breaking through the crust and the soft squelch pushing over my shoes, and then they were surrounding me. In silence, they watched me with their unblinking eyes, their massive bony heads seeming to plot some malevolent scheme. I waved my arms. "Yah!" I shouted, and the two in front of me shied and then came in closer. There was a nudge on the back of my thighs that made me cry out and stagger towards the cows facing me. I may have whimpered. I reached up to my neck but the locket and chain had gone, most likely whipped off by a branch during my rush down the hanger. The cow in front huffed out through its nostrils, and when I dared to take my eyes off them I saw Cara watching from the terrace. I put my hands out in front of me, positive that the cattle wanted me to fall beneath their hooves, and I cried out, unintelligible words that the animals ignored. From the terrace across the field and the parterre, I heard Cara calling:

"Go on, girls. Go on now." And the cows separated and let me go.

"Go on, girl. Go on," I say inside my head, willing myself along. I am ready.

I hear my door being unlocked. Two Care Assisters, or whatever they are called, come into my room, a man and a woman.

"How are you feeling, Mrs. Jelli-co?" the woman says. She is white and scrawny. I have seen them many times before. The man rarely speaks; he comes only when there is work to be done.

"We need to change your bedding," she says. "You know the routine, don't you, love? So no trouble now."

There are procedures in this place for moving people even if they are dying and too sick to feed themselves or sit up. Protocol. I understand, I don't mind, I thrive on routine. I know the drill. There must always be two Helpers in attendance.

They stand either side of the bed, and tip me onto my right side. The man rolls up as much of the dirty sheet as he can, into a sausage behind my back, and lays out half of the clean sheet on top of the plastic mattress protector. I am facing the woman but she doesn't look at me, she stares into the middle distance as though she can see through the wall.

"One, two, three," she says, and they roll me onto my other side.

"Trouble," I say. "When have I ever been trouble?"

The man laughs. The woman whips out the old sheet and pulls the clean one to the corners. All the sheets in this place have elasticated corners. Oh, if I'd had sheets with elasticated corners when I had to change the bed after Mother had soiled it. *It's wrinkled, Frances. I can tell you didn't bother to iron it. It's wrinkled, I can feel it. Frances? Are you trying to give me bedsores?* Praise be to Bertha Berman who patented the fitted sheet in the late 1950s, although I didn't see one until I came in here.

"All right now," the woman says. "All done." She tugs my nightdress below my knees where it has got rucked up, and lays the thin duvet with a clean cover over me. One day soon, they will bring it right over my head. The man holds me up while they insert a pillow which he has already squashed into a fresh pillowcase.

They pretend that it is difficult to change my bedding and that's why they need two of them, but it is an easy series of manoeuvres, one they are practiced in. I know that they work in pairs because the prison procedures state that they are not allowed to be unaccompanied when they manhandle inmates.

NINETEEN

I have often thought about how ironic it is that for the past twenty years I have been spied on day and night, through a judas hole in my prison door. I have come to know the footsteps of the different guards, the shuffle at the door, the slide of the plate, and the eye. The all-seeing eye. What has it seen? Nothing as interesting as the things I saw through the judas hole at Lyntons. But of course, the difference is privacy. The other women will complain and shout about being looked at without warning. But I think it is better to know when someone is watching rather than to live your life under an invisible gaze.

I check the throat of the person sitting beside my bed. The dog collar is in place. Victor has a piece of paper folded into the book he holds on his lap. He is using it as a bookmark. I thought the book was the Bible, surely it was the Bible a few days ago, but now I see it is a thin pamphlet of poetry.

"Would you like me to read you a poem, Miss Jellico?"

"No," I say. I have no use for poetry. "Read me the piece of paper."

"But it's nothing," he says. "It's an old bill that's been used as a bookmark, an invoice."

Pieces of paper are never nothing. "Indulge me," I say, and he does.

"Eastbourne June 25th," he reads. "To Mrs. Squilbin. From Messrs. J. Weston & Son, Artists and Photographers. 81 Terminus Road." He pauses to look at me and I nod, encouraging him to continue. "Eight sepia plates, six and a half by three and a half. Wedding gift. Two pounds, fifteen shillings. One pound paid on account. Overdue balance one pound, fifteen shillings."

If we were so inclined we could read all sorts of things into that note. That Mrs. Squilbin — what a name! — never paid the overdue one pound and fifteen shillings, never collected her wedding photographs because by the time the bill was due her new husband had already left her. Or, Mrs. Squilbin was the bride's mother. At the reception she fell out with her new son-in-law and refused to pay the balance. Notes can be interpreted in all manner of ways.

343

I remember the man in the wig — I can see him, but what was his title? — the man who read out my note in court. Deep voice, too full of himself, a bad actor.

Dear Frances,
Peter sends up his apologies, and hopes you won't hold yesterday evening against him. Please for goodness' sake, don't do anything hastily, I can imagine how much you must be hurting, just stay in bed for a while.

Yours,
Cara

It had been discovered in my suitcase.

"Are you the Frances addressed in this letter?" the wig man asked.

But there were many wig men, some on my side, some not. My wig man had told me I shouldn't take the stand, that it wasn't wise, that I would be ripped apart by the prosecution, but I had insisted. I had another agenda.

"I am," I said.

"Can you tell us who the letter was written by?"

"I can."

The first wig man sighed. "Please tell us who the letter was written by."

"Cara Calace."

"Cara Calace," he repeated to the group of twelve people, a few of whom looked interested, while others seemed to be asleep.

"Cara Calace, your friend?"

"Yes," I said.

"And who is the Peter mentioned?"

"Peter Robertson."

"Peter Robertson," he repeated with theatrical significance.

"Yes," I said.

"Peter Robertson with whom you fell in love?"

"Yes." The word came out as a sob, a genuine sob.

"Peter, it seems, has cause to apologise for something that happened the previous evening," the wig man said. "Something he did, or perhaps didn't do, that caused you pain. Cara is worried you will act hastily and urges you to stay in bed. Did you declare your love to Peter Robertson that evening, Miss Jellico? And were you rejected? Rejected by Peter Robertson and so hurt by it you were capable of anything?" The questions were rhetorical; he didn't require an answer.

Peter returned from London just as Cara and I were finishing an early dinner. Maybe it was Peter who encouraged our normal excess because we'd drunk only half a bottle of wine between us. She and I had reached a sort of truce, an understanding that we wouldn't speak of certain things. The front door slammed and Peter came racing up the stairs, his hands clasping bags and a small square case tucked under his arm.

"Did it go well?" Cara said, jumping up. "It went well, didn't it?"

I stood too while he dropped everything to squeeze hold of her, bend her backwards, and kiss her. I didn't think about it until much later but often when I saw them together it was as though everything they did had been rehearsed, not because they had me as an audience but so they could believe in a more perfect version of themselves.

"It went better than I could have imagined. But I am so tired." He flung himself down on the chaise longue.

"Can I make you a drink?" Cara said. "Did you have something to eat on the train?"

"I just need a bath and to go to bed. I'd forgotten how filthy London is."

"I should go up," I said.

"Presents first." Peter roused himself.

He had bought earrings for Cara: tiny

sapphire droplets and a necklace to match
— we still hadn't found any jewellery in the
Museum apart from the mourning ring —
and she ran into the bathroom to put them
on. There was a bag of pasta, cheese
wrapped in paper, and a whole salami. For
all of us he had bought a record player in a
case and long-playing records so we could
have music in the evenings: *Bookends* by
Simon and Garfunkel, *Astral Weeks* by Van
Morrison, *Five Leaves Left* by Nick Drake.
We had uncovered an old-fashioned gramo-
phone but Cara thought the records were
boring. She wanted modern music. And for
me, although I hadn't been expecting anything, a small gift wrapped in tissue paper.

"What is it?" I asked.

"Unwrap it and see," Peter said.

Cara came closer. It was a small gold case
for cigarettes and inscribed on the inside
was:

Franny,
To keep you on the straight and narrow
                                        Love,
                                          P

"What does that mean?" Cara said, at my
shoulder.

I laughed, for once understanding the joke.

"Just a silly thing," he said.

"I don't get it," Cara said, frostily.

He put his arm around her. "You know how Franny's cigarettes are always bent and broken."

"It's wonderful," I said. "But how did you manage to get it engraved that quickly?"

"I called in a favour at a little shop in Maida Vale."

When everything was unwrapped, I wished them goodnight, and even as I closed the door behind me I could hear raised voices. This time the argument didn't last for long. One door was banged and then another. Water gushed through the pipes as the bath filled in the room beneath mine while I brushed my teeth. And after I'd spat into the sink and rinsed, without stopping to consider, I lifted the board from the floor.

Below me, Peter put his hands on the sides of the basin, staring at himself for a minute or two in a mirror he had taken from the Museum. I lifted my eye away from the lens as he unbuttoned his shirt and then I moved back to see him go to the door, hold the handle as though trying to be quiet, and carefully turn the key in the lock. He returned to the mirror and stood sideways in front of it, his hand on his stomach, holding it in, and then lifted his arms in a champion's pose, smiling. He took off the rest of his clothes and I should have looked away then but I didn't, I continued to watch as he sank down into the bathwater.

I could see the hair on his chest, his penis floating, and his knees breaking the surface. He glanced over his shoulder at the door as if to check it really was locked, closed his eyes, and his hand went down. I should have looked away then too but I didn't, I couldn't. I thought about the things Cara had told me in the woods beside the obelisk, that Peter wasn't able to get an erection for her. His hand moved, and I studied his gentle face, his slightly open mouth, his full lips. He took his time and still I watched, saw him speed up and his forehead crease, saw him push with his feet on the end of the bath. At that moment when it was about to happen, when I could see it was about to happen, at that instant while I was watching his face, his eyes shot open and he looked up at the central point of the ceiling, looked up at me, and I looked down at him. I was convinced that somehow he knew I was there and that he was telling me, in the only way he could, that it would be different with me. And I understood that he loved me and that he knew I loved him back.

That night I lay in bed and imagined Peter, Cara, and Finn under the sea. I saw them floating gently in the current. The oranges which Cara had bought from the grocer's juggled sedately past, the pages of *Woman's Way* turned lazily, and the lid came off a tin of flour, a black-and-white photograph of Peter's dumpling wife emerging and rocking downwards until her face darkened. And through the middle of it all, I saw a cow: huge and white, jumping, and kicking her back legs in slow motion. Her mouth was open in a long bellow, and her tail high as if she'd been let out to pasture after a winter indoors. I made them dance, Peter, Cara, and Finn, coming together in a vertical chain with the baby nearest the surface and Peter at the bottom. Finn, with *my* hand now around his ankle, waved his chubby arms. I bicycled my legs as Peter dwindled below me, while the cow and the oranges disappeared into the murk. I let go of the child and above me, through the blue layers, I saw him ascending towards the light.

The weekend passed without us noticing it was the weekend. We ate and we drank and we smoked. We spent the rest of our time pawing through the things in the Museum as though twenty years ago we'd put them away in the attic and had only now remembered they were there. I came across a set of vellum writing paper and envelopes embossed with the Lyntons crest, the three oranges on a shield, and took them up to my room. A tea set came too and a small chest of drawers.

In a box labelled *Images d'Épinal,* Cara found fifty sheets of uncut cardboard models no child had ever touched. She lugged the box outside to the orangery portico. The pictures were of famous Italian buildings: St. Peter's, the Leaning Tower of Pisa, the Colosseum, the Pitti Palace. The paper was yellowed and the colours muted by time but she cut around each shape, folded the tabs, and stuck the pieces together with glue. Her work was rough and the edges jagged. The two-dimensional people that had been included to place around the outside of the buildings — a plump priest gazing upward with his hands clasped behind his back, a mother and two children, a single woman in a long dress, all of them smiling — sometimes had their heads or feet snipped off by Cara's haphazard scissors. But for a couple of days at least she was dedicated to the task and soon the orangery steps from the top down to the parterre became a little Italy, filled with three-dimensional cardboard buildings.

On one of the evenings when we had drunk more than our usual quantity of wine we decided it would be a good idea to bring the stuffed grizzly bear into the house, but didn't get it any farther than the library. We had danced it around the shelves and it had seemed hilariously funny. In the morning, I found the bear face down on the torn pages of the books, both of its arms ripped from its torso. It was a desecration I hardly believed us capable of, and the grotesque sight of the dismembered bear brought tears to my eyes. I sat on the steps below the main portico and wrote a letter to Mr. Liebermann, telling him that we had discovered some items which belonged to him, in a secret room. And then I thought about the wine I had drunk from Lyntons' cellar, the food I had eaten which I knew had been bought with money received from the objects Peter was selling. I thought about the steak dinner he had treated me to, and the paper I was writing the letter on. I took the gold cigarette case from my dressing gown pocket and read the inscription, as I did every time I opened it. I lit a cigarette, held the match up to the letter, and set it alight.

TWENTY

"Hello?" I heard someone calling from the carriage turn and when I went to see, Victor was there, pushing his bicycle through the weedy gravel. "That's a lot of potholes and uphill all the way." He was sweating and I could see an angry rash spreading from under his dog collar.

"Hello," I said, surprised to see him.

"I thought I'd take you up on your invitation since you haven't been to see *me* for a while."

"Haven't I? What day is it?"

"Monday."

"I've missed two Sundays?"

"You should see my congregation graph. Dropping by the week."

I wasn't listening, I was thinking about how I could avoid taking him upstairs where he would see the furniture and everything we had pilfered from the Museum, or how I could keep him out of the library where the bear still lay. By chance I had closed the doors and the shutters on the portico side so that I didn't have to see the poor creature myself. When I didn't return his smile, Victor added, "That's if your invitation still stands?"

"Of course," I said, finding my manners. "Let me make us a pot of tea."

"A glass of water would be nice as well." He stuck a finger under his collar to scratch and then removed his bicycle clips.

I led him around to the portico. "Why don't you sit here and catch your breath, and I'll go and put the kettle on."

When I returned we said various polite things about the good weather and the pleasant view, and he complimented me on my dressing gown. I poured the tea and Victor gulped his water and then he said, "Is your friend or her husband at home today?"

"No, I think they must have driven into town. At least, the car's gone."

Victor finished his water. "I have something for you." He took an envelope from his jacket pocket. "I got dragged into sorting through Dorothea Lynton's belongings. The woman we buried last month? The do-gooders couldn't agree on what should go to the jumble and what should be thrown away. I was called in to arbitrate. And I found this."

I took the envelope from him and pressed the yellowing paper where it bulged. It was addressed to Dorothea at a house in the town and it had been opened. Inside was a folded note and compacted at the bottom were tiny scraps of blue and white, each smaller than my smallest fingernail. I opened the note. A looping hand had written, *Sorry,* nothing else.

I took out a few of the pieces and turned them over in my palm. "What are they?"

"Can't you guess?" He lifted one from my hand. "I have to admit it took me a while."

"I have no idea."

"Peacocks' eyes."

"From the wallpaper!"

"Whoever cut them out must have had a guilty conscience and returned them. I thought we could try and put them back. And in case you didn't have any glue . . ." From his other pocket he produced a small pot with a pink rubber top.

"You've thought of everything," I said.

I took him in through the front door. I was hoping for the same effect that Peter had wished for when he'd first shown me around. Victor gazed upward.

"Can you see?" I said. "One side of the gallery is real."

"I think I remember something about this. Something about someone falling. Another of my uncle's stories." He shook his head trying to remember. "A dog, or a child. That's why they boxed it in."

We went through to the blue drawing room. The shutters were always open now, and the doors. He was staggered by the room's beauty just as I had been. He stood with his back to the mirror while I fetched the stepladder from the orangery where Cara had left it.

I took the glue and Victor the envelope of eyes, and we worked from bird to bird.

"Is there a word for inserting a new eye?" I said. "The opposite of enucleation?"

"Not that I know of. They'd be tricky things to put back. I don't think it's ever been done, or not successfully. The optic nerve is part of the central nervous system."

"Didn't you say you were a doctor, in the war?"

"Oh, no. I never got that far. A medical student only."

"Where did you study, in London?" My fingers were tacky with glue: I had never been good at craft projects.

"London, yes." He paused, a peacock's

356

eye on the tip of his index finger. "But just for a few years. I never qualified."

"Oh, really?" I said, not paying attention to his tone. "Surely you weren't conscripted? Wasn't medicine a reserved occupation?"

"Actually, I withdrew, dropped out; isn't that the phrase they use these days? A dropout." He said it with such self-loathing that I stopped my gluing to look at him.

"I was an impostor. Pathetic. Useless."

"Oh, I'm sure not. No. Surely not . . . useless."

He slid his back down the wall until he reached the dusty floorboards, and I sat beside him. "I knew I wasn't cut out for medicine almost as soon as I began my training, but the idea of going to fight was even more horrific."

I picked at the glue on my fingers. I could tell he wanted to talk. The way he spoke was different from how Cara told her stories. Victor was hesitant, stumbling over his words but not stopping, as though this was the first time he had said them and once he had started he had to get it all out.

"I was on the Central Line platform at Bank Underground station when a bomb fell into the booking hall, although I learned that later of course. I remember a woman with a suitcase waiting for a train. I suppose

357

I was staring, wondering where she was going, hoping she was getting out of London. We smiled at each other, just for a moment, you know that connection that you sometimes get with strangers, an instant, and the lights of the oncoming train lit up her face, her smile. And then there was the blast — the force of the air as it came down the tunnels lifted everyone up and flung us against the walls. The lights went out and I think I was unconscious for a minute or so, but I hadn't broken anything. I found my torch and turned it on. People had been using the platforms as an air raid shelter. Most of the tiles had come off the walls and there was a bit of debris, but oddly the platform wasn't that damaged. The people around me were though, I could see that, and hear it, hear them begging and crying. I shined my light down onto the track where the train had stopped halfway along the platform, and the woman was down there under the train, I saw her suitcase, and . . . well. An ARP warden put his torch on too and began calling for a doctor or a nurse, shouting it over and over while he tried to do whatever he could. And I . . . I turned off my light, and I crouched by the wall, and I said nothing."

I put out my hand to Victor but didn't touch him.

"I still wonder, if I'd managed, if I'd been strong enough to speak up, whether more people would have lived."

"Not many, by the sound of it."

"But one more life would have been worth it. Wouldn't it?"

I looked at him as he stared back and I understood what he needed was the truth. "Yes," I said.

We were silent for a while, looking through the open doors at the cloud shadows moving across the garden.

"Thank you," he said.

I offered him a cigarette from the case and we lit them. "You joined the clergy after that?" I asked.

He exhaled. "After the war. A penance I suppose. I'm not positive it worked though."

"Have you decided what you're going to do?"

With the cigarette in his mouth and his eyes narrowed against the smoke, Victor shook his head. He took the case from me and opened it to read the inscription. "A gift from a suitor?" He sounded sad but gave me a teasing nudge with his elbow and handed it back. As I put it in my pocket, I said shyly, "Yes, something like that."

Victor and I were standing in the entrance

hall. We had said our goodbyes, I had made a promise to go to church, which I knew I wouldn't keep, and he had said that he would come back and visit. I held the front door open for him. He glanced up at the trompe l'oeil. "I just remembered the story," he said. He gave a sharp shake of his head as if he regretted speaking. "Thank you for the tea. What a nice afternoon."

"But you have to tell me now." I half closed the door and moved back into the room, looking up too.

"No, it's nothing." His face was washed-out and I assumed he was demurring for my benefit, that it was a story he thought I shouldn't hear.

"Go on. I want to know."

He looked up once more, turning his back to me. "It was a young man," he said. "An only child. He might have been Dorothea's nephew, Charlie? Charles? I'm not sure. He jumped. He'd just come back from the war, the Great War that is, and the family was simply glad to have him home when there were thousands who didn't return. He'd been back for a week or two. He stood on the bannister and jumped." Victor's voice was breaking.

We were silent, staring upward, when we heard the car driving fast onto the carriage turn and pulling up at the front door. The engine was turned off and before the car doors were opened we could hear Peter and Cara shouting. Victor and I glanced at each other and looked away.

"But the desk!" Cara said. They were just outside. "I thought you were going to take it to London."

"It was only a thought," Peter said, using his calming voice. "So she would have something to write on for the time being."

"And the cigarette case? I suppose you were going to ask for that back after a week as well, were you?"

I turned from Victor and looked up at the trompe l'oeil, my face burning.

"For God's sake, Cara," Peter said. "It was a gift. What's wrong with that?"

"Oh, Franny," Cara said, her voice deepening. "It's just a silly joke I thought you would like."

In the entrance hall, Victor and I continued to look anywhere but at each other.

"Oh, Peter," Cara continued, her voice a horrible breathy impersonation of mine. "It's wonderful. Oh, Peter, thank you."

I was mortified and wondered whether I could hurry Victor out through the blue drawing room and around the portico, but the front door opened, and Cara and Peter saw us standing there. Peter's face flushed but Cara's eyes burned as if it was our fault for eavesdropping.

"We weren't talking about *you*, Frances," she said. "You aren't that interesting."

For a heartbeat no one spoke and then Victor and I started at once.

"Miss Jellico was showing me the peacocks in the blue drawing room."

"Reverend Wylde stopped by for a cup of tea."

"Cara," Victor said in greeting, a required politeness, and nodding at Peter, he went to the door.

"Franny —" Peter began and put his hand out but I followed Victor outside and to the gates at the top of the avenue where he had left his bicycle. "I'm sorry you had to hear that," I said to him as he pushed his clips back over his ankles.

"And weren't you sorry to hear it too?" He sounded angry.

Suddenly I wanted to defend them to Victor, even though I knew Cara's impersonation was cruel and her words catty. "It was a bit of fun. Cara's always teasing, and Peter. They like to joke."

"Peter who gave you the cigarette case?"

I resented the moralising tone I thought I heard in Victor's words. A man who had made his own mistakes and was now contemplating leaving the church.

"A gift, as he said."

"I don't think Lyntons is good for you, Miss Jellico." He chose his words more carefully this time.

"It's fine," I said, knowing he meant Cara and Peter, not Lyntons.

"Is it?"

"Cara didn't mean anything by it. She gets jealous sometimes. It's schoolgirl stuff."

"Does she have a reason to be jealous?"

"No, of course not." I knew my face was reddening.

"They are married." It wasn't clear whether he meant it as a question or a statement.

"Well . . ." I started.

"I just don't think you should get into something you can't get out of." He climbed onto the bicycle. He wanted me to ask what the something might be but I was determined not to.

"They're my friends," I said.

Victor raised his eyebrows. "Thank you again for the tea," he said and pushed on the pedals. I watched him negotiating the potholes, his figure shrinking as he cycled down the avenue.

■ ■ ■ ■

When I went back indoors, Cara and Peter were waiting for me, sitting side by side on the grand staircase, both looking glum. Cara jumped up when I came around the corner.

"I'm sorry," she said. "It was a silly argument I was having with Peter. I was angry with him, not with you." She went to take my hands but I folded my arms across my chest. I looked at Peter and he nodded. "Of course you should have a desk," she continued, talking fast. Behind them on the half landing where the stairs turned was the small French desk that had been in their rooms. "Peter's going to take it up for you now, aren't you, Peter?" He stood, awaiting my instruction, and she nudged him with her hip. "It's a beautiful desk. You deserve it. Please Fran, say you forgive me." She pulled on my wrists until I released them, and she put her arms around me. "I won't be able to live with myself otherwise," she said.

She sounded so genuine. Over her shoulder, between the strands of her hair, Peter gave me a crooked smile. My eyes slid away from him and I brought my hands up to Cara's shoulder blades and returned her embrace. She laughed with relief.

I followed Peter, who was carrying the desk, up to my room, and he set it in front of the window.

"I'm sorry about that, earlier," he said. "Cara didn't mean it."

"It's fine," I said. "I know she's had a difficult time."

"I'll bring you a chair up later." He began to walk away.

"She told me about Finn," I said, and Peter stopped. "That he died."

"She told you that, did she?" He still hadn't turned.

"I'm sorry. And I'm sorry I misunderstood. That I thought he was given up for adoption. It must have been terrible for you when he drowned." I waited for him to open up to me.

"Yes, well," he said. "I'll go and see about a chair."

It was after we'd eaten, with less wine to accompany the food than before, and I'd gone up to bed, that I examined the desk, opening the drawers and checking the legs, and I realised it wasn't the one they'd had in their room — which had gone from behind the door — but the second of what must have been a matching pair. There was worm in this one though, dusty holes in the legs, a long scratch in the wood of the back, and the leather was scuffed. They must have known that if I discovered their duplicity I would never confront them.

I put on my nightdress and as I washed my face I smelled the smell again, the one that had been in the bathroom when I'd arrived and had induced me to remove the carpet: stale urine, old cooking smells, and this time, something too sweet; perfume that had been sprayed in a room to cover up the odour of something rotten. My fingers went to my throat and searched around for the locket before I remembered that I had lost it in the woods. In the bathroom, I got down on my hands and knees and, feeling idiotic, sniffed around the room. The smell was strongest next to the edges of the bath panel. Perhaps an animal — a squirrel or a rat — had become trapped and died under there. A vision of the dead fox came, its neck gaping open as though there were a second mouth below the first.

The bath panel had three screws along the top and three along the bottom. I fetched a knife from the bedroom — the Lynton coat of arms on the handle — slotted the tip into the groove on one of the heads, and tried to turn it. The knife slipped from the slot, fell from my hand, and knocked against the wooden panel. From the other side, from under the enclosed bath, I heard a muffled cry, not an animal but something human. I scuttled backwards across the floor, jamming myself under the basin, all of me straining to listen but not wanting to hear. When nothing came, I lunged and grabbed the knife, holding it out with my shaking hand as if it might save me from whatever was under the bath. "Plumbing," I muttered, water draining through the pipes. The timing of the noise a coincidence.

I stretched forward, the knife out. And twice I knocked its blade on the bath panel. Tap, tap. The sound came back from underneath, someone weak, moaning with effort.

I ran then, out of the room, slamming the bathroom door behind me. I pulled my blanket off the bed and left the attic, running down the spiral staircase to the ground floor. I went to the blue drawing room, where the envelope with the remaining peacocks' eyes inside — those we hadn't been able to reach even with the stepladder — had been discarded beside the mirror. I pulled the French doors and the shutters closed, and pressed myself into a corner with my back against two walls and my eyes on the door to the hall.

I tried to stay awake, listening to every creak and groan the house made, but after an hour or two my head nodded to my knees. The light crept around the edges of the shutters in the morning and the house breathed. Whatever had been there the night before had gone.

I walked barefoot down to the bridge and as I approached, a bird of prey took off from the balustrade, wheeling above me with a brown body and wide herringbone stripes on the tail and wings. When she dipped and turned over the lake's edges and I saw the flash of white on her tail before she disappeared at the far end, I guessed she was a Montagu's harrier. I leaned over the edge of the bridge where the bird had perched and I thought about how Peter had tried to convince me it was Palladian and how more than anything I had wanted to believe him. When the rising sun had warmed my back, I used the dinner knife that I'd brought with me to scratch my name, *Franny,* into the stone. After it was done I dropped the knife into the lake.

When I went back up to the house, although it was early, Peter was sitting on the portico steps and Cara had propped herself against a column. They straightened when they saw me coming through the rhododendrons; they looked like they'd had another argument.

"Frances," Cara called. "What are you doing out already?" She put down the cup she held as if getting ready to hug me.

"And in your nightdress?" Peter said as I approached the steps. He picked up the cup.

I must have been white, still shaken. "What's happened?" she said.

"There was someone —" I started. "In my bathroom last night."

She took a step down. "Are you hurt? What happened?"

"Like the person you thought you saw at the window?" Peter didn't sound as though he believed me.

I pulled the blanket tighter around my shoulders. "They were under the bath."

"What?" Cara said and Peter turned his head to look at her.

"I heard them," I said. "Moaning behind the panel."

"Moaning?"

"It would have been the pipes clanking. They're always clanking," Peter said.

"Crying," I said.

"You know it wasn't the pipes," Cara said

to Peter.

"Don't be ridiculous."

"I'm not being ridiculous," Cara said. "It's ridiculous to live like the only things that are real are the things you can see. You want evidence for everything, proof."

"That's right." His voice was rising. "I don't believe in ghosts, or devils, or virgin births."

"What do you bloody believe in then? Nothing! You're soulless." Cara tightened her lips and looked across the fields, and Peter came down the steps, put his arm around me, and squeezed. "You're overtired, shattered I expect." I would have liked to lean into him, have Cara and her disgruntled face vanish.

"I heard it though," I said.

"See," Cara said, unable to resist turning back.

"I'm sure it was the water in the pipes," Peter said again.

"There's something behind the bath panel."

"But there was nothing in the room next to yours in the end when you made me check. Was there?" He held me more firmly, reassuring a child.

"Something was moaning under the bath."

"All right. Maybe an animal did get in

370

there. Why don't I come up and take off the panel? What do I need — a screwdriver?"

"I already tried."

"You won't find anything," Cara said, petulant. "It doesn't work like that." She took her cup from him.

"It won't hurt to take a look," he said, his voice calm, but his body tense.

Cara shouted something in Italian, each word a barb.

"That's not true," he said to her, but he let his arm fall from around me. I wondered if they had been arguing about the cigarette case again, or the desk.

She waved her hands, shouted some more, and the dregs of her coffee splashed onto the stone, turning it darker where it fell. We watched her anger and then Peter took his wallet from his back pocket and I saw it was thick with money. He counted four one-pound notes and held them out to her so she had to come down the steps. She snatched them from him and strode off. I wanted to be alone with Peter but I wanted Cara to stay, to reassure me that I wasn't going mad. Perhaps Peter saw my concern because he said, "Don't worry. She'll go into town to buy some food. She'll have calmed down by the time she's back."

371

"Do you think she's all right going on her own?"

"To be honest with you, I don't care."

I took out the cigarette case and Peter lit two cigarettes.

Twenty-One

In the last twenty years I have learned to be more circumspect of people and their stories. It is an advantageous skill for one who is incarcerated. *I didn't do it* is often heard in here. But when I was younger I used to believe everything anyone said. *You're too gullible, too easily led,* Mother used to tell me. *Just like your father.* Her words were meant to hurt, to be an insult, but they would always take me back to a summer when I was eight or nine, at any rate to a summer when we were still living in the house on Lansdowne Road in Notting Hill. Mother could have been there that day but I don't remember her, I only recall my father in the communal gardens our house backed onto. I had taken my dolls' tea set to the lawn and laid out the tiny plates, cups, and saucers, and we — my father, my dolls, and I — were having a picnic. He was eating a slice of imaginary

Victoria sponge when we heard a man say, *What are you doing? I say, what are you doing?* again and again.

For a while we thought someone was playing a joke on us, hiding in the bushes around the perimeter of the garden, moving from one spot to another. We heard a woman laughing and saying in a breathy voice, *My God, my God!* My father was hurrying me to pack up the tea set, avoiding my questions about what was going on and muttering about calling a policeman, when he spied a bird in a tree, black with a yellow beak and a splash of white behind its eye. Eventually we caught the Indian mynah bird in a cardboard box and returned it to an old lady who lived around the corner. She gave me half a crown and my father a glass of sherry.

Mother would continue her tirade with: *No one says what they're really thinking. You should learn to read between the lines or everyone will say you're a mooncalf. Do you want to be a mooncalf, Frances?* But the world is a nicer place when you think everyone is telling the truth. There are no agendas, no hidden motives; no one lies for dramatic effect.

I didn't get it, not then. It wasn't until I was in court that I realised what she had meant and that it was duplicity that would get me what I wanted, even though what I wanted wasn't what anyone expected. I learned from the wig men that the law is not about finding the truth, it is about who can tell the most convincing story. It is a game that must be grasped swiftly if you want to win, even if to everyone else it looks as though you have lost.

"Can you tell the court what this is?" a wig man asked. An usher passed me the cigarette case, and I turned it over and over in my hands in the way that Anne Bunting had turned the library book. So familiar, an object of love. I would have liked to slip it in my pocket, but the court was watching.

Later, when I put in a formal request to the prison governor for the cigarette case to be returned to me and it was granted, I cried. I hadn't expected to see it again.

Cara was right, there was nothing there, under the bath. No marks in the dust, no dead animals, even the smell had gone. I felt foolish but I didn't want to stay in the attic on my own. I followed Peter downstairs and he went to the Museum to look through some rolled canvases he had found. I said I was going for a walk but I went to their rooms to search for something to eat. I discovered the heel of a loaf of bread and the remains of a packet of butter. It reminded me of the food I'd eaten when I had first arrived. The butter was on the turn but I was hungry and I gobbled it before either Cara or Peter returned. I had been grateful when Cara had first invited me to eat with them, but now, as I scrounged scraps from their kitchen, it occurred to me that it was a type of control; Cara could be generous when it suited her, or not, when it didn't.

I put *Bookends* on the record player. We would play all three albums over and over whenever we were in their sitting room, so that everything we did, eating, talking, laughing, was done to a background of music, until the lyrics infiltrated my dreams, and I would wake up humming. It was odd to be in that room with the music, but without Cara or Peter; the shame of spying even more intense than when I watched them through their bathroom ceiling. I sat and then lay on the chaise longue.

The sound of Cara coming in with the groceries woke me. She put the needle back to the beginning of the record and I stayed where I was, watching her sway to the music while she unpacked the shopping, singing about Mrs. Wagner's Pies. She didn't ask me whether Peter had found anything under the bath. She'd bought a whole salmon, two pounds of tiny pink potatoes, a bag of sugar, and half a dozen eggs. She held up each package to show me. She was happy again as she made mayonnaise, which she said was much nicer than salad cream.

I thought about getting up, finding an excuse to leave, but I remained there on the chaise longue so as not to tip her out of her happy mood. But I was cross with myself. I didn't want to have to consider every word before I spoke, as I had when I'd first come to Lyntons, concerned about how it might be received. A few weeks ago I had chased off the little voice of insecurity and now I didn't want it to climb back up to my shoulder.

"Can I pay something towards the food?" I asked.

Still whisking and pouring, Cara looked at me and I saw that she thought I should have offered weeks ago. "No need," she said, waiting too long to reply. "Peter's paying for it. I thought we'd have another picnic, on the roof."

I inched my way out of the attic window, one foot on the edge of the lead gutter that was filled with rotting leaves and twigs.

Thirty feet below me, I knew, the stone woman and Cupid were kissing in the fountain. I passed up the picnic basket to Peter and then the blankets, trying not to glance down. Behind him Cara was clambering across the roof.

"I don't know if I can do it in this," I said. I closed my eyes to stop my head spinning. I was wearing the dressing gown.

"Come on," Peter said. When I opened my eyes, he was leaning out from the roof, his arm extending down. I reached up and put my hand in his. "I've got you," he said.

The architectural landscape of the roof inverted the building's spaces, creating walkways between the tiled sections, with a dozen chimneys jutting up from the lead. We went up close to the outside of the glass cupola, now an immense vegetable-garden cloche, and peered through the broken panes to the grand staircase far below. The air was still and the clouds over the hangers had heads of bright cauliflowers and undersides of deep purple. The roof radiated heat through the soles of my shoes. From this height, I could see the far side of the bridge, the tower of the mausoleum, and the top of the obelisk.

We found a spot behind a wide chimney stack and Peter opened a bottle of champagne. I spread out the blankets and table-cloth we had brought up with us. Cara took three blue-and-gold plates from the basket and three napkins. We laid out the salmon and the tiny potatoes and salad, and a bowl of mayonnaise. Cara had brought two paper parasols and she and I held them over our heads, sitting cross-legged in our fine clothes.

We ate and drank, and Peter opened another bottle. Cara and I wedged the parasols into gaps in the brickwork and we lay beneath them with our faces in the shade. Peter was reading. Cara began to hum the song that had been on the record player earlier and he joined in.

"Pass me the cigarettes," Cara said and they both laughed. I knew they had got the words wrong but I didn't tell them. My cigarette case was in my dressing gown pocket as usual but I didn't want to remind Cara that it existed. Peter lit three of his own cigarettes and we were silent for a long time, smoking and drowsing. Everything was still and heavy.

I was almost asleep when Cara said, "I went to the post office this morning to see if we had any letters."

After a moment or two, as though making conversation were an effort, Peter said,

"And did we?"

Cara rolled onto her side, propping up her head on one hand. "Yes," she said. "There was one from Father Creagh, forwarded on from Scotland. He wrote to tell me that Dermod had died."

Peter looked up from his book. "Dermod? Oh, Cara. I'm sorry."

"Oh no," I said, sitting up.

"I can't believe it," Peter said. "Why didn't you tell us sooner? All afternoon we've been lounging around eating and drinking, and Dermod was dead."

"He died before this afternoon," she said.

"Of course, of course," Peter said. "What did Father Creagh say? How did it happen?"

I gave Peter a look, almost reached out my hand to quieten him. I didn't think we should speak about dying and death in front of Cara.

"I don't mind talking about it, Frances," she said. "He drowned."

We were silent, all of us, I supposed, contemplating the awful coincidence of both Finn and Dermod perishing under the water.

"He was fishing," Cara said. "When the tide went out they found the boat. It had sunk with him in it. They think he must have hit his head somehow, and got stuck."

Her voice seemed softer, her Irish accent creeping in.

"Poor man," Peter said.

"Will you go home for the funeral?" I asked.

"Home? To Ireland? Ireland isn't my home. And anyway, the funeral was today. The letter was at the post office for a week."

"That bloody postman," Peter said. "I don't know why he can't cycle out here."

"It's too far," I said.

"Cara manages to cycle to the village and back."

"It's five miles along the road, and he's old. It wouldn't be fair to expect him to come out this far."

"Jesus," Cara said, sitting up. "I don't care about the postman, all right?"

Peter and I looked at each other. "Have another drink," he said, our answer to everything. He poured the last of the second bottle of champagne into her glass and opened a third. She had seemed happy when she was making the picnic and all the time she had known Dermod was dead. It didn't seem possible.

"It was Father Creagh who wrote to you?" Peter said. "Not your mother?"

"Still not a word from Isabel." She finished her glass and held it out for more. She seemed distant, unconnected, but by then the champagne was making everything seem distant and unconnected. All I wanted to do was sleep.

"Do you miss your mother, Fran?" Cara lit another cigarette and the smoke rolled from her nostrils. The only sound was the ticking of the roof as it expanded in the late afternoon sun; even the birds were silent.

"I miss the mother I had when I was a child," I said. "But if you mean the mother I had for the years after that, then no." I surprised myself, and I wondered if I would be punished later for admitting this aloud, with another dead blackbird, more noises under the bath, or the smell of the bedroom we had shared. "It's good she's dead."

Mother had lain in our bed for a week after she died. I stopped sleeping beside her and sat every night in the armchair in the bay window with a blanket over me. They say that the person — the soul — leaves the body when someone dies and what's left is an empty vessel. But I didn't find it that way with Mother. She still inhabited hers; she was still in charge. Her body stiffened but she continued to tell me what to do. Her eyeballs blackened but she watched me. On the Sunday evening, I laid the tea towels under the kitchen window, moved the crockery from the bath lid to the floor, and ran the water, but her body was heavier than I had anticipated, literally a dead weight. And so I brought a bowl of water into the bedroom with the flannels laid on a towel and rubbed at the purple patches that had bloomed on her skin, worrying that the order in which I used the coloured flannels was incorrect. I brushed her hair as I had done for the past ten years and cut her toenails — following the curve of the toes, as instructed — and wrapped the parings in a sheet of newspaper before putting them in the fireplace to be burnt. I'd been doing it for so long, I couldn't stop. And then I dropped the flannels into the cooling bath-water and went downstairs to ask Mrs. Lee if I could use her telephone. She charged me four pence, although we both knew that was too much, and she stood in her kitchen doorway with flour on her apron, un-ashamed to be listening in to the conversation.

"My mother is dead," I said to the doctor. Mrs. Lee folded her arms.

"Are you certain she's passed away?" he asked, as though I were in the habit of telephoning and giving such news. I laughed. I had no doubts that she was dead from the way the skin on her cheeks hung from the bone, from the flies that had reached her although I'd kept the windows closed, and from the smell that no amount of washing with the flannels had erased. The doctor came, took one look, and called the undertaker's. He told me I should have telephoned him sooner but there was sympathy in his expression and he must have known that now I was alone. He prescribed pills to help me sleep but I didn't take them, I had no trouble sleeping.

On the roof, Peter said, "Sometimes that's for the best. When they've been ill for a while, if they've been suffering."

"I don't think that's what Fran means," Cara said, staring at me until it seemed that her eyes had pierced me: a thousand pinholes letting in the light, exposing everything.

"She was bedridden." I dragged my eyes from Cara's. "She hadn't left the house in ten years."

"Did you look after her on your own?" Cara asked casually. She stretched out her fingers and stared at her hand as if examining her nail polish. There was a tiny black line on one of her knuckles. She held it up to me. "Thunderfly," she said. The insect's rear end curled, the same action as a scorpion, and then it was gone. The light had turned odd, yellow like the film that kept shop-window displays from spoiling.

"Yes," I said. "I did everything. I cooked for her, helped her to the lavatory, washed her." I took a gulp of champagne and thought about telling them how it had really been in that claustrophobic room in Dollis Hill.

"She didn't have any friends or relations?" Peter said.

"A couple of old friends but no one who could help out. There was only me." I lay back on the blanket and we were all quiet for a long time. I closed my eyes. I had loved her though; I omitted to tell them that I had loved her.

Cara's voice woke me but this time she was shouting, not singing along to Simon and Garfunkel. "I'm not allowed to leave you, remember? We promised each other."

"But that was years ago," Peter said in his calm voice.

"And what? That means it doesn't count?" Cara was still shouting.

"No, of course, of course. But we're together now, here, aren't we?"

She staggered upright and knocked over the half-full bottle of champagne with her foot. I struggled to rouse myself from the fug in my head as the drink frothed out over the tablecloth and the remains of the salmon. "Bloody hell," Peter said. "Do you know how much this bottle is worth?" He reached for it, while I tried to move the food and mop up the wine, my hands not quite connecting with my brain.

"Cara!" I heard a small voice calling from a long way off. "Cara! No."

Peter and I, both on our hands and knees, stopped tidying and looked behind us. Cara was at the very lip of the roof, her toes over the edge, her body swaying. The voice came again as I scrabbled up, crushing a paper parasol with my knee, my shoes slipping on salmon and mayonnaise, and I fell forward to grab hold of Cara, just as Peter was doing the same. A man, far below, jumped off his bicycle when he reached the gates, letting it drop before he ran towards the house. It took me a second to recognise Victor with his hair loose, and wearing jeans and a tee shirt.

We were all standing on the edge that day, at the very rim of the precipice, staring into the void. Something inside us wanted to see what it would be like to jump, just to find out what would happen, an actual physical lurch that seemed so possible, except we all knew that once we had jumped there would be no way back.

I had thought I would like living life to the maximum, I had thought I would enjoy being unconstrained and reckless, but I learned that it is terrifying to look into the abyss.

Cara didn't fall. We grabbed her, Peter and I, and pulled her away from the edge. All three of us crashed backwards, a sprawl of arms and legs, Cara's dress torn, a red welt across Peter's neck, my left hand scraped to match my right. I don't remember us climbing through the attic window, although we must have — leaving the crushed remains of our picnic and the blue-and-gold crockery up on the roof.

We found Victor in the entrance hall, too polite to go farther into the house uninvited. "Are you all right?" he said to Cara. "I was worried you were going to . . ." — he looked at Peter for confirmation — ". . . fall," he finished.

"She's fine," Peter said to Victor, his voice frosty.

"What were you all doing up there?" Victor said. "It didn't look very safe."

"We were having a picnic." I went forward, forever the responsible girl who owns up in front of the headmaster. I was irritated with

Victor for the things he had said the day before and I didn't understand why he'd come again.

"Isn't it a nice day for a picnic?" Cara said, smiling. She was fiddling with the earrings Peter had bought her and I had a sudden ludicrous worry that Victor would ask her where she got them and how Peter could afford them.

Peter had put an ironwork table and three chairs on the portico, and I realised they were the ones from the photograph in the book I'd taken from the library. He went to fetch one of the old packing cases from the basement for a fourth seat and Cara went off to make tea. The light was still a sickening yellow, like it might be the end of times.

When Victor and I were alone he bent his head, his Jesus hair falling forward, and whispered, "You didn't tell her, did you? About the young man?" I frowned at him. "The young man who jumped from the gallery in the entrance hall," he said.

"Of course not."

"It's just I thought that might be why Cara was about to jump."

"She wasn't about to jump," I said. "She and Peter had been arguing. It was nothing. She was getting some air. It was very close up there on the roof."

Peter arrived then with the packing case and Cara came back to ask if Victor took milk and sugar, apologising that she didn't have any biscuits, saying that if she'd known he would be coming she'd have made some little chocolate-dipped orange madeleines because she had picked three oranges from the bitter orange tree. She described in detail how she would have beaten the eggs if she hadn't used them all for the mayonnaise, how she would have made a batter with them and the juice of the three oranges, and folded in the flour if she had remembered to buy more, and how it's most important to let the batter sit for an hour or two in the fridge before it's piped into the mould. She apologised for not having any dark chocolate that she could melt and dip the cooled cakes into. I didn't have the heart to tell her that inside, the oranges were probably dried up and useless.

Victor sat at the table looking as though he already regretted coming over. We made a half-hearted effort to talk about the temperature and whether there was going to be a thunderstorm. Peter sat with his arms folded, cross I supposed that religion had intruded upon his tea table. Cara returned once more, saying she was sorry but we didn't have any milk, so would the vicar like a slice of lemon instead. When she had gone again, Victor put his hand on the top of his head. "Good God! I completely forgot why I came."

"Not more peacocks' eyes?" Peter said. I hadn't realised he'd noticed the work we'd done in the blue drawing room.

Victor stood and pulled an envelope from his jeans pocket. "A telegram! I happened to be in the post office when it arrived,s and there was some argument about the delivery boy or the postman cycling all the way out here to deliver it, and I offered. I thought another ride out to see you, Miss Jellico, would be nice." I knew he was checking up on me but I wasn't grateful. I didn't need anyone to take care of me.

Before he could hand over the telegram, Cara was there with a silver tray, the Lyntons coat of arms etched on the surface, which the teapot only half obscured. "We haven't any lemons, I hope that's all right. I forgot that I used them in the mayonnaise and that's on the roof with the rest of the salmon and potatoes, although I don't suppose you'd want mayonnaise in your tea in any case." Only she laughed.

"It's quite all right. Thank you." Victor thrust the envelope forward, moving it in the space between Peter and me, and while

I was thinking it was odd that the telegram should be addressed to us both, Peter took it and opened it.

He looked ill, his face pasty. "Christ Almighty," he said.

"Oh dear," Victor said. "Bad news?"

"What?" I said. "What is it?"

Cara ignored Peter and the telegram, and poured the tea into the cups. She was smiling but her hands were shaking.

"It's Liebermann. He's on his way over."

"Here? From America?" I said, without thinking. Peter stared at the teapot. I took the telegram out of his hands and read it. "What day is it today?"

"Tuesday," Victor said.

"No, the date."

"Twenty-sixth."

"Of August?"

"Yes, August. Is that a problem?" Victor looked from one to the other of us.

"He'll be here tomorrow morning."

Peter continued to stare without saying anything.

"Haven't you finished your reports?" Victor asked. "Surely he'll give you a few days' grace?"

I thought of the furniture in the rooms upstairs: the writing desk, the beds and mirrors, the glassware and cutlery, the mahogany dining table and the rug and chaise longue — as well as the missing Reynolds, and the Egyptian cat I hadn't seen since the day we opened the Museum. I remembered how we hadn't done any washing-up for at least a week, and how the empty wine and champagne bottles that we had started collecting almost as keepsakes now lined the edges of Cara and Peter's sitting room. I thought about the clothes, the Italian cardboard buildings, and the bear. It would be impossible to put it all back and tidy up before tomorrow morning. Would Mr. Liebermann be able to work out what had been going on? I thought about my few sketches, my basic measurements of the bridge and the follies, my water-colours of the orangery, the rough notes I'd written for my report.

None of us said anything, although Cara was smiling. Victor stood and said, "Well, thank you for the tea. I should be getting back."

Cara and Peter didn't look up or acknowledge that they had heard him.

"I'll show you out," I said.

Beside the gates, Victor put his bicycle clips on without looking at me.

"Thank you for coming with the telegram," I said.

"Actually, that was just an excuse." Victor

picked up his bike; it was heavy and old, black with a little pocket hanging off the back seat, a lady's bike with the chain covered and no bar across the middle. It was clean and rust-free, and I could picture him spending his Saturday mornings with it upside down in the vestry. "The real reason I came was to tell you I've decided I'm leaving the church."

I was ashamed for not having been kinder, for not listening. I wondered if it was too late to make amends. "Oh Victor. I'm sorry. I could come over later . . . or tomorrow . . . or when Mr. Liebermann has gone."

"Whenever you feel you have the time."

He pushed the bicycle out of the gravel and onto the avenue. "Victor," I said and put out my hand but he had gone too far from me. He had his legs either side of the bike and was ready to push off before he turned back.

"As I said yesterday, I don't think this is a good place for you. I think you should leave. Go back to London, or somewhere else."

My sympathy and guilt were replaced by defensiveness again. "I don't see how you believe you have the right to say such things." I would have gone on if I could have found the words fast enough, but Victor cut me short.

"Because I thought you and I were friends, Miss Jellico. And that's what friends do, look out for each other." He pushed off and I watched him go, steering around the holes, giving a little pedal now and again to help the bike along.

TWENTY-TWO

When I got back to the portico Cara had gone, the teapot and cups left on the table. Peter was disappearing into the rhododendrons. I called to him and he stopped to wait for me, and together we ducked under the yellowing leaves. Neither of us mentioned that we were leaving Cara on her own.

Nothing moved and the air was oppressive. I would have welcomed the threatening thunderstorm.

"Maybe there's enough time to put everything back," I said, knowing it was hopeless. "Or we apologise. Just say we've been using some things for a while, borrowing them."

"And the reports we should have almost finished?" Peter said. He ran a hand through his hair. "And the things I've been flogging?" It was the first time he had admitted what he had been doing. "But it's not just that. Not even the things I've sold have touched the debt I'm in. Two wives are bloody expensive." I didn't point out that he wasn't married to Cara; it wouldn't have made any difference.

We walked beside the lake and crossed the bridge. Even there we didn't pause but continued single file along the far bank, the grass flattened where we had trodden it down over the summer.

"Cara went upstairs to squeeze the oranges.she picked," Peter said. "They're all the food we have left in the house until she goes shopping."

"If she manages to get any juice out of them, she'd better mix it with plenty of sugar," I said, wondering what we would eat for dinner. I was hungry.

"I'm going to have to take her to London again to see a doctor," Peter said.

"Because of Dermod?"

"Because of everything."

"It does seem like an awful quirk of fate, a terrible coincidence for there to have been another boat accident."

"What?" Peter said.

"She told me what happened. About the boat sinking, losing everything, and Finn drowning. It must have been horrible for you. I haven't been able to stop thinking about the noises she said the cows made —

like human children crying."

"What? Wait." He stopped on the path, turned. "She said there was a boat and that it sank?"

"Well, yes. She said you were going to Scotland, although apparently she thought you were all on your way to Italy."

"No, Franny. No. There was no boat. We got on a plane and we did go to Italy."

"Italy," I repeated.

"Italy," he said firmly.

"I don't understand. What about the cows?" I said lamely, unable to comprehend this different version.

"The ones that sounded like crying children?"

"Yes! She said she dreamed about it for years afterwards."

"That was her mother's story," Peter said. "When their house in Ireland — Killaspy — was set alight she heard the horses in the stables. She was sent to the end of the drive to wait until the fire was put out. But she heard the horses. They sounded like human children. For years the crying would wake her and she'd have to look out of her bedroom window to check for flames. She told me the story herself."

"There was no boat? You didn't go to Scotland?"

"Later. Later we went to Scotland."

"I don't understand."

Peter stared over the lake and began walking again.

"Why would she lie to me about it all?"

"Because . . . because she's worked you out, Fran. She knows you'll believe her, lap it up. She's a damn good storyteller and all she needs is an audience. If she tells the story well, you'll think she's someone different than the person in her head. Who wouldn't want to rewrite their past, if it means it will change their future?" The path widened and we went side by side. He didn't look at me while he spoke; I thought he must be reminding himself of what had happened. "When I'd saved enough money, I bought us plane tickets to Rome — the three of us: me, Cara, and Finn." He walked fast, making me take extra little steps to keep up with him. "Finn was three months old. I booked us into a hotel, and Cara was so excited, amazed to be finally in Italy. We went out to celebrate, had a few drinks, a meal. She wanted to see everything, taste it all. And Finn was like her too — his huge eyes taking it all in. It was late when we got back to our hotel. Even that was beautiful to her — I don't think she'd ever stayed the night in a hotel before. I loved seeing her happy for once but I was tired, and we argued. I don't remember what about now. She started running a bath, and I'd had enough, so I went out to a bar. We didn't have a proper bath in the house we'd been renting in Ireland, only a tin one in front of the fire. And when I came back, she was asleep in the bath. She'd had the baby in her arms and she'd fallen asleep, and he had slipped into the water and drowned."

"Oh Peter." I stopped, but he was striding ahead. He picked up a stick and hit at the tops of the bulrushes along the bank, the male flower heads bending and swaying and sending their clouds of yellow pollen eddying into the still afternoon.

"She keeps talking about heaven and hell, and wanting to know where Finn is now. It's all a load of rubbish. The boy is dead." He choked on the words, and then gathered himself together. "And she goes on and on about it being a virgin birth."

When I caught up with him, I said, "Are you sure it wasn't?"

He looked at me as if I were mad. But for the first time amid all the lies and half-truths, I wanted to make up my own mind and stop being led one way and then another. That Finn had no father, the most nonsensical story of them all, seemed to have a nugget of truth, a glow about it, that if polished well enough would shine through.

"It's just about piling on the guilt and wanting a penance extreme enough to make it all go away," Peter said. "It's never going to go away, but she doesn't realise that. And I, I only want to help her get through it, but it's tiring, it's so bloody tiring. I should be there now, up at the house keeping an eye on her, making certain she's safe."

I didn't suggest we go back.

Beside us, the lake narrowed and the weir crossed it. Here, some of the water had been diverted and slowed into the grotto to form a pool within a man-made cave. A stone shelf had been created around the edge on which it was just possible to stand, or to sit and dangle your legs, if you were brave enough, into the water. If the sun was out and the time of day was right, the light reflecting off the surface danced around the walls like the sun spinning off the glass Peter had hung from their bedroom window, and it shimmered across the low ceiling of knapped flints and pieces of mother-of-pearl set into the mortar.

On other days, I had imagined us sitting inside the grotto with our legs in the water and our fingers touching. It was a romantic place, somewhere appropriate to tell Peter that I loved him, and that I knew I could make him happy, and for him to say he loved me too. I had often thought about when Peter had told me he didn't mean to hurt Mallory by falling in love with Cara, and I supposed that my father hadn't intended to hurt Mother by falling in love with her sister. It was easy to justify how I felt.

But the reality of the grotto was chilly, and we stood at the side with our shoulders hunched and our heads jutting forward because of the low roof, and when we looked in the pool, the water was dark and we had no reflections.

"What about George Harrison's fur coat?" I said.

"What?"

"Nothing. It doesn't matter." I was embarrassed to have mentioned it. So trivial compared to the loss of a child.

"George Harrison?"

"She said she met him in Ireland, before she met you. She told me his fur coat was in your bedroom up at the house."

"How could it be? A coat saved when we lost everything on her imaginary boat, including our son?"

I had no answer. I tried to consider the

401

sort of person who would make these things up. I imagined Cara in the sitting room, sawing through one of the bitter oranges she'd picked, with a blunt kitchen knife, one of a set from the Museum. Peter had promised to sharpen them but he hadn't got around to it, and every mealtime when Cara was preparing the food she would complain that he had sharpened the garden tools but couldn't sharpen a kitchen knife, and Peter would promise he'd do it soon. I pictured her now, grinding the two halves of the orange against our jade glass orange juicer maybe getting a drop or two out.

Peter and I climbed to the top of the grotto where the grass was short, cropped by rabbits. The roof had given way a little and there was a shallow dent in the ground, the length of two bodies side by side. We sat down in it, with the air motionless around us and the noise of the cascade beside us, as the water flowed out of the lake. Peter lay back on bent arms and closed his eyes, and I stared at him, so beautiful and tired, and deserving of someone other than Cara.

I wanted to make him happy. I wanted to tell him that I loved him, certain he felt the same way, but I hadn't got any further in my ruminations than the kiss that might happen after our mutual declaration. What

402

then? Would he tell Cara immediately? Where would we go, the two of us?

On top of the grotto I turned to him, all of me aware of the beat of my heart. He sat up, rested his elbows on his knees, and propped up his chin. Beside him, I knelt, trying to make myself say the words but struck dumb. Instead, I untied the belt of my dress — the dressing gown — and let it fall around me.

"Franny . . ." he said without moving.

The air touched my skin.

"Franny . . ." he repeated, and moved back as though to get a better look at me. I remember smiling.

"Fran," he said and I waited for him to take me in his arms. He sat up fully but didn't move towards me, so I took his hand and pressed it to one of my breasts. I held his wrist and felt how cool his skin was compared to my own while I pushed his hand onto my nipple and his fingers spread out and away as if they were rearing back in fear. "Oh no," he said. "No." He retreated, shuffling on his knees and pulling his wrist away from my grasp. "Please, Frances. I'm sorry. I think you've misunderstood." He took hold of the dressing gown from around my thighs and bottom and brought it up to my shoulders to wrap me in it, pulling it forwards where it fell back. "I'm so sorry," he said again. He must have seen the terrible disappointment in my expression, the tears coming, because he added, "But we can still be friends. We'll always be the best of friends. Franny?" And then in pity I supposed, or so he didn't have to continue looking at my face, he drew me to him and put his arms around me and held me, and I felt the firmness of his body against my soft one.

I wanted to tell him that it would be different with me, that we both knew it, but his body tensed and then he pushed me away. I turned in the same direction as his gaze and saw Cara, staring at us from the concrete jetty across the lake.

"What does the Bible have to say about impotence?" I ask Victor, the pretend chaplain. "Sexual dysfunction?"

He blushes, shuffles, scratches the crook of an elbow through his shirt.

"I'm asking for a friend," I say, and smile, and for the first time he puts his head back and laughs. It surprises me, his laugh: it is deep and rich and envelops me in happiness.

I would like to ask him more about the bomb in the Underground station — what

he told me has often been on my mind —
but perhaps a requirement of his content-
ment is forgetting.

"I have read," I say, "that scientists are
working on a pill which if taken no later
than six hours after something bad has happened will mute one's memory of that
event. The accident or catastrophe, or
whatever, will be less painful to recall, like
watching someone else's memory I suppose,
or a film. Would you take the pill, Victor?
Would you have taken it when you left that
Underground station?"

He strokes my hair and doesn't answer, or
I haven't spoken. Perhaps he believes that
pain as well as joy makes us who we are.

I remained there, sitting on top of the grotto
with the dressing gown falling off my shoulders, while Peter got up without looking at
me or saying another word and went across
the weir and Cara turned to go back into
the trees. I could only suppose that they
met under the rhododendrons and walked
up to the house together. I didn't know how
much she had seen.

I didn't want to return to Lyntons straight
away. I went to the mausoleum thinking I
would spend time with the two wives but
the place was gloomy, the flowers on the

chests of the women were dry and colourless, and I noticed the smell of urine in the
corners of the tomb. Hunger drove me back
in the end, hope that I might find some food
somewhere. The storm that had threatened
hadn't materialised, and the sun was low
over the hangers, elongated into bands of
apricot and red. The cows had gone from
the field but the sweet fetid smell they left
behind lingered under the cedar. I should
have walked a different route and gone
around by the front or the portico because I
couldn't resist looking up at Cara and Peter's rooms. Already it felt like it was the
end of something. Many of the building's
windows had been closed and the lowering
sun reflected on the uneven glass so that
behind each pane a fire seemed to roar,
consuming the house unnoticed. Only Peter
and Cara's sitting room windows were open
and I saw Peter lean on the sill and look
out. He had a glass in his hand, a tumbler. I
could hear that album on the record player,
the one we always had on — *Bookends* by
Simon and Garfunkel. I stood beside the
cedar, and in the half-light I must have
blended in with the tree, but I thought Peter saw me because he seemed to raise his
glass as if in a toast, perhaps of forgiveness
or apology. I raised my hand in salutation

but even while I hoped, I knew things wouldn't be the same, couldn't ever be the same.

If I had gone to their rooms then, would the ending have been different? But I was too ashamed, the embarrassment of rejection was too raw, and I didn't know what Peter might have told Cara. He could have said that I'd undressed and pressed his hand against me; maybe they had laughed about it. But then I remembered that Cara had said I wasn't that interesting, not worth talking about. I went in through the side door, then up the spiral staircase to the attic.

They were quiet in the rooms below mine. I leaned out of my window and looked down, but saw nothing. In the bathroom, as I packed my toiletries, I heard the water in the pipes again, the splash of their bath. I changed out of the dressing gown and put Mother's underwear back on, and my skirt and blouse. They were tighter than ever. Everything I had still fitted into my two suitcases. Gathering it all together didn't take long; the only items I packed which I hadn't arrived with were the cigarette case Peter had given me and Cara's note. I considered whether I could just leave, or if I should say goodbye, but if one of them was in the bath I would have a while to wait. I sat on my bed and watched the shadows in the garden lengthen.

Then I was taken with a sudden need to hurry, an urgent desire to get away from Lyntons as fast as I could. I checked my watch — if I was quick there was a bus I could catch from the main road to the railway station, otherwise I would have to pay for a taxi or stay overnight at the Harrow Inn. I didn't have any real plan of where I was going, except back to London.

I put my handbag and raincoat over my arm, picked up my two cases, and walked down the spiral stairs. I could have carried on to the bottom, let myself out of the front door, walked around the fountain and along the avenue. But at the small passageway I hesitated, took a step down and back up, then elbowed my way through the baize door on to Cara and Peter's hallway. Outside their room I put down my cases and folded my raincoat over the top so it didn't touch the floor. I pressed my ear to their door, but heard nothing.

I tapped, embarrassed, hoping they wouldn't be there and I could leave another note and creep away. No one answered, there was no noise. I turned the handle and stepped into the room. Dirty saucepans and bowls that Cara had used for cooking the salmon and potatoes were still on the table, and a woven basket contained the dry end of a morning roll. One of the wine glasses we used was on its side, a puddle leaching into the mahogany. The record continued to turn on the record player, the speaker giving out a repeating crackle. In the kitchen area Cara *had* been squeezing the oranges: four pulped and hollow halves with clean edges lay on a board. A third, pitted and lumpy, sat alone in a latticework bowl. Blue and gold to match the dinner service.

"Hello?" I called out. "Cara? Peter?" Their bedroom door was shut; the place was too still, too silent. I stood in the middle of the room, listening, and then rummaged in my handbag for a pen and piece of paper. I heard a noise from the bathroom, the sloshing of water in the bath. "Peter?" I called again, and Cara came out into the sitting room, leaving the bathroom door partially open. Her evening dress — she had changed into the silk one with the thin straps and the feathers — was a darker green across the front, as though she had spilled something down it.

"Cara," I said. "I didn't realise you were here." I took my hand out of my bag and went forwards. Her arms were wet, her hanging hands dripping water where she stood, the loose green cloth puddled around her feet. She stared at me. "Is Peter about?" I said. "I came . . . to say goodbye." I wasn't brave enough to ask what she might have seen from the jetty. She continued to stare. And although Peter might have been naked in the bath, something made me shift around her so I could see into the room. Suddenly Cara came out of her trance-like state, and in one quick movement took the key from the other side of the door, closed it, and locked it. But not before I glimpsed something, someone, in the bath, low down under the water, blondish hair floating. "Is that Peter?" I said to her as she stood away from the door and I jiggled the handle. "Is that Peter in the bath?"

She stepped backwards, almost stumbling over the dress, righting herself before she tripped, but dropping the key. We both dived for it, grappling on the floor and bumping heads. I had my fingers on its metal shaft and then Cara got hold of it, and while I was still down, Mother's underwear digging into me once again, she stood and flung the key out of the open window beside us. "No!" I cried, but by the time I was kneeling on the window seat, the key had gone — it wasn't on the terrace, and considering the force with which she'd

410

thrown it, must have been lost somewhere in the box hedges.

"You can't go in there," Cara said, standing in front of the bathroom door. "This is nothing to do with you, Frances."

"What have you done?" I shouted, pushing her aside and rattling the door handle, shouting Peter's name through the wood. "Let me in!" There was no response. "What have you done?" I said again. "Peter's in there, isn't he?"

I pounded on the door with my fists while she stood, impassive, watching. "Is there another key?" I asked, knowing there wasn't. I looked out of the window once again as though it might have reappeared. I hammered on the door some more, looked at Cara, and then threw my weight against it, but like all the doors at Lyntons it was solid, well made. I only bruised my shoulder; the door didn't move.

She sat sideways on the window seat in her old position: feet pressed up against the frame, staring out of the window. "Don't go anywhere," I said, and she turned her head to look at me, but didn't reply. I left the sitting room, ran along the hallway past my suitcases, and switched to the spiral staircase, down to the basement. I put the light on and one hanging bulb after another illuminated the corridor. Here I paused, trying to control my breathing and force myself on, to the butler's room where Peter kept his tools. The sledgehammer sat beside the chest. It was heavier than I had anticipated and I had to hold it out in front of me, my shoulder muscles complaining before I even reached the stairs.

When I burst back into their sitting room, Cara was standing in front of the window with one foot up on the seat, as if painting her toenails. She twitched when I came in, perhaps expecting me to have been gone for longer, maybe to fetch the police. I dragged the sledgehammer behind me, furrowing the rug as I went, and when she saw it she took one step from the window to stand in front of the bathroom door again.

"Get out of the way," I said when I was facing her.

"You can't go in there," she said. "Just go home, Frances." I didn't know where she meant.

I pushed her and tried to swing the sledgehammer at the same time, but the two of us became tangled in the green dress and when I pulled the hammer back, she also had hold of the handle. "Let me get in there!" I screamed at her. "This is about that stupid pact, isn't it? What have you done? What

412

have you done!"

"No! Let go," she shouted. She pulled hard on the heavy end of the hammer, she was stronger than I had expected and the shaft slipped from my hands. The weight of the hammer end almost carried her with it, through the open window behind her. But at the last moment she twisted and the hammer fell out and down. We heard it land and I shouted her name or some other word. She was half out of the window, tilting back, her legs still inside the room. Only the tips of her fingers, clinging to the sides of the frame, and my foot pinning the hem of her green dress to the floor, kept her from falling. The orange sun framed her beautiful face and hair in a perfect halo, a golden nimbus fanning out around her, and for a second I was reminded of Victor's sermon about light and transformation. There was an instant when our eyes met and I saw she was calm, all the anger and the anguish gone. Then she released her fingers and the dress ripped away from under my foot, and she fell backwards with nothing to stop her. I heard the heavy thump, the crack of a skull and a cry that was only an exhalation of breath. I covered my face with my hands, stuck to the spot for I don't know how long, until I had the courage to look out.

■ ■ ■ ■

The silence in the house was absolute. For the first time, I was alone. I knew what I was going to find, but still I went up to my bathroom and removed the floorboard, and for the final time looked through the judas hole, at Peter. My love. The bathwater was pink, and my sample knife was on the floor, although I knew he hadn't done this to himself. There was nothing to hurry for any more. I watched him lying on his back, his arms by his side. His eyes were open, but they seemed to focus beyond the spot in the ceiling where I looked down at him, to a point above the roofs of Lyntons, and up into the evening sky. He was motionless, as if he too were a gisant, carved and placed on top of his own tomb, his body alabaster. I willed him to get up, to push his hands on the edges of the bath and rise dripping, from the water. I lay beside the removed floorboard and I cried for him.

After a time, I went down to the terrace, not to make certain Cara was dead — I had known that as soon as I looked out of the window — but to collect the sledgehammer. All my muscles were quivering, my body shaking, but I dragged the hammer from under her head. From the light falling out of the windows I saw that one of the right-angled edges of the hammer end had hair and skin sticking to it, but by the time I had dragged it across the dirt under the rhododendrons it had rubbed off. The shaft, though, was sticky with blood.

The hammer bumped behind me down the steps, gathering grass when I passed the chicken sheds and cutting a fresh groove in the earth beside the lake. When I reached the bridge, I lifted the hammer in both hands at the very end of the shaft and swung it at the stone. I don't know how much damage I did, not enough to have it all fall into the lake as I wanted. When I couldn't lift the hammer one more time, I left it there and walked back up to the house, under the portico, across the drive, and along the avenue to the church. I don't remember, but I was told that this was where Victor found me, in the vestibule with blood on my hands.

TWENTY-THREE

My father came to the trial, turning up on the first day in the public gallery amongst the journalists and general gawkers. It took me a second look to recognise him, an old man, still a stranger. Luther Jellico. I'd thought of him often although I hadn't seen him for almost thirty years. When I was young and idealistic I imagined scenarios where he arrived at the Dollis Hill apartment and understood everything without me even speaking. He would take me to live with him — my aunt out of the picture — in the big house in Notting Hill, although I knew in reality it had been sold. Later I looked for him in antiques shops, at antiquarian book fairs, and in libraries, rehearsing what I would say.

I might have carried around the guilt of my parents' separation like a bad meal in my belly, but it was my aunt whom I considered to be the real villain. It was she who had made me choose between the fox-fur stole and the truth. It was from her, as much as from Mother, that I learned that the truth isn't always the right way. When, after we had lived in the apartment for a couple of years, the Christmas cards and birthday presents stopped coming, it was my aunt I blamed for making my father abandon me. The wicked stepmother I never saw. And after she died, although I was an adult by then, I waited for my father to return to Mother and me. I waited but he didn't write, or telephone Mrs. Lee downstairs, or call at the door. I didn't see him again until that day in court.

Now his hair and his moustache were white, his neck scrawny, but with just one look, all the love and anger came rushing back. I couldn't take my eyes off him. When I should have been concentrating on what the wig men were saying, making certain I got my story straight, I was staring up at the gallery, while he averted his gaze. *You've come!* I wanted to shout. *Too late! Too late!* I couldn't wait for that first day to be over so I could be passed his note, or his request for a private visit. I tried to work on the strength I would need to tear it up in front of him or deny his request. A muscle I exercised while the day dragged on. I asked

417

the officer who took me back to my cell in the breaks to double-check, but there was no note, no request.

My father came every day, sitting in the same place with his eyes downcast or closed. Perhaps he too carried some guilt for the way I had turned out. Or maybe like the rest of them, like me in the end, he was a voyeur.

"Are these your sleeping tablets, Miss Jellico? Benzodiazepine, commonly known as Valium? Prescribed to you by a Dr. Hunter at Dollis Hill Surgery in June 1969," the wig man asked.

"To help me sleep after my mother died."

My father's eyes snapped open. I, though, wasn't surprised that the wig men wanted to ask me about the Valium I'd been prescribed. The prosecution had been obliged to disclose all relevant evidence before the trial started. I had been able to deal in private with my shock and dismay at what Cara had done.

"And you took them with you to Lyntons?"

When had I last seen that glass bottle with the wad of cotton wool in its neck? As I had packed my toilet bag before I left Dollis Hill for good? I couldn't remember unpacking the bottle when I'd put out my toothpaste and talcum powder after I arrived at Lyntons.

"I suppose."

"You suppose. Yes or no?"

"I don't remember."

"Did you take any benzodiazepine when you were staying at Lyntons?"

"No."

"Where did you keep them when you were living in the attic rooms?"

"I don't remember, I don't remember having them with me."

"Can you explain how they were found in Miss Calace's and Mr. Robertson's kitchen area?"

"No."

"And can you explain how traces of benzodiazepine and orange juice were found in a glass in their kitchen area?"

"No." I thought about the face at the attic window when I had returned from London, and Cara, the storyteller, denying she'd been up there.

"And also in Peter Robertson's stomach?"

"No." There was an ache under my breastbone and a sting in the bridge of my nose when I thought of Peter's body in the bath and, afterwards, cut open by the pathologist's knife.

My father was late on the seventh — the

final — day and there was shuffling in the gallery before a space could be made for him. I had stopped willing him to look at me. I wondered if he was hoping for a reconciliation on the steps of the courthouse when I was found not guilty. I wasn't planning on being found not guilty.

I had tried to practice my expression in the cell below the courtrooms but there was no mirror. I decided on a smirk of arrogance during the prosecution's closing speech. But what does a guilty expression look like?

This wig man was good, reminding the jury that I had admitted I was in love with Peter and had been rejected by him, that he gave me gifts and led me on, that I had been prescribed the drug used to sedate him, and I owned the knife that cut him. This perhaps had been my only surprise from the pretrial meetings with my solicitor. Whatever Cara had seen Peter and me doing across the lake, it hadn't tipped her over the edge as I had presumed; instead she must have been planning her actions for days. The wig man came close in a way. He claimed that I had attempted to make my double murder look like a double suicide. If I couldn't have Peter then no one would. He told the jury I had drugged Peter and slashed his wrists with my sample knife — the only sharp

420

knife in the house. After a fight with Cara where she attempted to get the key to the bathroom, I had pushed her out of the window, and then gone down with the hammer to finish off the job.

I had never been more nervous than when the jury returned from their deliberations.

"Do you find the defendant guilty or not guilty of the murder of Peter Robertson?"

I liked that Peter was first.

"Guilty."

A gasp from my father.

"Do you find the defendant guilty or not guilty of the murder of Cara Calace?"

"Guilty."

A cry of "No!" from the gallery, and I couldn't help myself, I looked up to see my father with tears on his cheeks.

I smiled at the verdicts, not because my father was there, that was incidental, but because I hoped it would get me a longer sentence. Life for a life. Penance, that's what I craved. I wondered if my father remembered the rules he had taught me before he'd left, or at least one of them: payment will be due for any wrongdoing. By the time I heard the judgements I knew I would be strong enough to veto any demands for a retrial and to turn down any requests my father might make to visit me in prison.

■ ■ ■ ■

I received a solicitor's letter five years ago saying my father had died and he had left everything to me: his London house, his belongings, quite a large sum in the bank. Possibly he hoped it would be useful for when I was released, I don't know; he didn't provide any further instructions or a note. I, in turn, have left most of it to a niche charity that restores historic bridges. And so, I lie here and think of fathers. My own and Cara's, and Finn's of course. It no longer matters who his biological father was, whether indeed he even had one. Peter was all the father he needed for his short life. Children need a loving, familiar face, a constant.

Perhaps I am a child: a creature of habit who likes routine. No alternative consequences for one action versus another, no *what ifs*. Prison lunches are served at twelve noon. Before they moved me to the end-of-life unit to die, I queued for the food behind Ali Shaw and in front of Joan Robyns. Mashed potato was served with an ice cream scoop into the top-left indentation of my compartmentalised tray, baked beans in the middle, two pink sausages bottom right.

No squeeze of tomato ketchup, no thank you. I've always been polite. I would have had mustard to help take the taste away, but they don't allow it in here, or pepper. Five years ago, a prison-rights organisation decided that serving food to prisoners on trays was demeaning and we should have plastic plates. I broke two chairs and Joan's nose, and I refused to eat for three days. I was transformed when I put myself in prison.

There's been a lot of money spent on this place, not like some prisons that the transferred women used to talk about: rats and drugs and fights. Out of control. No, I wouldn't like that. I want to know where I am. They sent me to see a psychiatrist every month, after I started eating again. I told her how once I had stood on a bridge over a lake and thought about the fact that when I was dead I would soon be forgotten. I didn't seek notoriety, I had no choice, it came along with the court's decision. She asked about Mother and my father. I told her some things, but not all of it of course. I never told all of it. I told her how happy I had been when I was a child, I told her about Mother's illness and the routines: when I fed her, when I helped her with the bedpan, when I washed her private parts with the flannels. For the first thirty-nine years of my life I knew what would happen when. The funding for the psychiatrist stopped after a year, but in my twelve sessions I never said all of it. I never told it all.

"What would you have told, Miss Jellico?" Victor leans in. Today his breath reminds me of picking berries in the kitchen garden with Cara. She plucked a mint leaf, tore it in two and put one half in her mouth, then held the other up for me, and smiled. It smelled perfectly of summer. I opened my mouth and she put it inside. The leaf was rough and hairy, tough and dirty-tasting under the sharpness. When she wasn't looking I spat the chewed green ball into the brambles.

"You would have made a wonderful doctor," I say to Victor and hope I have said it out loud.

"Miss Jellico?"

I like my routine. That summer I was out of control, we all were. I couldn't wait to be back in a place where I knew what would happen next. A rhythm, that's what I need. Mother always said that I was a girl who liked order, to know what would happen next. That's why I was happy when they said *guilty*. And because of the penance, of course. I deserved to be locked away: there

424

was a payment to be made for what I did.

"Miss Jellico?" Victor whispers. "What did you do? We were friends once, remember?"

Now I understand that Victor loved me, but it is too late. It is all too late.

"If you don't say," he continues, "it would be a miscarriage of justice, and that would be wrong. You know it would be wrong."

I squeeze his hand. A hand in mine. Is that all we need?

"Not long now, Mrs. Jelli-co," the Nursing Sister says.

At four o'clock I brought in the tea on a wooden tray. China pot warmed, shop-bought Garibaldi biscuits arranged on a plate, with two napkins inside silver rings. *If food is worth eating, it's worth eating properly.* I put the tray on the bedcover and got the spare pillow from the top of the wardrobe where it was kept. I put it behind Mother and helped her sit up. We drank our tea, she ate a biscuit. *Not hungry, Frances? That's not like you. Not today, Mother.* I told her what had been happening outside the window on the street. Who had walked past, who hadn't.

When she finished her tea, with a shaking hand she offered me the plate of biscuits. *You're putting on weight,* she said. *Around the jaw and around the middle. You want to watch that.* And all the while she held out the biscuits like a trap, bait to hook me with and reel me in. I tried to be quick with her plate and teacup, but despite her fragility she was faster. She pinched me through my cardigan and blouse, on my waist where no one would see the purple fingerprints. Her grip was still strong. Mother read her book and I took the tray to the kitchen to do the washing-up. I ate the four biscuits on the plate and then the rest of the packet while I cried over the sink. *She is an old ill woman,* I told myself, *and I love her.*

I try to hum a tune, that one about Mrs. Wagner's Pies. How does it go?

"I think she's singing."

"Shhh, Mrs. Jelli-co. Everything is fine. If you're ready you can go now."

At five o'clock I went back in. I marked where Mother was in her book, closed it, and put it on the bedside table. She was dozing. I turned on the bedside light, went to the window, and glanced out. There was no one in the street. I drew the curtains. Mother sighed. There was a particular order, we liked our routine. I went around to the other side of the bed and lifted her shoulders to take the spare pillow from behind her head. I didn't put it back in the top of the wardrobe where it belonged. Not straight away. She struggled and moaned: she was stronger than I had expected.

Afterwards she looked as though she were sleeping. So peaceful. "I'm sorry, Mother," I said.

There is water coming under the door of my prison hospital room. It rises around the legs of Victor's chair and wets the hem of the duvet. In a corner, the white cow bellows. I have never liked cows. The blackbird sits on the curtain rail, its droppings staining the window. It watches the fox leap onto the bed and run in circles over my covered feet. The hare, though, sits silently on my chest. The water comes, pouring in through the window now, until we are all under the waves. I lie in bed and watch the hare, the bird, the fox, and the cow swimming around my prison hospital room, where none of them belong.

Victor sits on the bottom lip of the stone tomb, a little to the left, leaving space beside him, and watches Christopher King, the gravedigger, at work. He is a young man, surprisingly young, Victor thinks, for a gravedigger. The sun is high and the grave-yard is even more overgrown than when he last saw it, twenty years ago. The inside of the church brought back more memories, as well as feelings of inadequacy and indeci-sion. He'd gone into the vestry when he ar-rived — the vicar had said it would be unlocked and that Victor could borrow anything he required. He had paused at the Bibles and the Book of Common Prayer, taking in the old smells of beeswax, musty vestments, and flowers past their best, and then he had filled a glass with water and taken it outside into the light.

Christopher lays the boards around the edge of the hole, followed by the sheets of butcher's grass which he knows don't fool anyone but he thinks make a grave look neat and tidy. He dug the hole yesterday and normally he'd return, to do the backfilling, only after the coffin's in and everyone's left. This time though he's been asked to hang around for the whole bleeding service. Still, he's being paid for it.

"Mr. King?" a voice says and Christopher jumps. An old man is standing behind him, holding out a hand. Christopher wipes his own down his overalls and then shakes. "Victor Wylde," says the man, whose skin is flaky and red. "I used to be the vicar here, used to be a vicar in fact. I hope you don't mind staying on, I know it's a bit of a strange request. It's all been arranged with the reverend." Christopher nods, although he's not heard of a funeral being done by a non-vicar before.

They stand side by side looking into the empty grave until the man says, "She asked to be brought down through the old back gate, along the avenue," and when Christopher glances at him he sees the man's eyes are swimming and he looks away, embarrassed.

After another minute Christopher says, remembering, "The yews and limes were felled a couple of years after the house was blown up."

"Blown up?" Victor says, although he knows this, had heard about it from someone or read it in the local paper before he left the area. He takes a handkerchief from his trouser pocket and blows his nose. He won't cry in front of the gravedigger. He'd like some water but realises the glass is on top of the tomb where he left it.

"Lyntons was a ruin and no one wanted it, after you know what," Christopher says.

"Yes, well," Victor says, so that Christopher is stopped before he is able to say more. They stand silently. Victor thinks that digging graves might be a good job: fresh air, physical exercise, not many people you have to talk to.

"Pall-bearers will be here soon," Christopher says. "Better get changed." He goes off down the path and through the lych-gate to where his van is parked.

As Christopher strips off his overalls beside the passenger seat and puts on his wedding suit — the only suit he owns — he remembers when, as a boy, he climbed with the Savidge twins over the wire fencing and watched Lyntons being blown up.

The twins already knew the house and the parkland. In the summer they showed him how to dive into the lake from the piers

430

which were all that remained of an old stone bridge that had been dismantled. The three of them lit a small fire in a room with bird wallpaper and fed it pages from the books they collected from the room next door.

A couple of weeks later, Christopher was still hanging around with them, hiding behind the old cedar in the field. There were four or five blasts that sounded like shots from an air rifle ricocheting off the hangers, and the house exploded, brick and rubble thrown into the air, and a plume of smoke shooting straight up, twice as high as the building. They whooped and cheered as the ground shook, and a cloud of dust spread outwards and the bits of stone, wood, and plaster came down and the dust rushed towards them. Even the Savidge twins had been scared then, running back to the fence, but the cloud overtook them before they could start climbing.

They crouched together with their hands covering their heads. When the dust settled, their clothes and exposed skin were grey while their teeth and the whites of their eyes gleamed. They walked home laughing, shoving each other, and arguing about who had seen what.

The rubble was used for the foundations of a nearby housing estate.

Victor sees Christopher smoking by the lych-gate and wearing a suit that is shiny and too tight for him. When the undertaker's cars pull up he throws down his cigarette and stubs it out. Victor waits on the path looking up at the church, anywhere but at the coffin. The feeling of everything being too late, pointless, and wasted threatens to overwhelm him. He goes to the edge of the grave and waits, telling himself it isn't Frances inside the box, Frances, the woman he loved, who might have loved him back if things had been different. She is gone.

When the coffin is lowered into the hole and the pall-bearers have left, Victor stands beside the gravedigger again and tries to remember the things he has thought about saying. None of them come to mind.

Christopher bows his head and clasps his hands like he's seen mourners do, and waits for Victor to speak. While he waits he remembers the time he went back to Lyntons on his own, the day after it had been blown up. He climbed the pile of rubble and poked through it with a stick, searching for something interesting he could take home. He picked up a smooth flat object, licked the surface, and rubbed it on his arm to clean away the dust. A piece of china was revealed: the edge of a dinner plate with a blue-and-gold rim, and a crest made up of three circular things — they may have been oranges. He thought it might be valuable. It had sat on his shelf in his bedroom for years.

Christopher realises that Victor has been speaking, saying something about difficult old birds and how someone or other was right, this is a heavenly place to be buried, although he hasn't been paying attention. When Victor stops speaking the silence is awkward and eventually Christopher tugs on the lapel of his suit and goes to his van to change into his overalls.

Victor picks his way back to the tomb and drinks the water, which is warm now. He sits on the lip of stone again and watches the gravedigger work, moving the soil, spade by spade, into the hole.

ACKNOWLEDGEMENTS

There are lots of people I want to thank: India Fuller Ayling, Henry Ayling and Tim Chapman for their patience, support, and time. Louise Taylor, another early reader of *Bitter Orange*. All past and present Taverners, especially Judy Heneghan, Amanda Oosthuizen, Sarah Wells, Isabel Rogers, Rebecca Lyon, Richard Stillman, and Paul Davies. All of the Prime Writers for their moral support. All Friday Fictioneer writers around the world. Everyone at Fig Tree and Penguin UK, especially Juliet Annan, Assallah Tahir, and Poppy North. Everyone at Tin House, especially Masie Cochran, Nanci McCloskey, Diane Chonette, Sabrina Wise, Anne Horowitz, and Priscilla Wu. The whole of the Lutyens & Rubinstein team, especially Jane Finigan, Sarah Lutyens, and Juliet Mahony. The lovely David Forrer. And the amazing Caroline Pretty. My family — Ursula Pitcher, Stephen Fuller, and

Heidi Fuller. And for help with research for *Bitter Orange:* Malcolm Gibney, Patricia Oliver, English Heritage, The Grange Estate (in particular Richard Loader), David Brock, Tim Knox, Christian House, and John Harris (and his book *No Voice from the Hall*). And finally, Leonard Cohen for my writing soundtrack.

ABOUT THE AUTHOR

Claire Fuller's debut novel, *Our Endless Numbered Days*, was published by Tin House in 2015 and went on to win the Desmond Elliott prize in the UK and was a finalist in the ABA Indies Choice Award, an IndieNext pick, and chosen as a Goodreads Debut Spotlight.

The employees of Thorndike Press hope you have enjoyed this Large Print book. All our Thorndike, Wheeler, and Kennebec Large Print titles are designed for easy reading, and all our books are made to last. Other Thorndike Press Large Print books are available at your library, through selected bookstores, or directly from us.

For information about titles, please call:
(800) 223-1244

or visit our website at:
gale.com/thorndike

To share your comments, please write:
Publisher
Thorndike Press
10 Water St., Suite 310
Waterville, ME 04901